RELEASING ME

By

Melissa DeDomenico-Payne

In gratitude for Mimi and the believers…

CHAPTER 1

The small waiting room held a video camera, 3 plastic white chairs, and a rack of brochures highlighting community services and charities. I spoke through the interior glass window at the short, dark-haired woman with wire-rimmed glasses.

"Is Otis Johnson here - I was told he would be here after 4 p.m.?"

"Hold on please," she replied as she picked up the phone and dialed one number. After briefly speaking into the telephone and hanging up, she returned her attention to me. I heard a loud buzz and a click.

"Go through the lobby door and wait for an escort," she directed me. I entered into a small hallway, where a glossy oak bench provided temporary respite for my 20 minute wait. I studied the slate gray concrete walls and the cherry-framed pictures highlighting a sea of tan uniforms capped with eager faces and crew cuts. Eventually the dark-haired woman returned.

"You can follow me now," she said and began slowly walking down the hall. "What is this about?"

"I'd rather not say," I replied.

"I'll find out anyway," she said, as though I was ridiculous for expecting any sense of confidentiality.

She sat me in a small interview room, where another oak seat awaited me. I sat and was immediately joined by Otis Johnson. An obese man, he bustled into the room slightly short of breath. He glanced at me briefly with kind brown eyes and swept a lock of curly blonde hair away from his mildly sweating brow.

"Hi. Are you here about the Remingville Cemetery?"

"No," I answered, briefly wondering what was happening at the cemetery. "Why are you here?" he asked.

I had a rush of thoughts. *Because my mother said she was going shopping for antiques. Because she's not leaving him. Because my friend told me that my step-father was cheating on her and I want to give her one more chance to escape. Because the Commonwealth Attorneys' office told me there was no statute of limitations for child abuse. Because I was told you would be the person to help me.*

Somehow I began a response and the words flowed faster and faster as I described the years of pain that had led me to today's visit. When I was finished, Otis covered my small, excited hands with his dry and pudgy hands.

"You will be o.k." he consoled me.

"I just never wanted to be seen as a victim," I said. He chuckled.

"You have every sign of being a victim."

I didn't realize at that time that overachievement could be as much a sign of victimization as a list of negative behaviors. I never missed a day of school. I was voted "Most Popular" and "Best Leader" my senior year of high school. My grades were good. I had achieved two bachelor's degrees in four years and a master's degree in a year and a half. I had only slept with two men in my life -- husbands. I had never done drugs, didn't abuse alcohol, and had a good work ethic. The problems I did have -- eating disorders, depression, anxiety, insecurity -- I could keep primarily hidden. Just as I had generally been good at hiding the abuse that riddled the last 8 years I lived with my parents.

"I guess my mother felt she had to stay to take care of my brother. But now that he is almost out of high school, she can leave."

"She's co-dependent," Otis said matter-of-factly. I had no idea what he meant, but made a mental note to try to find out what that meant.

"What will happen to him?" I asked.

"What do you want to happen to him?" Otis slid back in his chair, with his arms crossed over his stomach.

"I don't know. I don't want him to go to jail. I guess I would just like some sort of apology -- some sort of admission of guilt -- and counseling, maybe. Can that happen? I just want to make sure that he doesn't do this to anyone else. Pedophiles don't change, from what I understand."

"He's not a pedophile. There's just something about step-fathers and step-daughters -- I don't know what it is."

I was confused, but I didn't push the matter.

"What do I need to do now?"

"I need you to write out a statement." Otis handed me a yellow lined pad of paper and a black ball point pen.

"Would it be possible for me to type it? I type much more quickly than I write."

"Sure, follow me." Otis led me to another small

room and sat me at his desk. The room seemed dark compared to the fluorescent illumination of the hallway outside. Otis brought in an old manual typewriter and several sheets of flat white paper. I lifted the clasp to the typewriter, guided in and advanced the paper, and set the clasp. I drew my hands to the home row of keys and began to click.

October 2, 1996 -- Statement:

I would like to state that on an evening in May, 1979, I was sexually molested by my stepfather, Mickey Walter Williams. At the time, I was ten years old. He came into my bedroom soon after I went to bed (it must have been sometime around 8 or 9 p.m. since I was not asleep yet). He put his hand on my leg and then moved his hand so that he was fondling my vaginal area and penetrating it with his fingers. I kept my eyes shut because I didn't understand what was happening. There were no public service announcements then (i.e. during the 1970's) that I can recall and therefore, I had no idea what to do in that situation (not even to say no). He did this for a period of time and then left. Later (I would say an hour or so later) he came back into my room, but this time when he put his hand on my leg, I opened my eyes. I caught a glimpse of his face. It had a very "mean" expression on it - an image which I can still see in my mind, but which I cannot adequately describe. His expression then changed and he told me to go back to sleep. After he left the room, I rolled over on my stomach. I guess I thought that if he came back, this position would prevent him from doing anything to me. It did not. He came back later that night (actually I believe it was sometime after midnight or between one and two in the morning) and again fondled my vaginal area and penetrated my vagina with his fingers as I stayed on my stomach.

It should be noted that during the first incident, my mother was in the kitchen washing dishes. I'm not sure where she was when he came back the second time. I believe she was in bed during the third incident. After he had left my room after one of the incidents (I don't recall which one), I heard my mother ask him if I was asleep. So I'm not sure if he fabricated some story about why he had gone in my room (ex. Like he heard me cry out, or that I had had a bad dream, etc.).

Sometime after that, I was riding the school bus home with my friend, Katie Foster (now Katie Walters). I told her about the incident. She told her mother, Valerie Foster (now Valerie Morrison). Her mother told her to tell me to tell my mother. So one afternoon, while my mother was feeding my baby brother Jessie, I told her what had happened. I described the incidents in detail. I remember asking her if something like that had ever happened to her and she said no (shaking her head). I remember that she told me that I should never tell anyone, especially not my grandmother (we are very close). I didn't mention to her that I had already told some people. In support of my mother, I think that she was in a very difficult position. She had had to leave my real father when I was only two years old. And in this situation, my brother was only a few months old and she was not working. She probably couldn't bear the thought of getting another divorce and raising another child without a father. I never told her about anything else that happened throughout the years.

While no other physical incidents occurred throughout the years, other forms of abuse did occur. On more than one occasion, he would tell me things that were inappropriate to tell children. For example, he told me that he had once killed a cat by smashing its head with a brick so that he could see what it looked like inside. He also told me that he had used LSD (we were watching a movie where some people in the movie were using LSD).

Suddenly I jerked my fingers back from the typewriter. My heart pounded. I thought I heard my mother's voice in the hall. I couldn't breathe. I froze in my seat, listening intently to the voices outside. A woman was laughing and as Otis began to read marriage vows to the couple in the conference room next door, I realized that the lady was not my mother and I could resume typing my statement. My mind went to perhaps the next most traumatic time in my life.

He would also encourage me to talk about things that I was learning in sex education class (junior high school). There also was a time when I was in the eighth grade where my boyfriend and I had engaged in some foreplay activity (kissing, touching each other). My parents found out about this and while both were not pleased, my stepfather seemed to take great pleasure in bringing up the matter to me on several occasions. The first night that he found out about it, he asked me very explicit questions regarding the matter (i.e., "Did his fingers enter your body?").

When I was in the seventh grade, Katie's house caught on fire. While her family stayed with relatives, I fed their animals for them. One day I could not find her dog. My stepfather went with me to look for it. He took this opportunity to tell me that he didn't think that we had gotten along well recently and he said that he thought he knew why and he thought I knew why. And he apologized. I cried. But then he threw a twist on it by asking me if I would give him a kiss.

Even though this apology occurred, other things happened after it. On at least three occasions that I can recall, he would come into the family room in his underwear in the morning before he went to work and I went to school (and no one else was up). He would have his penis hanging out of his underwear, or parts of his testicles. Then after a few minutes, he would say "Why didn't you tell me I was hanging out of my pants." I don't recall my response. I just remember always trying to ignore the situation and to comment as little as possible. I can remember him also occasionally coming into the bathroom while I was taking a shower. He would open up the sliding glass doors and say "Excuse Me" and remove something in the shower (like soap or something). Of course, he got full view of my body. I don't remember any exposures which I had prior to the molestation, except for one time when I was going into the bathroom and I looked into my parents' bedroom and saw him standing completely naked in front of the full-length mirror. He also would sometimes come into the bathroom when I was in first grade to see if I was o.k. if I had been in there a while.

Often when I was a teenager, he would tell me things like I had a nice body and if he were in school, he would want to date me. He also would ask me to massage his back and if I didn't, he would try to lay a guilt trip on me (like "don'task me to do anything for you then"). While I was massaging his back, I usually sat straddled across his back.

When I was in ninth grade, my stepfather's father died. I had never known anyone who died and was shaken at the funeral home when I saw the corpse. My stepfather took on the role of consoling me and eventually worked me up into going to see the corpse. He kept encouraging me to kiss the corpse until I did.

The only other negative things I can remember about him is that he drank a lot of beer, had a terrible temper, and would often be mean to animals (kicking or smacking at them). He had no qualms about cussing someone out (i.e., a stranger) if the opportunity arose (for example, ifsomeone was driving too slowly). These were behaviors I observed since we moved in with him when I was in first grade. Prior to the molestation incident which occurred when I was 10, I cannot remember anything negative except what was previously stated. We often spent time together while my mother worked and he was usually nice to me. It was after the birth of my brother that it all changed.

Otis popped his head in the door. "How's it coming?" he asked, smiling.

"Fine," I replied. "I'm almost done."

"By the way, would you be willing to take a lie detector test?" he asked.

"I guess," I said. "But I don't really believe in them. I'm the kind of person who can carry language to the extreme. If you ask me if I've ever stolen anything, I'm going to think about that pack of gum I took from the department store when I was three."

"You are a perfect person for the test, then. But we'll see what happens." I returned to typing.

I am not making this statement for any other reasons other than relief from carrying this burden for many years. I think that I have done better than a lot of victims, however in some ways I carry the issues with me. For example, I have not come forward to authorities because I thought that he was a good member of the community and I didn't want to ruin his reputation, nor my mother's, nor mine. It's a humiliating experience. However, recently I have found that he is not necessarily highly thought of in the community and I have come to grips with the fact that child molesters do not reform and my believing that I'm the only person with one incident is a form of denial. And not reporting it could do damage to other children out there. I've been hoping all of these years that my mother would just leave him, or he would get in trouble for something else so that I could benefit. But the reality is that this is the only issue in my life that I have run from and I'm tired of running away from it.

Maybe getting this out in the open will help him to relieve the guilt I believe he is troubled with.

-- Meredith A. Pearson

I signed my name and drew in a sigh. I picked up the papers and stuck my head out the door. Otis was no longer within sight and I found my way back to the original interview room. Otis returned. I handed him the papers. He began to read, occasionally shaking his head. I tried to be discreet as I looked for reactions in his face. When he was finished, he put the papers down. He asked me if I had ever been to counseling for this issue. When I told him no, he gave me the name and number of Miranda Marco.

"She's very good. I've gone to her myself. I think it is really important that you get into counseling right away."

"I will. What is the next step?"I asked.

"I'm going to call him in for questioning. In the meantime, try to gather whatever evidence you can for me -- witnesses who can speak to your character or to his behavior, diaries, anything at all."

"Who has access to this information?" I asked.

"What are you thinking about?" He asked.

"My stepfather is friends with someone at the police department –- Barry Wolfe. Do you know him?"

Otis shook his head. "We're really separate from the police department, so he won't have access to the information."

I could only trust that he was correct and honest. He stood up and led me to the copier, where I made copies of the simple statement that was going to change my life.

Then he walked me out through the echoing hall, the buzzing door, and the barren lobby. As we entered out into the warm October afternoon, he told me to take care and held his arms out to me. I hugged him. It was nice, but foreign to me to feel this sort of platonic warmth from a man. As I walked away from the stucco building and the sea of brown cars decorated with large gold stars, I felt fear set in. And I knew where I needed to go next.

CHAPTER 2

I pulled up in front of the red and black brick house with black shutters on Spruce Peak Drive. It had always been what I considered home.

As the story goes, my grandmother happened to call New York and find that my mother was in anguish. My father was gone again and my mother was getting ready to go on welfare. My grandmother told her that they were coming to get her. They drove to New York, packed the car with our personal items, and drove us back to their home.

At that time, they thought drugs were at the root of my father's problems. He approached drugs like people approach buffets - sampling everything, lacking self-restraint, and returning often despite the consequences. As the one Sicilian male with three sisters, he had felt enormous pressure from his family and fell far short of their expectations. He often took unannounced trips -- traveling as far as Florida and Haight-Ashbury in California. After a long interchange with hospitals, he was finally diagnosed with schizophrenia. No one knows whether it was the drugs that created the condition (he had "dropped acid" by his own account over 300 times) or whether he actually had the condition and was self-medicating. His condition was just starting to worsen at the time we left.

My mother had quit school when she became pregnant at 16. My parents married slightly before I was born. My grandparents, unhappy with many events that had unfolded in New York, took the opportunity to move when a job offer came up for my grandfather. Unfortunately, after they moved to Virginia, my grandfather was laid off. It was hard for them to cope with the disappointing changes, but rescuing my mother and I seemed to offer them hope and opportunity to rejuvenate.

My grandparents' life was in stark contrast to the life that I experienced during the early years of life. They were typical of the "Great Generation." Grandpa had served in World War II and when he returned, they married. At that time, he was a handsome and lean man with a striking combination of dark hair, dark eyes, and endless wit. My grandmother was the perfect beautiful match with the popular short hairstyle of the time, friendly brown eyes, rosy cheeks, and a wide smile reflecting cherry red lips and white teeth.

Nanu often proudly announced that she was a virgin when she and my grandfather were married. They raised two daughters. My grandmother worked in the cafeteria while her children went to school. She set the table and had a well-balanced dinner on the table every night by 5 p.m. They attended church every Sunday. They volunteered with the Elks, the Masons, and other civic groups.

When I was a child, she always found time for me. She helped me make mud pies, played "bounce the ball" with me, played endless games of Yahtzee and Trouble with me, took long walks with me, and provided answers for all my questions. As I grew up, she became my friend.

My mother and I lived there until my mother married my stepfather. I was in first grade when we moved out. But many, many days and weeks I took opportunity to stay there. When I was 18, I returned to live there for the first two years of college. I was married briefly for one year and it was to my grandparents' home that I returned the night I left my husband. At one point, they converted their living room into a one-room apartment for me. Their house represented everything that means "home" to me -- warm, comfortable, strong, safe. But this sanctuary had been one more place where silence was perpetuated.

When I had moved into my grandmother's home at 18, I told her what had happened to me. She comforted me, told me how strong I was, and cried. She said many times over the years that she wanted to confront my stepfather and my mother. She was adamant that a woman should always choose her children over her husband.

But the downfall of the "great generation" is that they wanted to maintain the image for which they had worked so hard. The confrontation never really materialized. My mother spent nearly every lunch hour at my grandmother's house, but soup and sandwiches don't seem to be swallowed well with conversation about molestation. Because of the close relationship that my mother had with my grandmother, I knew that it would be important to tell my grandmother what had happened before anyone else did.

My grandmother and I had a little routine. Even though I had a key, I liked to pound on the thick hickory door and tuck the clanging doorbell switch back and forth many times. She would stand at the door and stare at me through the window. She would take a long time to open it, asking me "what do you want?" as if I were a stranger. Then we would typically sit down at the small round imitation brown marble kitchen table and enjoy whatever healthy snacks and tea were available.

Today I sat down and told her, "I've got something to tell you. I just came back from pressing charges against Mickey for child abuse."

Nanu, as I called her, was shocked. I explained to her that I had recently been visited by my friend Katie, whose uncle worked with (and despised) Mickey. Katie had told me many stories. How Mickey would come into the office and tell the young receptionist that he had had dreams of her the night before. How he would disappear at lunch with other young girls. How he was inappropriate at a company party and my mother stormed out of the party, embarrassed. And the worst -- how Katie's mother suspected him of harassing her after Katie's father died.

We were in Junior High when a number of tragic events were faced by Katie's family. Her mother had been stoking their woodstove with pine logs that ignited the flue and caught the roof on fire. As a result, Katie and her family lived amongst relatives and friends for several months. Katie stayed with me often during this time. It was also during this time that Mr. Foster developed Hodgkin's disease. After about a year or so of suffering through chemotherapy, he died at age 39. Shortly after his death, strange occurrences began to happen around the Foster home.

We lived in what someone recently called a "hollow." Now Linden, Virginia has become a yuppie countryside retreat for transplants from Northern Virginia and Washington D.C. But when we were growing up, the graffiti on the rocks at the entrance of Blue Mountain across the road described it accurately as "Hell Town." At that time, I didn't realize that this was a proud nickname for many small Virginia towns.

In Linden, there were several clusters of homes joined by a haphazard design of paved, gravel, and dirt roads that often provided only one way in and one way out. Most of the people at that time were related to one another. My family and Katie's family were the only "outsiders" in our neighborhood -if you can even call it a neighborhood. Her house was several acres behind my house. Once a makeshift elementary school before the organization of the public schools, her home large and bordered by a rippling freshwater creek, a large grassy yard, and a spattering of woods and brush which provided significant camouflage for the home in the summer. Mostly isolated woods, farmland, and orchard land provided the other borders for her house.

On more than one occasion, Katie's mom (Valerie) returned to her house to find certain things out of order. She strongly suspected that someone had been in and around the house while she wasn't there. One night in the middle of the night, a loud screaming noise awoke the family. And one day, she received a phone call. "Is Robert there?" the male voice on the other end of the line asked. Then he laughingly said, "Oh, that's right ... he's dead." Valerie had recently confided to Katie that she had recognized the person on the phone that day as my stepfather, Mickey. And she suspected him of tampering with the house.

Years later, Valerie remarried and moved to Staunton. One day in the mail, she received an anonymous card. She only described it as "disgusting," and destroyed it. Katie's uncle had mailed something to Valerie from his office. Now they thought that perhaps it was possible that Mickey had seen the address and used it to mail the offensive correspondence. Katie's family was very old-fashioned, religious, and good. They weren't the type of people to gossip or embellish the truth.

When I originally heard this information from Katie, I began to believe it was time to press charges. I asked Katie to talk to her stepfather, a retired law enforcement officer, about what to do. Through Katie, he encouraged me to press charges, and referred me to Otis. The day we -- my mother, grandmother, and I -- had been visiting in her kitchen a few weeks ago, my mother had said she was going "antiquing." And it was these trivial few words that spoke volumes to me -- after everything she knew and everything that she didn't know -- she wasn't going to leave on her own.

I let Nanu read the statement I had provided to Otis. When she finished, she just shook her head. I told her that I didn't know when they were going to arrest Mickey, but I thought that they were going to move rather quickly with the case. It was Wednesday and I expected an arrest by the weekend. There are many traits my parents have passed down to me. One of the most prevalent is delusion.

CHAPTER 3

It was Friday. My step-sons Terry (age 12) and Justin (age 9) were with us for the weekend and we were enjoying our typical Pizza Hut specials. I happened to look out the window at the Crown gas station across the street. I saw the black Ford 4x4 first and then my step-father. My heart began to thump and I wondered if he knew yet. He looked rather unassuming as he fueled his vehicle.

My weekend went on with normal activities of cleaning and watching T.V., joined by nightmares, and obsessions over what was going to happen. On Sunday, the phone rang and I looked at the caller i.d. Caller i.d. had meant the elimination of the prank phone calls that had plagued me since I moved out of my parents' home. For many years, I suspected that my step-father was at the root of the calls. On one occasion, soon after I got caller i.d., I even received a hang-up phone call from Shenandoah Quarry, my stepfather's workplace. Today I recognized the number on the display as my parents' number. In a normal household, this would mean nothing -- it perhaps is an average and expected occurrence. But my parents almost never called me and I knew that the phone call meant they knew. I didn't pick up the phone and they didn't leave a message.

I called my grandmother immediately.

"Did you tell Aunt Cathy that I had pressed charges?"

"Yes," she replied.

"Why?" I asked.

"Because I thought she should know."

"Well, she apparently called my parents and now they know. So when the police call, he won't be surprised."

"Well, I'm sorry. I didn't know she would do that."

I did. Aunt Cathy and I had had a volatile relationship for as long as I could remember. She was the eldest of my grandmother's two daughters and some of the issues between us seemed to be originated in jealousy (on her part). Years of hard living and turmoil had turned the once-vivacious, olive-skinned GOGO dancer into a pudgy, gray-haired squawk.

At one time, she also lived with my grandmother at the same time that my mother and I did. My first memory of her is when she was packing to move out. I asked her where she was going and she said that she was getting married. It wasn't long after that her daughter Rachel was born. I remember riding home in the car with her from the hospital. The baby was crying and to the baby she asked, "Do you want a hamburger?" It is funny how silly little things like that stick in your memory. I remember she always had a revolving door of vehicles -- 1970's hotrods or 1950's derby cars. Her husband was well-known within the town -- well-known because of his altercations with the police. Within a couple of years of Rachel, Randy Jr. was born.

As I child, I was only vaguely aware of what went on in the Pearson household. In the middle of the night, Aunt Cathy would gather her sleepy children into the jalopy of the day and cruise through town in an attempt to find their father. He had at least one girlfriend. There was one time when my mother and I visited Cathy. She had a black eye and had asked Randy Sr. to leave. He was only gone briefly.

Nanu and I often joked about Randy Sr. He never came to any family functions -- not even Christmas. He was a man of few words -- so few that one wondered if he could speak. But my grandmother felt that he was a decent financial provider –- citing the money and gifts that he contributed to his children on birthdays and holidays. But it was quickly apparent that for at least one of his children, money and gifts would not be enough to satisfy what was really needed.

I remember Randy Jr. having behavioral problems from a very early age. Aunt Cathy worked as a cashier at the local Safeway -- earning quite a reputation for her lack of customer service people skills. Because of her shifts, it was necessary for her to schedule a variety of family members to serve as daycare providers. My grandmother was scheduled quite often. She was dismayed at the children's behavior -- they would fight constantly and instigate mischief.

Randy Jr. was nearly 18 months old when he climbed onto a card table and fell off, cracking his skull open. For months, his blonde hair remained shaved short, displaying a wide scar. His chronic cough, mucous-laden nose, and generally indecipherable speech presented a few clues that he would face tremendous barriers in his later life. There was a statistic I once heard that indicated that one third of all men in prison suffered a head injury at some point in their lives. By the time Randy Jr. was age 3, I knew he was on his way to jail. And I was only 9 years old.

By age 3, he learned to express his anger by grabbing a knife out of the kitchen and threatening to stab me. In Kindergarten, he would get under the table and try to bite the teacher. Although his intelligence was there -- he won a school-wide math contest in 2nd grade -- his scholastic intelligence was overshadowed by what he was learning socially at home. As a teenager, I spent at least one summer babysitting Randy Jr. and Rachel. I spent most of my time raiding the refrigerator, stocked well from my aunt's savvy couponing in the days before it was in vogue. Other time was spent watching "Days of our Lives" and playing Pac Man with the Atari game system my cousins had received from Santa. I allowed Randy Jr.to run in and out of the house so that we would have minimal confrontations. At the time, I believed this was good enough supervision and survival on my part for the hourly dollar wage.

By 8th grade, Randy Jr. was no longer allowed to come to school. He did attend an alternative boy's outward bound program, but was asked to leave. The reasons were never confirmed to me, although my mother at some point mentioned that the words "homosexual acts" were used in correlation with whatever had occurred. He had private tutors until he graduated.

Holidays were especially taxing for all of us. We all gathered around the polished dark maple table that was stocked with a warm fresh buffet and provided comfortable seating for our 9-person gang. Following grace and good tidings, the meal and conversation would commence. The talking escalated in volume and speed and before long, Randy Jr. would say something and Aunt Cathy would fire back a retort. Then Randy Jr. would respond with a shout and storm out the front door. Aunt Cathy would huff and then dinner would resume to a calmer atmosphere, with general silence about what had just occurred.

Counseling was recommended many times, but Randy Jr. would spend his counseling sessions in silence. Randy Sr. refused to come to any family counseling sessions. And Aunt Cathy focused much of her energy in blaming the school system. At Christmas, Aunt Cathy always searched to ensure that her children had the latest, greatest gifts. She meticulously priced out their gift lists to ensure that they were provided with exactly (to the penny) the same value of gifts. But she did not put that same energy into finding the help that Randy Jr. needed. Eventually he was diagnosed with a personality disorder. Following graduation, he began to be involved with a crime circle that typically engaged in petty theft and grand larceny. Eventually, he took up fairly regular residency in jail until age and fatherhood provided more distraction.

Rachel was a stark contrast to her brother. She had the dark hair and olive skin of her mother, but a very quiet demeanor. As a teen, she also found refuge at our grandmother's house. One day, she became significantly distraught and locked herself in the bathroom at my grandmother's house. My aunt's screams and my grandmother's pleas were met with Rachel's cries to leave her alone.

The local mental health crisis counselor was called and tried to coax her out. Later, it would be apparent that this incident was probably a result of pregnancy. During her senior year, Rachel became pregnant. As she grew larger and larger, she swore that she was not pregnant – just gaining weight. She denied the pregnancy until she was 6 months along.

Meanwhile, I grew up hiding abuse through overachievement. I was congenial, pleasant, and intelligent. I made excellent grades. I was actively involved in civic groups, school activities, and leadership opportunities. The press covered my activities well. And I became the first and only one from my immediate family to graduate from college.

Because of my relationship with my grandparents, I seemed more like their last child than a grandchild -they were in their 40's when they were actively involved in supporting and raising me. I reaped all of the joys of being the first grandchild - although in actuality, I was not. When they lived in New York, Aunt Cathy was briefly married. Many times I snooped through my grandmother's personal papers – trying to find clues to my father and other aspects of life that I feared were being kept from me. At some point, I found evidence that Cathy had abandoned her infant son and left him with her first husband, who was of questionable character.

It seemed that Aunt Cathy's jealousy could have originated out of modified sibling rivalry, the comparison between her children and myself, the loss of her own child, and/or issues of which I wasn't even aware. I did have some fond memories of being a small child and cruising with her in her jalopies. And I certainly appreciated her personality when I needed support. But these were counterbalanced by many times when her boisterousness and hasty judgments left me silent or distraught. It was quite common for her to refer to local girls as "whores" and to find fault in the local school system, the police, and any other individual or group that she felt had failed her.

Before I married the first time, all of the women - Nanu, my mother, Aunt Cathy, Rachel, and I -- went shopping for bridesmaids' dresses. For most of the day, Aunt Cathy kept nagging me about the importance of getting payment for the dresses from the bridesmaids. While on the surface this sounds trivial, I felt that she was really attacking my friend Jenny – the only non-family-member in the wedding. The confrontation built to a point where I broke down in Manassas Mall, crying uncontrollably and yelling at her to stop. My mother tried to calm me down. My voice echoed in the open airway outside of Leggett's and the small crowd resting on the public benches stared with interest. At that time, I didn't care. I found out later that Rachel defended me, telling her mother that she had pushed too much.

Aunt Cathy's advice to me came neatly hand-written on the card with her wedding gift: "Marriage is <u>a lot</u>

of give and take." Ultimately, I came to realize that this statement probably held more significance for her in her life – I would never fully know what she had given up in her life. Once bright and attractive, my aunt was now abrasive and bitter. But she would serve some very important purposes over the next few years. She would force me to stand strong in my convictions to bring the abuse out in the open. She would serve as the support system for my mother. And she would be the link between my mother and grandmother while all other communication between them was severed.

CHAPTER 4

I spent the next week digging deep into my treasure chest to find the diaries and journals that could capture any of the events relevant to my charges. I searched frantically for the diary I remembered very well -the 5-year diary that I had received in 4th grade (the year I was molested). It was cobalt blue with a tiny lock opened by an imitation skeleton key.

At this particular time, I still had every card, every letter, every scrap of meaningful correspondence for my entire life. But I couldn't find my diary. I did find the one-year diary that covered my very painful junior high years and the journals that gave insight into a mind that was depressed and at times suicidal. However, nothing specifically alluded to the molestation.

I also contacted my two friends -- Jenny and Katie -- who I knew would be willing to come forward and make a statement on my behalf. In actuality, there were many people who knew about the abuse, but few that I felt comfortable contacting to burden with involving in a process of criminal prosecution.

Katie and I were riding on the school bus when I told her. Later, she approached her mother, who sent message to me to tell my mother. In those days, this was quite a proactive response and Valerie's mother thought my mother would handle the situation. The following year, I made a new friend, Deena. She spent the night with me a few times and I shared my experiences with her. In Junior High, I shared my story with two of my friends, Kathy and

Melanie. The year I graduated, I broke down in my Communications class after watching a show on suicide and shared my experience with the entire class, including the teacher. I told my friend Jenny in college and my friends Patty and Tara at my first job. I told my first husband, Jackson, just before we began to date. I also told my current husband, Warren, just before we started to date.

For all those whom I told, there were probably twice as many who perhaps could have realized the situation if they had just paid attention and asked the right questions. Looking back, there were many subtle signs. I stayed gone as much as I could - staying at friends' houses, being involved in as many activities as possible, staying at my grandmother's house, working.

In retrospect, I think that I was an easy target for men with predatory tendencies. I remember visiting the Washington Zoo with my elementary class when I was young. As I looked at displays, I suddenly felt a man pressing up against me from behind. I moved to another display. He followed me and did the same thing. Eventually, I was able to distance myself from him.

At the Country Club pool, Katie and I had noticed a man sitting by the side of the pool with his legs positioned so that his penis was revealed to us on several occasions. I approached my friend, Carson, who was working at the pool that summer.

"Carson, who is that man sitting by the pool,"I asked. "That's my dad. Why?"
I was shocked and grinned in a combination of

embarrassment and defeat.

"No reason," I said. Carson gave me a strange look and then let it go.

I varied between reclusive behavior and somewhat sexualized behavior. One of my friends and I chose to do a mock strip tease for our "planet". For activities and schedules, several classes at the intermediate school were grouped and named for each planet. I had the same teacher in 5th and 6th grades. Mr. Krepske was a kind man with light brown hair and a full beard who constantly encouraged me in my school work. I insisted on giving back massages to him, as well as a few of the boys in my class. Besides this being a strange and inappropriate classroom activity, it should also have been unnerving that a 5th or 6th grader would know how to give a massage so well. In another situation, I sat across from a young man, Richie Tharpe, who I allowed to make "vroom vroom" sounds as he pressed his foot on an imaginary gas pedal between my legs.

Shortly after the abuse, I spent a lot of time drawing. If my grandmother or anyone else in the family had been more observant about what I was doing, they would have noticed that all of the Indians in the tribe I was drawing were naked and that I spent a lot of time perfecting the details of their private parts.

In high school, I was frequently called a 'tease'. It was nothing for me to flirt and imply a potential relationship with someone, only to stop the line cold. It was before the era of phone sex and sexting. And so it was typical for me to engage in writing detailed sexual fantasy letters with a few of my close male friends -- again, fantasy that didn't end in any sexual reality. Through these tactics, I could remain preserved and in control of my own body and relationships.

As a teenager, I suffered frequent headaches and what I now know was depression. I was intrigued by death and the supernatural – the world beyond made more sense than the world I lived in. In 8th grade, we were assigned a project of collecting and analyzing newspaper articles with a certain theme. I chose the theme of "death."

That same year I also grew my hair very long. A boy running down the hall chose to grab my attention and a fistful of my hair as he ran by me. I felt a clump rip from my head and then melt to the floor as if I had been a victim of radiation poisoning. I felt nauseous. As I began to date, I often chose "bad boys", different boys, or boys with problems -- feeling that I could save them or take care of them.

For several years, I and my fellow 4-Hers in the county would take the four hour journey by bus to Virginia Tech to attend what was called "4-H Congress". 4-Hers from around the state came together for competitions, seminars, and recreation. Many formed romantic relationships for the week. I chose to date a boy whose hair was dyed white in the middle but remained dark on the sides. His nickname was "skunk." I thought he was cute and unique.

In another instance, I decided to go out with a boy

named Winston who asked me out when I was visiting the local Caverns. He was a tour guide and his soft curly hair and insecurity appealed to me. Later, when I shared with a friend that I was going to go out, she told me that her father said he had the worst reputation in school and wondered why I was going out with him. I felt like Winston had a good heart. Because of what my friend said, I regretted my decision. Rather than cancel the date, I went with him and two others on a double date but chose to be rude and closed off.

Another boy of interest was an artist with perfectly winged blonde hair and deep blue eyes. I flirted with him and constantly positioned myself near him during school until he finally kissed me and asked me out. The night we went out, he had a party and ignored me for much of the party. Before taking me home, he chose to take me parking. He made a game out of jerking my head back by my hair so that he could forcefully kiss me.

I also made insane choices regarding my safety. My first job was at a bowling alley, where I worked as the snack bar attendant. It afforded me a wealth of education -- probably similar to that afforded to a bartender --about the diversity of our human race. It also afforded me some freedom from home because of the flexible late night schedule. Every Friday night was "Moonlight Bowling,"where bowling went on until the wee hours of the morning.

I was working the Moonlight shift one night when two young guys approached me. I knew them somewhat from school -- they had a reputation of doing drugs and being generally on the fringe of what would be considered acceptable teenage behavior. They told me they were hungry and asked me if I could go to their house after I got off of work and fix them a pizza.

My shift ended a little earlier than usual and I took them in my beat-up primer grey Mustang Ghia to Apple Mountain. At that time, a number of houses were just being built for the local commuters who were finding their peace in woodland retreats. I walked into their house. There were people sleeping everywhere -- on the couch, on the floor. And there were two small children -- a toddler and a pre-schooler awake watching T.V. in the dark. I popped the instant pizza in the oven, set the temperature, and instructed them to remove the pizza in 20 minutes before I left their house. I had told no one I was going there – if they would have acted on ill intentions, it would have been difficult to trace what happened to me.

My first husband and I dated for several years before marrying. We had befriended two men in their 40's through the bowling alley. Raymond Forrest was a burly man with a ZZ TOP-inspired beard and skin that was hardened from years of construction work. His standard costume was a polo shirt, tennis shorts, and knee socks that clung to his permanently sweating body. He was known for his body odor - but it was something I didn't notice. He also was one of many men who liked to keep a little bottle of Jack Daniels in his locker to inspire his bowling. At that time, the bowling alley didn't serve alcohol. Raymond had been married a few times and had a teenage daughter living with him. Junior was his best friend. Junior was petite, bald, and wore simple black-rimmed glasses. He had never been married and lived quietly alone in one of the few low income apartment complexes.

For several years, this odd pair became our good friends. Raymond actually bowled with my mother and me on a team together during my first year in college. My ex-husband and I often visited Raymond's small two-bedroom house or Junior's apartment. We often played rummy or just spent time talking and watching television. And on more than one occasion, we watched pornographic movies that they had selected. When I left my ex-husband, I distanced myself from the couple and lost track of them. Sometime later, I heard that Raymond had suffered a stroke and eventually died. Junior remained working as a clerk at the local pawn shop until it went out of business. I wonder now at the relationship we all had together -- was it loneliness, general dysfunction, or perhaps just another rare connection of people that can't be explained.

Another bowling alley regular, Russell, took an interest in me. He was a short, African American man in his 40's who seemed marginally employed and unattached. He lived in the next village over from Linden. One evening I was returning home from the moonlight shift. Russell was stopped at the post office with his car hood up. I stopped to see if he was o.k. He said he was just checking his car and wanted to talk to me anyway.

"I wanted to see if you wanted to come back to my

place and have a few drinks with me."

"No, thanks, I really don't drink and it's pretty late. I need to get home. Besides, I really don't think that my boyfriend would like that." Finally, by age 17, I was learning to pay attention to my inner warning bells.

"Jackson? Well, I heard that you all were having problems."

"No, we're not having problems."

"I heard that he beats you."

"What? Who told you that?"

"I'm not going to say, but that's what I heard."

"Oh my gosh, that's not true!" I exclaimed.

Finally, he accepted that I wasn't going to go with him. I eventually told Jackson, who laughed before becoming furious and confronting him. Russell never approached me like that again.

On another occasion, I was leaving Jackson's house where he lived with his parents until our marriage. It was night and I saw a young man who was sitting near the parking area next to the railroad tracks. His car hood was up. Knowing it could be quite a long time before another car ventured by, I stopped my car and asked if he needed help. He told me his car was broken down and asked if I could take him to his relative's house. The address he gave was on one of the more deserted roads outside of town. Again, I escaped what could have been a potentially terrible situation had the rider had other intentions for me.

Another of my bowling alley relationships was with Calvin. Calvin was around 6 feet tall, a stocky man in his early 30's. He had soft, thinning, auburn hair, a wild go-T, and various missing teeth. He always tried to talk rather gently to me. He and I started riding around town after my shifts at the alley. He would share all sorts of stories with me. He had a rather predominantly arched stiff back that seemed to end rather abruptly just above his hips. He told me that when he was a baby, his father had bent him nearly in two. He also told me about his relationship with his wife. They had an on-again-off-again relationship and he claimed that she cheated on him with a man that beat her. He said that for years, she wouldn't allow him to ejaculate inside of her and that he would keep a towel handy for this purpose after sex. He claimed that every morning he left a fresh rose on her pillow. His wife eventually found out that we were riding around together. One day I entered the 7-11 where she worked and she said to her co- worker, "Calvin wants me to have a baby." I'm sure she was saying it for my benefit, but I ignored her. I had already found excuses to stop the rides with Calvin.

There were so many older men who seemed to take an interest in me and provide me with attention. Another man brought his child with him to Moonlight Bowling so that she could see me. At two years old, she had a full head of thick and curly black hair which was often knotted. Her father would put her on the counter and I would hold her, talk to her, and brush her hair. She quickly became attached to me and would often cry when he would try to take her home. With tears in his eyes, he would say, "I wish you were her mother." He was a short, bald-haired, unemployed married man in his 40's. His wife was the primary breadwinner, supporting the family through her work at a local convenience store.

At that point in time, I was enjoying all of this attention. I thought that these men trusted me with their stories. I felt good and important that they were seeing me as an attractive and mature person (even though I was significantly younger than them). I felt kind and helpful because I was able to listen to them, provide them with attention, and validate their feelings. Today, I wonder how many of them would be classified as sexual predators.

In college, one of my degrees was English and I earned a reputation for proclaiming a sexual interpretation for many of the readings. I also had many writings and my poetry in particular reflected my subtle torment. Poetry was safe -- it could release the emotion but offer an elusive story so that the blatant details of my abuse experience remained hidden. My first year in college, I entered a poem in the annual college contest.

Childhood

I.   *Innocent child*
         With wondrous eyes
         Looks unprejudiced at the world.
         You offer your small, pudgy hand
         Easily, trustingly
         To those who beg of it.
         Your soft, smooth skin
         Is pure cream;

No wrinkles or scars
Hinder the tranquility.
You have simple satisfaction.
Your heart mirrors love.

Innocent child
Clings to mother's full bosom.
Seeking attention if not love.
Your hair, soft, true
Shines in new knowledge,
Glimmers in misinterpretation.
Your tears are physical,
Delicate, sweet.
You dream of slow maturation,
Though childhood is happiness.

II.   *Dark man*
Torments by evils inherited,
Focuses his cold stare intently
Upon the innocent child.
Your memory rewinds
Past empty wallets,
Past female exploration,
Past primary glandular confusion.
The pain of your childhood
Thunders through your body,
Haunts your mind,
Puppets your hands.
Dark man

Realizes the sin, but helplessly
Continues the terrible tradition.
You beg forgiveness;
Living daily hells.
Your victim rewards you this,
But never forgets –
Your poking, prodding fingers
Permanently enthrust
Lifelong agony.

III.   *Tormented child*
With pained eyes
Looks confusingly at the world.
You withdraw your still-smooth hand
From those who beg of it.
Your soft skin
Is still smooth,
Yet hidden scars
Replace the tranquility.
New questions kill
Your once-easy satisfaction.
Your heart is no longer transparent.
Innocent child
Still clings to mother's bosom,
Though she ignores your sadness.
Your hair, still baby soft,
Has grown dark with new knowledge
That was thrust upon you.
Your tears are now mental,

Angry, depressing.
You were forced into adulthood
Into wonderment of what you will pass on.
Childhood is our recurring nightmare.

It didn't win. In addition to needing some work, I suspect it was a probably too heavy and unsettling for the judges.

As I entered the workforce, I found myself more than once the victim of sexual harassment and I had no skills to deal with this other than avoidance and so I would quit the jobs.

Despite all of this, the abuse essentially remained silent. While I received a good deal of empathy and support, I lacked the guidance and resources to stop the abuse. A true end to the silence would have begun with words that would confront my family -- the words I was now finding.

CHAPTER 5

I placed all of my documents in a large manila envelope, along with the contact information for Katie and Jenny. I also enclosed information for an additional contact -- Richard Monroe. Richard had been a friend of my step-father for many years. He owned a small-time catering restaurant and had been recently released from jail. He had taken the fall for a local drug dealer and his reward was a small country estate. While renovating, he had unwittingly hired my husband to install tile throughout the house.

Frequently the men engaged in conversation. When Richard realized the connection, he asked my husband, "Did you ever hear anything about Mickey doing anything to Meredith?" My husband said no, but conveyed the information to me immediately. The information could only have come to Richard through Mickey and I wondered why Mickey would talk about this. I had no idea of what Richard had heard, but I would be interested to see what the police could find out.

A little over a week later, Otis finally called me with news. "I met with your step-father. I'd like for you to come in."

I reunited with Otis in the little interview room where I had first shared my story with him.

"What did he say?" I eagerly asked.

"Well, he didn't admit to anything. But he skirted around the answers. For instance, he would say things like, 'Well, I might have accidentally thrown a brick and it hit a cat in the head...' I asked him if he would be willing to take a lie detector test, and he said he would have to think about it."

I held my breath as I asked, "What did you think?"

"Oh, he's definitely guilty. No question about it."

I felt so validated by having an outside stranger hear the two stories and believe me. His next words would deflate me.

"A few days after I questioned him, I received a call from John Gerard." John Gerard was a local attorney. Otis continued.

"Mr. Gerard told me that unless I was prepared to press charges, I was not allowed to question his client (Mickey) any more, or your mother. I tried to see if I could at least offer the option to your mother to voluntarily talk with me, but her attorney indicated that she didn't want to talk about the incident."

"What did you think about my journals?" I asked.

"Well, I probably read more than I was supposed to. You do write well. Some of these parts that you call "free" or "random" writing really give insight bow you were feeling. I saw where you got "A's" all of the time on your writing -- I'm not sure I ever got an "A" in my life."

"Did you speak to Richard Monroe?" I asked.

"I did, but he said he doesn't know you and doesn't know what you are talking about."

"Did you tell him that my husband did a tile job for him?"

"I think so, but he just doesn't want to talk."

"So what happens now?" I asked.

"If you can get your friends to come and make a statement, then we'll give all of this stuff to the Commonwealth Attorney and go from there. I'm going to need a statement from you -- something that tells about the effect that the abuse has had on you. You know what I mean."

Because I was volunteering at the women's shelter at the time, Otis presumed that I knew about victim impact statements and what was needed for such a statement. I had no idea what he needed or what would be helpful, but this is what I created:

Statement

I have been asked to provide a statement explaining why I am now coming forth to press charges against my stepfather, Mickey Walter Williams, for sexual molestation which occurred when I was 10 years old I find it extremely difficult to write this, partly because I know that what I say has a definite bearing on whether or not the case makes it to court.

There are several "logical" reasons why I am doing this now. First, I have accepted the fact that child molesters do not change. I believe that given the opportunity, he would engage in some sort of abusive behavior toward another individual. My silence would indirectly make me an accessory and I would not want the guilt that this could happen to someone else and I didn't do all I could to prevent it.

Second, I have "grown up" and finally realized that

he is not the upstanding individual in the community as I once thought. I had always rationalized that maybe what happened to me was only an isolated incident and that if I brought it out in the open, I would ruin his life. I had to come to terms with the fact that the molestation was the least of the issues surrounding the abuse. I suffered emotional and mental abuse for years which is enough justification to press charges.

Third, I thought that pressing charges against him would somehow alleviate any guilt which I believed he was feeling for his actions, as well as relief for myself. Because he has denied the charges and his attorney is not allowing questioning for him or my mother, I am now angry, disgusted, and disillusioned. I thought that this would give both him and my mother the opportunity to redeem themselves. I was naive.

Emotionally and mentally, there are several other reasons why I am now coming forward. I was always a model student in school. In the years following the molestation -when I was a teenager and suffered the frequent mental/emotional abuse (i.e. manipulation, inappropriate conversation, sexual harassment) – I threw myself into school. I probably owe my exceptional academic record to my parents. My self-esteem was so low at home that I took great satisfaction in the instantaneous rewards which school provides. The constant verbal and written words of encouragement kept me going through the years. I became involved in several extracurricular activities at school -- anything to keep busy and stay away from home. I can remember two things very clearly from those years: I couldn't wait to turn 18 so that I could leave home and I hated any time when we were off from school due to bad weather or holidays. I lived for school. I realize now that it was probably my latching on to school, as well as the positive relationships with my grandparents, that saved me.

The bitterness really settled in when I was 14. My boyfriend and I had been doing some "heavy petting" at my home on a few occasions when my parents had gone out. I had told my friend, Katie, and out of concern that I might get pregnant, she confided in her mother who in turn called my mother. After a grueling interrogation where my stepfather seemed to get great pleasure out of finding out all of the sordid details, I was grounded for 8 months with no T.V., no phone, and minimal attendance at clubs in which I was involved. What I still remember about this was how often he took the opportunity to remind me that he could press charges against my boyfriend for statutory rape. For many months, I felt like trash. I became very religious and began to view sex as evil. What angered me was that I had consented to what I did with my boyfriend and at the time, loved him. Yet what my stepfather did to me was not consensual and there appeared to be no punishment for that. The night of the interrogation, I took 7 Tylenol. The following night, I took quite a few (although I think it was less than 7). I always have remembered it as a suicide attempt, but I'm not sure that I really wanted to die as much as I wanted the problems to go away. I told my friend Katie about this. I'm not sure if it was through this route or by clear observation Tylenol were missing that my mother found out about this. She confronted me about it and I never did it again. I have not disclosed this information to a great number of people. It is not something of which I am proud. I am only disclosing it now so that you can get a sense of the hopelessness I felt at that time and at many other times throughout the years -even though I never tried it again.

It took me many years to find words to describe the situation with my mother. "Betrayal" is the first word. For years I rationalized why she didn't leave my stepfather. I believed it was because she had been married before and didn't want to face another divorce. I believed that she was staying in the marriage for my brother (even though choosing one child over the other is wrong). I believed these things up until a month ago, when I found out that my parents had refused questioning on this matter. Now I know that my mother may be staying with him just to remain in the comfortable life she has created. It takes a lot of work to leave any marriage. I guess it's not worth the effort to her and that hurts me. I believe it's a blatant betrayal of me to stay with him. And I have decided that it is unacceptable to include anyone in my life who openly betrays me -it's like saying "It's o.k to treat me like trash." It's not o.k., no matter who it is.

I have never understood the concept of "unconditional love" by a parent. I have experienced great love and support by my grandparents, but they are not my parents. I am 27 years old and this is the time when ideally most women are growing close to their mothers. I remember when I divorced my first husband, I was doing the deposition. My mother was serving as a witness for the deposition. The attorney was asking her how long she had known me. He made a comment somewhat to the effect that she had known me all her life, sometimes I went to her house and sometimes she came to my house to visit. We testified to that fact - although "sometimes" was a stretch. I have lived in my new house since April. My mother has not been here since I moved in. I lived in my house in town for three years. I think my mother may have been there two to three times. I believe that I have been to her house less than 5 times since I moved away from home when I was 18.

I look at other people with envy. I remember I had a friend whose mom was at every school function and always looked so proud of her daughter. I had no doubts that this woman loved her daughter. I had doubts all the time that my mother loved me. I remember my boyfriend and I discussing the abortion issue when I was in high school. I thought that my mother had wanted to abort me, but didn't because of my grandparents. I thought that maybe she should have because it was obvious she didn't want me. When I spoke to my grandmother about this, she reassured me that my mother had chosen to keep me and get married.

When I was 18, I would have been willing to have 10 children. I think that I wanted so many children because I wanted people in my family who I knew would love me. As I grew older and began to see the complex issues surrounding children, I realized that I wanted to be as prepared as possible to be a perfect parent before I had any children. My delay in having children is due in part to my continued education and career aspirations. Underlying issues remain. How would I explain to my children the relationship I have with my mother and stepfather? How would I explain to my children that they could never spend the night or stay alone with my mother and stepfather? And now, how would I explain to my children where their grandmother is (since she's not speaking to me or my grandparents)? I don't want deception for any lives I create.

In the past few years, I have been working on resolving all of my issues. I was reunited with my father, who is mentally ill. I was in a minor car accident which scared me. I had to have an AIDS test (which fortunately came out negative) because one of my former clients bit me. All of these things combined with other experiences have given me this sense of urgency regarding my life. I don't know how long I will be on this earth. I am not going to waste a single minute doing something which I don't want to do. I also am going to resolve all of my issues so that my conscience is clear and I can go forward with my life.

For years I had to sit through family functions knowing what had happened and pretending everything was o.k. It is a family pattern within my family to smile and make everything appear o.k even when something is dreadfully wrong. Unpleasant things are swept under the

*rug. I have adopted this for most of my life. For years, I
wasn't in touch with my emotions. I always kept a wall up
and pushed the anger and hostility down. I only broke
down once publicly (that I remember). It was in my last
year in school and we had watched a movie on suicide.
Moved by the movie (especially because a friend of mine
had tried to commit suicide that year), I raised my hand. I
was barely able to get the words out, but I said something
to the effect that I hated it when no one believed me
(referring to the abuse). I also gave a speech that year on
how I lived with a stepfather I almost hated. I still do keep
an emotional wall up, in many respects. I have detached
myself from a lot of the emotions connected to the
memories – I still have the fear that if I were to let go
completely, I would never stop crying. I guess it was
through taking Family Therapy class and analyzing my
own family as a project that I began to see our family
patterns emerge. And I realized that I needed to face my
issues head-on in order to break the cycle.*

*For 17 years I have carried this burden. I kept
telling people along the way, but it seemed that no one
helped me. I know that ultimately, I needed to be the person
to resolve the issues. I don't really know what I would have
liked for anyone to do. I just know that I don't like the way
the situation was handled by anyone, including myself. I
have these lingering feelings of abandonment. I have
turned into a very controlling person. I try to keep my
career, education, and home in order. Since the only
person I can trust 100% is myself, I have learned to rely on*

myself for most issues and have tried to build a strong support system around myself.

I resent that I have to give out all of my personal information for examination and judgment. I don't like to be viewed as a victim. I don't want to blame all of my mistakes on my stepfather or say that my parents are responsible for my actions. However, I realize that the only way to have people believe me (unfortunately) is to show them the emotional scars. I recognize that there are definitely some patterns of behavior that came out of my situation. I also recognize the physical ailments that may be attributed to the situation. I have suffered headaches (sometimes as many as 4-5 a week), stomach problems, and chest pains during times of high stress. I also have eczema, a skin condition which flares up at times of high stress.

I have always been proud of the fact that I have been a positive member of society. I work 50-60 hours a week (some of which is volunteer). I went farther educationally then most people in this county. I've not gotten in a lot of trouble with the law (with exception of a few speeding tickets). I'm generally nice to people. I keep a nice home and work hard at my marriage.

I have made a lot of mistakes, though. Throughout my teen years, I was scrambling for love wherever I could find it. I especially was attracted to boys who had problems (I liked to help them out). I also was attracted (and still am) to men with large families (I guess it allows me to become involved in the "family I never had"). I married a man for the wrong reasons when I was 20. I had rationalized that if

I first moved in with my grandmother when I was 18 and then married when I was 20, I really wouldn't be marrying to get out of the house. Wrong! My first husband drank too much. We were sexually dysfunctional. We quickly moved into a cycle where I also participated as a non-supportive person. The marriage ended after a year. I don't think I can blame my parents entirely for my failed marriage. However, isn't it ironic that the first man I married drank a lot and I suffered mentally and emotionally? I think so. What is also ironic is that the primary reason that I left him (besides the realization that I loved him, but wasn't "in love" enough to stay with him) was that he wouldn't have sex with me on a regular basis. It may be related to the underlying issue that I used to see almost all men (except for my grandfather, father, and a few others) as having relationships with me that included some level or element of sexuality. My husband not relating to me sexually was a foreign concept to me.

For the past 17 years, I have been busy trying to settle my life. I'm sure people look and say "Why Now?" Things are finally calm enough for me to have the courage to take action. I am scared to death of the repercussions which may come out of my actions. But I really believe that bringing it out in the open like this was the only way to deal with this issue. Anything less would have been sweeping it under the rug again. Also, I have had to deal with an enormous amount of guilt throughout this whole process. I never was neglected financially by my parents. My mother paid for several things for me throughout the years, including my divorce and portions of my two weddings. I always got very nice gifts at Christmas time. But I always felt that it was like "hush money" and that I would be acting ungrateful to create problems for her by exposing what had happened. My stepfather also did several nice things for me. But that could be attributed to the cycle of abuse. My grandparents are having difficulty with the situation. My grandmother's blood pressure is up and my grandfather (who never knew anything until recently) is having difficulty accepting what happened. Both are being very supportive to me, but I know they wish this mess would all disappear.

I keep telling myself that regardless of the outcome of this situation, I will know where I stand and the situation will have closure. However, I do hope that it goes to court. It angers me that I have waited until I was "together" enough to come forward and that may be what is held against me. If I had come to the authorities 17 years ago, he would have been locked up without question. I wouldn't have had to go to the lengths I'm going to now just to be taken seriously. Even if he is found not guilty, at least I will know that the court heard my case. Otherwise, I will view it as one more example of someone not listening to my story. I'm not doing this for money. I'm not doing this for revenge. I'm not doing this because I've finally "snapped" into mental illness. This experience has been nothing short of painfully exhausting for me and many days I am not sure that the rewards (i.e., emotional relief, closure) are going to outweigh the costs.

I have to mull over an issue completely before I make a decision. I do this when I write poetry as well -- I think about the topic for months sometimes before ever writing it down on paper. So to everyone on the "outside," it appears that all of a sudden I create something hastily or make a snap decision. In reality, I have been thinking about it for a very long time and have finally built to action. In this case, because of the depth of the issue, it has taken me 17 years to prepare myself and bring myself to action.

My mother commented to me on more than one occasion that some kids could go through a tough time and still make it out o.k. I often thought she was indirectly disclosing what she thought about me. I think she thought that because I turned out to be a fairly decent person that some of her guilt could be relieved. She didn't see the invisible scars. I don't think she knows about all of the abuse that occurred. I gave this analogy to my grandmother the other day: Sometimes a person may break their arm. It will heal, regardless of whether or not it is set properly. However, if it is not set properly, then it will be ugly and deformed and will necessitate a re-break in order to set it right. Breaking the bone again is very painful, but it must be done if everything is to be done properly. I'm breaking the bone of my family because it has healed in an ugly way. I'm tired of looking at its deformity. I'm going to set it right, no matter how painful it is.

-- Meredith A. Pearson November 13, 1996

CHAPTER 6

I received a phone call from my grandmother's house. She said, "I want you to talk to someone."

A young male voice said, "Hello." It was my half-brother, Jesse. Jesse had been born on my 10th birthday. I had wanted my parents to have a child so badly and was so excited when he was born. I remember how grown-up I felt as my mother would allow me to hold him while she prepared dinner. She would carefully place him in my arms so that his neck was supported and both he and I felt secure. He slept a lot in the early days, but occasionally would look at me with his big blue eyes and offered accidental smiles with his small perfect lips. He provided some joy for me at home, but eventually also additional despair as he encountered some of the same rage from my step-father.

I remember that when I was restricted to my room for 8 months, I spent a lot of time playing with him. One time, he and I were in the bathroom together -- playing some sort of silly game, nothing with nudity, sex, or anything like that. My step-father told me that we needed to get out of the bathroom -- that it didn't look nice for us to be in there together. I remember becoming so enraged that he would accuse us of being deviant when we were doing nothing wrong. On one occasion, my brother picked up a maxi pad out of the closet and put it between his legs. Instead of coming to the conclusion that perhaps he thought it was a diaper, my step-father accused me of changing my pads in front of him.

Siblings living in the same household can have parallel lives, or really experience the same household very differently. It was hard to know how he perceived our common experiences, and what he had experienced when we were apart. Upon returning from 4-H Congress one year, my mother picked up Katie, myself, and Katie's brother from the Greyhound bus stop.

"I've got something to tell you," my mother said. "Patches is dead."

Our first calico cat Tiger had been run over by a motorist -- more than likely by a tourist going to the nearby apple orchards on a crisp October day. There was a general resentment we all had toward the "Apple Pickers", and the accident further incited our negativity. Tiger had been Mickey's cat since before he married my mother and her death was devastating for the family. We soon looked for a replacement pet.

I acquired two kittens from a friend at school. "Ebony" was the black kitten and "Patches" was multi-colored with soft orange, brown, black, and white spots. I asked what happened to Patches and my mother said, "I'm not sure –- I wasn't there when it happened. But I think that Jesse sat on him." I never talked with Jesse about the incident and have wondered to this day what really happened and how it may have impacted him.

We eventually replaced "Patches" with a snow white kitty we called "Ivory." This was followed by Snuffles, a beagle mix. At that time, there were no leash laws where we lived and animals typically frolicked in packs throughout the day until their owners returned home in the evening. The sweet little 6-year-old ran to me for comfort when all his father could offer him was, "Well, that's what happens -- he wanted to chase those other dogs out in the road." I hugged him and cried with him, sad not only for the death of our pet, but for the despair of our life.

Although we were separated by so many years, I felt very close to him when I lived at home. My mother returned to work when he entered kindergarten, and I became his main babysitting source. We were typical siblings in that we loved each other and fought with each other. When I moved out of the house, I became a little more envious of him, as he was beginning to have more luxuries and freedoms than I was offered. He attended a private religious school. My parents often left him with little to no supervision at home. He was showered with clothes and toys -- the benefit of being the only child at home in a two-income family.

In high school and college, I still picked him up on occasion and took him out with me on dates. When I left my first husband, I became a little more distant. On one occasion, he stayed the night with me while I was living with my second husband (before we were married). We were having some issues at the time, and I took Jesse to school early. He was having stomach pains and appeared to be having anxiety. He told me that his father was yelling at him a lot. I felt guilty -- almost like I abandoned him to be at the mercy of our parents.

Now on the phone, our conversation was brief before he asked, "What do the police want with my father?"

"How do you know about this?" I asked.

"I heard Dad playing the messages and an officer left the message that he needed to see him at the police department regarding a situation with his stepdaughter."

"I don't want to talk about this over the phone. Can we meet in person?" I asked.

We arranged to meet at the park-in-ride just outside of town at 5 p.m.the next day. I was surprised to see him pull up with a young girl in the car. She had jet black hair and a slender build. His blonde hair, as usual for these days, was now dyed in a collage of different colors.

"Let's go to Grandma's," I suggested.

When we arrived, I told him that I had contacted the police and maybe the best thing would be for him to read my statement. I took it out of my purse, where I was keeping it for safekeeping. He quietly read it and then laughed at some parts.

"What are you laughing about?" I asked.

"Just the part about the cats. He does tend to knock the cats around."

When he was done reading, he leaned over and began whispering to his girlfriend. She spoke briefly to him. It was all very odd.

"Well, I believe you," he said. He motioned to his girlfriend. "It happened to her, too."

I was shocked at this response. I told him that I had

worried about him and asked him if anything like this had happened to him.

He laughed sarcastically. "No, I would kill him." He then went on to say that recently he had had car trouble and had fully expected to receive a lot of grief from his father when he called to get help, but it was actually his mother that had given him a more difficult response. He said that they often went out together antiquing and that he had no interest in that. He said that they were often gone from home and he barely saw them. His tone varied between cynicism and sarcasm.

I tried to reassure him. "You know, this was my experience. But this is your father and if he was good to you and that has been your experience, then that is o.k.and that should be what you focus on."

"Will he go to jail?" He asked.

I told him that I wasn't sure what would happen, but I didn't think that my stepfather would be going to jail. As he exited, we agreed to keep in touch. I began to worry about his future -- how he would cope knowing that his father was a child molester. I began to realize that the only future I could affect was my own. And I needed to cope knowing that my stepfather was a child molester and that my mother failed to protect me.

The first time I called Miranda Marco, my call was met with an answering machine greeting.

"This is Miranda Marco. Ifyou are experiencing an emergency, please call 911. If you are calling regarding an appointment, please leave your name, number, and a convenient time to call you."

I quickly struggled to find words to leave in a message that indicated my desire to meet with her. Within a day, she returned my call.

"Hello, Meredith. This is Miranda Marco. You wish to schedule an appointment?"

"Yes. I am going to court to press charges against my step-father for abuse and I need to go to counseling." I told her a few details regarding the situation.

"That's very difficult. It sounds like you may be experiencing some depression. I'm happy to meet with you and talk."

"Well, I think I'm probably experiencing more anxiety than depression, but I'm glad we can meet." Somehow in my mind, anxiety held less of a stigma than depression. She and I worked together to set the appointment time.

As I prepared to leave work earlier than usual, my co-worker pressed me to tell her where I was going. Nadia was an attractive Swedish woman with a heavy accent and a light heart. Four year ago, she had met an American while on holiday in South Africa. They married after a whirlwind romance returned to America. He began to be abusive and she was very isolated by the culture and the language.

Eventually, she found the courage to leave him. She was a nurse and had been working as a supervisor in a group home for the mentally retarded prior to working with me at the mental health crisis center. We had both been hired to serve as the coordinators of a new adult program.

We grew close as we went through training together, began hiring our employees, and recruited our clients.

"Come out for a smoke with me," she said when we had opportunity for a break. We took the elevator down to the lobby area and between the visitors coming in and out, I told her a little bit about my situation. She shared with me her story, as well. When I told her I was going to counseling, she asked who I was seeing. When she heard the name, she immediately laughed.

"Oh my God," she said. "That's my shrink. She is very nice. Lindsey sees her also." Lindsey was one of our new employees. Lindsey was a very kind woman who had migrated here from England. I began to feel more comfortable with these references.

I drove into downtown Winchester to the 2-level colonial townhome. I entered and sat in the quiet waiting room, which was set up like a typical living room with a 3-piece beige velour furniture set. A woman came down the stairs and walked out. Soon, another woman followed.

"Are you Meredith?" she asked. I nodded.

"Follow me." She was an attractive woman in her late 30's, with a casual bob hairstyle controlling a bushy bob of black hair. Her demeanor was confident, yet relaxed. She wore an unassuming long flowered dress with ankle boots.

I sat in a large arm chair in her office. She sat across from me in a stylish wing-backed mauve chair. I told her that I was there because I had pressed charges against my step-father and that Otis had referred me. She talked lovingly about Otis. She said that he had a special place in his heart for these issues. She told me that we could meet approximately once a week over 12 weeks and she reassured me that I would heal. She asked that I keep a dream log and bring it with me each week. She also suggested that I read "A Courage to Heal."

I followed the instructions. I went to the library and checked out "A Courage to Heal." I read nearly all of it in a weekend. I hadn't read like this in a long time, practically devouring the pages. I found it so validating and it gave me so much insight into myself and my situation. I also felt challenged. When I got to the chapter that dealt with dissociation during sex, I found that I kept falling asleep. I tried to read it several times, finally getting through it. It was then that I had the realization that this was one of my survivor issues -- during sex I often was mentally somewhere else, thinking of anything but what was going on. And now that I identified the issue, I began to make a concerted effort to overcome this.

CHAPTER 7

My dream logs captured the mental and emotional struggles with which I was dealing.

Dream Log: Wednesday night - November 20, 1996: I went to a counselor (she was Indian -like my eye doctor). She wanted to check my employment references because she didn't believe I worked at the women's shelter.

Dream Log: Thursday night –- 11/21/96: In part of the dream, my grandfather was talking about a son that had died. He said that he (grandpa) had been on T.V. and the son saw him and said, "DaDa in TV." He told about how he takes him to work with him. I remember feeling very sad about this son and also sad that my grandfather had not dealt with the grief because he was referring to the child as still here. My grandmother also was there. I'm not sure who Grandpa was talking to -- perhaps his brother Don. Later, I was very thirsty and kept drinking everywhere I went, but nothing satisfied the thirst completely. I then dreamt that I was in New York City. Grandpa was talking about how you could see celebrities anywhere. Bo Diddly had a place on 68th, according to Grandpa (actually on 66th). I was going to go or did go see him. At some point, I was in an outside area (like a concrete foyer) and a bunch of nurses were there on lunch break and they told me I could eat with them. I think I was with another female. I thought that was nice, but knew that I probably wouldn't. I dreamt that Nadia and I were at a banquet (informal) and were both flirting with a man with whom we work. I noticed my wedding ring and felt guilty. We parked our car at

Judy's house (Judy is an acquaintance through my husband's family). I drove down a snowy road and all of my husband's family was there and a family friend and some children. My sister-in-law Bea was babysitting. I was worried about driving the car on the ice between two ponds. I got out of the car and was worried about falling on the snow. Also about the banquet -- the Executive Director was there and he found papers where I had doodled. I explained I did that on the phone and gave other excuses (he was asking me what I did all day).

Dream Log: Friday night (11/22/96): I dreamt about a bear being against me and several animals. I vaguely remember this dream. I do remember we sort of formed a semi-circle around the bear. I don't remember whether or not I was an animal or what most of the other animals were. I remember two of the other animals on the semi-circle physically quarreling. Both were small. One was a scorpion. I remember wondering why the scorpion didn't sting the bear. I remember dreaming that I was in a warehouse. It was Thanksgiving Day and a lot of people were there. A phone call came from the Independent Living Center and a staff was asking where their client was. So I went around to see. I walked up the stairs (everything was wooden and very broken-looking). When I made it near the top, I saw that one of the stairs was broken. I looked down and there was one of my clients in a pool of blood. I ran down a long ramp and out into the main area. I was so upset that I couldn't speak. I just motioned for someone to call for help. I ran back to him. Three cars (at least 2 of *which were new and red) escaped from the scene -- leading me to believe they had done it. I remember thinking one was his brother. When I approached him, I noticed that his hair had gotten longer and he had a slight beard. His back was contorted. When help arrived and we started speaking to him, he was suddenly able to get up and he was o.k and smiling. I remember that I felt so bad about this incident because it was like we had forgotten him before. The police came to investigate and made an announcement from what seemed to be a ski lodge on a mountain across a valley from this area (we could hear him fine). He basically said that I had been through a personal crisis lately and that's why I had reacted this way (and hinted that it was inappropriate). We were sitting around a table like my mother-in-law's and my friend Katie came in. Behind her were my first boyfriend and his wife. He appeared older, shorter, and stockier. His wife appeared more sophisticated and slender than she is in real life. They came back in this kitchen area and we talked. He talked about his high school football career. So I brought up my husband's sports career. One of the girls didn't believe me. Later, they left and my first boyfriend hugged my husband and kissed him on the lips -- which I thought was unusual. Then he was just going to shake my hand, but I hugged him and asked why I didn't get a kiss. So he said to go ahead -- that he dared me. So I did.*

Dream Log: Saturday (11/23/96): I was in some sort of rock cathedral and I was opening cabinets to see what was inside. Most of the contents were modern items (dishes, etc.) even though the cathedral was old.

Dream Log: Sunday (11/24/96): I had some sort of interlude with a young man in a furniture store. He had felt my bare breasts. Unfortunately, he became famous for his partying habits and the store videotape was put on T.V. Because I didn't work for the store, the store people hadn't identified me yet, but were looking for me. A lady with whom I used to work knew the truth. I was talking to her on the street corner by Cracker Barrel and saw my parents in their red Camero. I quickly turned away -hoping they didn't see me. They drove on very slowly -so I'm not sure whether or not they saw me. I remember having an interview with my old supervisor -- hoping he wouldn't know about the furniture incident. I remember some good things about my former clients had been in the paper, but I searched and searched and couldn't find the article/picture. I remember being in a prison courtyard. Two young boys fought and somehow one escaped -- leaving the other to take the rap. But this other one climbed over the fence (wire with barbwire at the top) and into the brush. There were two black men in a beat up car with some other people. These black men had already previously escaped. The young boy came back -there was nowhere to go right now.

Dream Log: Monday (11/25/96): I was sleeping at the women's shelter. A blond-haired woman got up and went out the door and started screaming. It was early in the a.m. and she was not doing this because she was upset. She was doing it for attention. I went after her. I remember that I called her a "nut" but then felt guilty about it. My

*husband's ex-wife pulled up in her red jeep-like car. I
began feeling angry because she was trying to be nosey
about this situation. I remember telling her that I worked at
the women's shelter and trying to get the point across that I
knew what I was doing.*

*Dream Log: Tuesday (11/26/96): I was with my
sister-in-law Susan walking down my childhood friend's
driveway. Susan was becoming very ill and said she needed
sugar. We went to my neighbor's house. They opened up the
door. From inside their house, I could see a lot of
commotion at my mother's house next door. There was at
least one van out front. My brother was dressed up in a Boy
Scout uniform and was getting on with other boys dressed
this way. I remember hoping they didn't see me, but
suddenly the neighbor's house became like a van or bus, so
I'm not sure whether they could see or not. Later in the
dream, someone's child had been kidnapped. We had
entrusted one of our clients to wait for this child -- we were
to give her Tic-Tacs for this. She had to wait 14 minutes for
this child. At some point, I found the Tic-Tacs in my pocket
—which meant the client didn't wait and the child was lost.
But somehow it was both Nadia's and my fault. The child's
name was Rose. We spoke to her aunt and her aunt didn't
mention anything about the child, so we thought maybe she
was o.k. Later, I was at the police station filling out papers.
I saw my stepfather come out from down the hall. He had
been talking to a guy affiliated with the health department.
This man motioned that Mickey had told him something,
but that he couldn't tell me. My step-father did see me. I*

was afraid and told Monroe at work He said if he came to my work, they would remove him. Monroe came to where I worked. He and his girlfriend and two kids had been taking a tour outside by the pond. I offered to take his shoes off for him. They were black sneakers (like Adidas) and very ugly. I remember that his feet weren't wet and didn't smell bad. After that, he hopped along the counter on all fours with his knuckles curled up like a cat. I also remember that one of my workers was reading something I wrote and was making fun of the writing (like it had mistakes). I told her I was an English major, so don't argue with me (in a joking way). Nadia asked me why I said that and I told her that was my supervision style – but joked about it. One of my workers also came in with a rubber penis and was joking about it. I didn't find this too amusing.

Each morning I woke up and immediately wrote into the spiral bound notebook in this format. I had always been in touch with my dreams, finding that in many cases, what I would dream about close loved ones and friends would eventually come true. The year I was molested, I remember dreaming twice in a row that I had been kidnapped -- once by a clown that dragged me under the bed. Over the years, I had had recurring dreams in which I couldn't breathe, or needed help and couldn't yell out. I also was occasionally prone to sleepwalking. My mother told me of an occasion where I once sleepwalked out into the livingroom and just stared at my parents.

Occasionally, I would have dreams that reached far

into the psychic realm – especially as an adult. One early morning, I remember dreaming that my bed was rocking and shaking back and forth. When I woke up shortly after this, I turned on the television to find there had just been an earthquake in another part of the world. What I knew most about my dreams is that I rarely had anything but nightmares and that my sleep was chaotic and disturbed. I hoped that therapy would find me relief in this area.

CHAPTER 8

Just before Thanksgiving, my Grandparents were going to celebrate their 50th wedding anniversary. It was customary in our community for couples celebrating long-term marriages to have large family parties, or at the very least, a card party where friends and relatives would shower them with cards and gifts. The crisis facing my family was going to halt any attempt at celebration. But a special gift was delivered by my aunt -- a gift from both my mother and my aunt – a white stone 50th anniversary picture frame with pictures of my grandparents at their wedding.

The picture displayed a wedding party that was in contrast to the typical white wedding dress surrounded by an entourage of supporting theme-matched tuxedos and gowns. My grandmother was dressed in a blue dress suit adorned a large corsage of wide leafed white flowers. My grandfather wore a sharp tan suit with a white carnation boutonniere. Their wedding ceremony had been civil, with one couple serving as the best man and matron of honor. They had dinner following the ceremony at a posh restaurant in the hotel where they spent their first night together. That simple event sparked a bond that had now lasted 50 years.

Shortly thereafter, my grandmother mustered the courage to call my mother at work.

"Christy? I want to talk to you. How are you?" my grandmother asked.

"I can't talk right now. I just feel like I've got an axe over my head."

"Why haven't you come and seen me?"

"I just felt like you would take Meredith's side," she said.

"You are right," said my grandmother. Their conversation ended. My grandmother was devastated.

Meanwhile, it seemed that the case was taking forever to resolve. I had hoped that everything would be resolved before the holidays, but this was not going to happen. My friend Katie visited for a weekend and delivered a type-written statement:

I, Katie Foster Walters, do testify to the best of my recollection the following:

Sometime between the ages of eight and ten years, during the Spring season of the school year, I remember Meredith A. DeAngelo-Pearson telling me of a recent incident in which her step-father, Mickey Williams, had entered into her room on several occasions during the same night. During that time he molested her by touching her genitals. She also stated that when he entered the room, he looked closely in her eyes and face, as if to see if she was sleeping. She knew this only because she could smell beer on his breath. Then he proceeded to touch her genitals with his fingers. She stated that she was too afraid to wake up and really did not know what to do. She stated that she hoped it never happened again and that she really was scared. Meredith told me that Mickey had entered the room more than one time that same night.

I, Katie Foster Walters, also remember Meredith asking me to talk to my mom about the situation to see what she thought Meredith should do. I spoke to my mom, and she suggested that Meredith should tell her mother, Christy Williams. My mom stated that Meredith needed someone to help her and that her mother would be the person. I told Meredith what my mother had said and that she should tell her mother. Reluctantly, Meredith told her mother, and Meredith told me that her mother had instructed Meredith not to dare tell anyone. To my knowledge, Meredith's mother never helped her in any way.

Katie showed me the statement before she took it to the police.

"My mother said not to *dare tell* anyone?" I laughed.

"Well, maybe she didn't exactly say it that way, but that's how I remember it." Katie laughed also. Katie had been my best childhood friend and no matter how distant the years or miles, we always were able to easily fall back into our friendship.

"I also don't remember the beer," I said.

"I do remember you telling me that," Katie said.

"What's your husband saying about me calling so much?" I asked.

"Well, he did ask. But I just said, 'If I tell you, then I'll have to kill you,'" she laughed. "That's what we used to say in the military. It works."

I was surprised that I didn't remember this detail, but not surprised about the alcohol. My step-father had a long-standing relationship with his alcohol. I remember that he was always well-stocked with beer and had it quite often

-- particularly when he was working outside. Drinking would begin early in the morning and continue until the night. I distinctly remember that he drank Miller beer. As a child, it wasn't unusual for me to be allowed to take a sip from his can. In the 1970's, it seemed like kids could do things like that without too many repercussions. He also had a convenient stash of liquor -- vodka and whiskey -- in a small cabinet behind a mirror in the laundry closet. In Junior High and High School when my parents weren't home, Katie and I would take an occasional sip of the alcohol and replace it with water to the level matching the small line drawn on the outside of the bottle. We were never confronted on this. I can only presume that by the time the liquor was accessed, my step-father had already had enough beer so that he didn't notice the watered-down taste.

I also suspected that he used drugs. On occasion, there would be people who stopped by the house for a few minutes and he would take out a brown paper bag to them. He would refer to them – black and white men I had never seen before or since -- as "friends" yet they never made it past the garage door. Two of his friends that he actually did spend time with also served time in jail for drugs. Another lifelong friend and business owner was heavily rumored to have earned his fortune through drug dealing. And of course, I had the confession he had given me about his drug use.

I was young (maybe 10 or 12) and we were watching a movie at his mother's house. We did this often -- this was when HBO first came out and his mother lived in town, where she could get cable channels. At our house, we had five television channels, and only two came in clearly most of the time despite our fancy antenna perched on the roof. In the movie, the characters were taking LSD and "tripping." I don't remember the name of the movie, but I still remember the hallucinations depicted in the film - particularly where a woman watched her hands turn into bird wings and fly into the air. Mickey took opportunity to share with me that he had tried LSD once and how this had affected him. My parents went to parties often and camped by the river. As I got older, it seemed that they began to encourage me to stay with my grandmother. I suspect that this would protect them from any observations I might make.

I also have strange memories where I am not quite sure what was happening. For instance, for a period of time we frequently visited friends of my parents who had a little girl slightly younger than me. They lived in an old farmhouse just out of town. One evening, the father – Greg- - couldn't remember his name or who he was. My parents spent a significant amount of time trying to tell him who he was before we left for the evening. I wonder now what Greg had taken that resulted in such a devastating loss of memory.

On another occasion, before my brother was born, I walked into the livingroom and my stepfather was sitting at the desk. He kept asking me "You didn't see what I was doing, did you?" To this day, I wonder what he was doing.

He always had pipes and burned incense. A couple of times a week, he would pick me up from school to take me to receive allergy shots (amazingly from a doctor who later was rumored to have relationships with young boys). Once he was very late and I called my grandmother from school. He came before she did, and when I told him that I had called her, be became livid - yelling at me. I wonder now what had made him so late and what had evoked such a strong reaction from him.

As a victim, you spend a lot of time wondering why someone did this to you. I had heard stories that when he lived in Roanoke, he was only 3 years old and was allowed to walk across the small city from one grandparents' house to another's. I wondered if he had been molested along the way. Once when his mother was babysitting my brother and I, I remember her running her fingers over the lower part of my brother's stomach, just under his diaper. He would laugh and she would comment about how this was tickling him. I wonder now if this was just innocent, or if she was doing something inappropriate, and had she done this to my stepfather.

I had found yearbooks that covered the period he was in high school. He had served as a class officer, and had been actively involved in a civic group in town. The pictures showed a friendly-faced, neatly dressed, attractive young man with blonde, wavy hair. What had happened to this bright, attractive boy? Was it drugs or alcohol?

Perhaps he had had beer on his breath the night he molested me. But in the mornings when I was watching

T.V. before school and he came in to sit down and eat cereal while his penis and/or his testicles hung out of his underwear, he had not been drinking nor doing drugs. And what did it mean that when we first moved in with him, he boldly stood naked in front of the full-length mirror in his bedroom? It seemed this was a purposeful display for my 7-year-old eyes that could easily see him through the wide-open bedroom door.

Now I was analyzing everything and everyone. I wondered if all men were child molesters. I wondered what had happened to my mother to react the way she had. Had she been molested? There was a story that one time my mother was a small child and they found her asleep on top of the dresser. No dresser drawers were out -- the joke was that she floated up there. My grandfather had narcolepsy, which created all sorts of issues and often made him have very similar traits to an alcoholic. Had something happened in that house?

And there was a story about my aunt, as well. She had apparently told my grandmother that she had had to visit the hospital for vaginal bleeding and the doctor told her this was caused by "rough sex." My grandmother had told her that it sounded like she had been raped. She denied this, but today I wonder. I asked my grandmother if anything had ever happened to the girls, but she said no. And she told me that if it had, that she would have stood by her children. "Your children come first" was her standard statement.

Thanksgiving came and went. I began what would

become my pattern for the next several years. We visited my husband's family first. Then I would call at the end of the day to make sure the "coast was clear" (*i.e.,* that my grandparents were alone) and my husband and I could come visit. There was still no word from my mother, stepfather, or brother.

I went to my second session of therapy. This time, Miranda started out much more confrontational. She told me that while she had understood me to tell my circumstances and who had referred me, she had not heard that I wanted to be there. I reassured her that I wanted to be there. As we proceeded through our session, she told me how unusual it was that I remembered the first incident of abuse and asked me if it was possible that I had been victimized before that. This thought astounded me. It was not something I had even contemplated. But just as I was now wondering all of the reasons why my stepfather did this (and realizing that I would probably never fully know these reasons given that during the one conversation we had had about the abuse, he never offered a reason), now I also began to wonder what had made me such a victim.

By the time the abuse occurred, I had already well-established myself within the victim role. It is said that your first memories that you can recall are indicative of the significant issues in your life. My very first memory is of standing in my crib at my grandparents' home (I must have been nearly two years old). My mother was lying in the bed in the same room and telling me to lie down.

In another early memory, I can recall swimming in

the above-ground pool at my great-uncle's house in Maryland. I'm not sure exactly what happened, but my head immersed under water and I remember seeing my diaper floating up to the top of the pool surrounded by rays of sunlight. To me, this represents ultimate helplessness.

I remember being the victim of teasing and occasional cruelty from friends and relatives. At one family reunion, a cousin dumped an entire pail of sand over my head. And then came the incident that I jokingly refer to as the "kidnapping."

My great-grandmother had colon cancer and my grandmother took me to visit her often in Ohio. She and I would make the long 8-hour drive in her brown 1972 Chevelle. I would lay my head on her lap and watch as the high mountains changed to flatlands.

One summer following my first grade year in school (the same year my mother had married my stepfather and we had moved), my grandmother took me again for a visit to Ohio. By that time, my great-grandmother had moved from her fancy apartment in the retirement complex into my great-aunt's house. The brick ranch was in a nice neighborhood and in those days, it was not unusual for people to let their children play outside within the neighborhood.

While outside playing, I met a girl who was smaller than me and perhaps one year younger. We played well all evening and started again the next day. I visited her house two blocks away. She took me into her basement, where we found an old out-of-tune piano. I showed her how well I could play due to the lessons I had been taking.

We then went on to other activities, playing well for a long time. Then her personality turned. She went out of her room and came back with her father's belt. She called me a "Son of a Bitch" and told me to get into the closet or she would beat me with the belt. I don't remember now whether or not she actually hit me, but I remember that I stayed in the closet a very long time, hidden from family and friends who came in the room.

I was scared and intimidated by her threats. I could hear her outside the closet moving about. She would peek her head in the closet ever now and again to ensure I was still there and remaining hidden. Eventually, it was dinnertime and the little girl went out to eat dinner with her family. She ordered me to stay in the closet.

During dinner, I heard the phone ring. The little girl's father answered and I heard him say, "Meredith? She left a long time ago."

I jumped out of the closet and exclaimed, "No I didn't" and took opportunity to run out of the house and back to my great-aunt's house. To this day, I am baffled at why I would allow myself to be so intimidated by another child. I don't know if there were things I saw in my early years between my mother and my father, or some other incident that I can't remember or comprehend. I've also always wondered what path that little girl took in her life.

I took speech therapy for several years for my inability to correctly pronounce the letters s and r. Children on the bus called me "tongue" for years. I had a tendency to dissociate during times of trauma -- most of the time just trying to appear as if nothing were bothering me until the incident was over, or I broke down.

For instance, in 3rd grade a couple of boys trapped me behind the coat closet and wouldn't let me out. They were laughing and viewing it as fun. Eventually, I broke down crying and they realized they had gone too far.

In those days, our area of Virginia was often blessed with long and snowy winters. Many days I braved the cold and knee-deep drifts in layers of long johns and jeans so I could sleigh ride with Katie and any others who would join us on the looming orchard land behind her house. On one occasion, one of my neighbors tackled me and kept throwing snow on my hand. I tried to ignore that this was bothering me. When I got up, it took several hours before I had any feeling in my hands.

In the 4th grade, Katie and one of her friends, Patsy, convinced me to go to the principal's office with them to report that our bus driver had been allowing the high school kids to smoke on the bus when she first started the route. In those days, smoking was allowed at the high school and many children of all ages smoked. But smoking was not allowed on the bus.

The bus driver was subsequently fired. She was related to some of the children on that bus and when she was replaced with a black woman, it was the ultimate betrayal in the eyes of the hollow children. Of course, in my child's mind, I thought that it was our report that had resulted in the firing of the bus driver, but who knows the whole story. And although it was three of us who sat in the principal's office that day, it became known that I was the person who went to report.

I was tormented by teasing, isolation (many children would put their foot across the seat or move away from the seat to avoid sitting with me), and cruelty. I was often pelted with snowballs as I walked home in the winter. Then, at the end of the 4th grade year -- the same year I had been molested -- I received the ultimate punishment.

I was walking home from the bus stop, which at that time was just outside the small cinderblock post office. Suddenly, I felt a hard hit at the back of my head.

"Got her!" the red-headed teenager, Junior Mansfield, cried out. He laughingly picked up speed on the small bike he was riding and headed back into the hollow. He had cracked eggs on my head. I became hysterical and ran into the post office, where the Carolyn, the soft-spoken pctitc office attendant consoled me. She called my parents and had them pick me up. My parents may have called Junior's parents -- I don't recall. But I do recall my mother telling me that eggs were really good for my hair. Somehow, that didn't calm my fears.

That same year, I remember that my 4-H group held a wedding shower for a local couple. He was a handsome young man, with a boy-next-door look of short brown hair and gentle demeanor. The bride-to-be had long hair and wore glasses. Later they were married and within a period of time, the bride disappeared. For days, the bus driver talked about the missing girl. One day, we found out that she had been abducted from a local laundry mat. As a nurse, she had to do laundry in the wee hours of the morning. She was taken to a cabin outside of town, tortured, and killed. I remember the story and I remember her name -- Hope. As I grew older, I would often walk through the local cemetery and try to catch a close glimpse of her headstone that was carefully enclosed in a locked family plot within the larger cemetery.

CHAPTER 9

My therapist reviewed my dream log and commented that I dreamt differently than most people - with much more detail and movement. She told me that as I continued with therapy, I could expect that my dreams would get healthier with less nightmares, better colors, and better themes.

Dream Log: Thursday, November 28th (Thanksgiving): I dreamt that at work I was preparing for the move to New Market (where my new program would be housed). I told Nadia that we should go through a box of donations that was there. We found a lot of Indian moccasins (which I have always liked since childhood). I said that I and my clients could wear them in the program. I also found a tablecloth with little red and blue designs with matching napkins that I thought would go great in my kitchen. Nadia and I wanted to take it home. Nadia and I discussed whether I should or not. She suggested that I should ask, but I didn't want to do that in case the answer was no.

I remember it was very gray outside. The roads were very confusing, but all paved (like highway roads). People had given me advice for the quickest route and told me to get on the right-hand curb and turn my blinkers on like I needed help so that I could go around traffic. But there wasn't any traffic and I didn't want to do this anyway. I remember that the road signs didn't list New Market, but I remembered coming this way and felt it was the right way. To my left was an old building like the back of Main Street in Front Royal. I was walking now and this was where I was. I heard my name called from an upstairs window a couple of times before I looked up. This building was full of apartments. I knew that it was a boy with whom I had gone to school, but now I couldn't see him. Apparently he was living with his parents. One of the neighbors was asking who was yelling. He was a big overweight man. I talked with some of the other apartment residents, but I don't remember Chris (the boy) coming down. I had the feeling he was trapped up there. A horror film had been filmed in the basement of that building. I also dreamt that two ladies (young and pretty) were going to open some sort of business in this one place on Main Street. My husband and I were in there -- it was like a hotel room and we were going to fool around. But I remember that the curtains were open slightly. I got up to close them before I undressed. I saw a bar across the street. Dan, a boy with whom I went to high school, was dressed very scraggily and was in the bar drinking. Another boy I knew from school (also a year ahead) -Mark - was working construction on the street. I remember that I had started my period, so I was going to do more to my husband than he was to me during our sexual time together.

Dream Log: Sunday, December 1st: The only thing I remember is sitting at my dining room table and in a plastic bag were mice that had been frozen. Some were so small I didn't know where to put them, so I searched until I found bigger ones and put the other ones back. I was going to let them unfreeze. I think my sister-in-law Jenny was *with me. She told me that they sometimes use a blow-dryer to unfreeze theirs. The mice had a little blood on their backs. I also dreamt I was on a school bus. For some reason, the bus was letting off kids very late -it was almost 10p.m. at night. A girl I knew from school, Becky, was taking afriend (Diane) back after she had stayed Thanksgiving. I remember thinking that she had taken Arlene, a black girl, home with her. I also dreamed my father-in-law had to meet with a committee because he had been in some trouble. He was talking to a lady at a little store about this. Then my husband and I were at the same store. It was busy. The lights were bright inside, but it was getting dark out. We had a tab there, but my husband gave me $3 to pay the bill. He got upset over something there (not with me) and left. I walked out the door for a moment and the waitress called out two names -- one of which I answered to and told her I'd be right back. A man outside made a comment to my husband that they didn't know us here. I went back inside to pay. The store looked like a diner.*

Dream Log: Tuesday, December 3rd: I had a dream that my 1st husband (at first it was my 2nd husband, but then he turned into my 1st husband) and his friend David were going to take the SATs in the round conference room like the room at Shenandoah University. I said I had already taken the test, but then wanted to take it because I wanted to see how much I had learned. Then I was at my parents' home. My husband's ex-wife was sitting on the couch in the family room. I had given her 2 books which I *had written -one was about my childhood. She said she liked the other one better. She smiled at me and I felt good that she had read my books. I remember I looked in my underwear drawer. A lot of my underwear was missing, but there were some maxi pads in the drawer.Some were used (neatly rolled up in toiletpaper). I thought this was disgusting and wondered why they were there and threw them out. I also remember my stepfather in the dream. I remember making the connection that he always made me clean my plate and that's why I overeat now.*

As my brain worked overtime through dreams to process the stress and anxiety of the situation, I took time to work on my physical health. I went to the dentist for the first time in many years and began to complete needed dental work.

I went to the gynecologist for a regular exam. While I had been mentally prepared for cavities, I was not prepared for an abnormal result from my pap test. I had never had an abnormal pap smear. I was going to have to have a follow-up test.

The pressure of waiting for the outcome of my case was weighing on me psychologically. Therapy helped me to put things in perspective. However, I was suddenly afraid of my step-father somehow sneaking to my house and sabotaging my home. The therapist helped me to realize that while this might be possible, it was unlikely. My dreams were displaying the torment of my psyche during this time.

Dream Log: Saturday, December 7th: I got out of *bed with my husband and looked in the mirror. I was breaking out in a terrible rash. I had welts all over my face, lips, back, and chest. Then I dreamt that I was having a bad dream and I was trying to cry out to my husband so that he could wake me up, but he didn't hear me – I couldn't find enough volume in my voice and could only whisper with struggle. In reality, I was able to finally holler out to him and I woke up and was very scared for a while. There also may have been a part of this dream where I didn't have a shirt on and was embarrassed that people might see me. I was in my living room.*

Then I dreamt that I was in my house and my sister-in-law Jenny stopped by. I remember that I was mad at my husband and made the comment that I was going to leave him. She came over and said that it would be o.k if I did. I began to cry because she didn't understand me. That wasn't what I wanted to do – it was just what I said when I got angry. Then we were outside a church, but the church was more like a pavilion. They made an announcement for a certain group of people to come at 7:30 a.m. mass (I don't remember the name of the group). I remember I wondered why they were only making the announcement for the 7:30 mass --it may have been for those who wanted to take communion. The church had many pews and it was like an outdoor pavilion with concrete floors. Jenny sat somewhere else and then I was with two of my ex-sister-in-laws. I hadn't realized what time it was and decided to go to this mass so I wouldn't have to go later. I chose to sit down in what was like a booth. Across from me, but separated by the top of the booth (to the left) was my former sister-in-law Sarah. But I did not care. My other ex-sister-in-law Beatrice sat with me.

The mass was very confusing. The priest kept stopping and music (like gospel) was played. At one point, I wondered where the priest went during the music and I saw him return from the bathroom. At the end of mass, I left, but then realized I hadn't received communion -- he hadn't given it out. I was driving a jeep with other people in it. I had to park on a hill (on ice, I think) and I put the emergency brake on. It was a stick-shift vehicle. When I went back to take communion, almost everyone else had taken it. But the priest encouraged me to come up. I had gum in my mouth. I tried to stick the gum under my tongue so that the priest wouldn't see it and would give me communion. He did give it to me -- with a cookie. I remember some of the crumbs fell on the floor. The McDonald's was also part of the church. My friend Katie was also there.

Dream Log: Monday, December 9th: I remember dreaming that I was talking to a case manager, John, on the phone. He was telling me about one of my clients at the women's shelter (I was doing an overnight at the shelter). However, due to confidentiality, I couldn't draw out very many details easily. The end message was that this woman might attack me while I was sleeping/doing the overnight and I shouldn't trust her. I remember that the conversation was very pleasant and I really enjoyed talking to him. Clients also were walking around a lot during the time I *was on the phone.*

Dream Log: Tuesday, December 10th: I vaguely remember having some sort of confrontation with my aunt Cathy. She wanted to discuss some issue with me. I told her that she hadn't wanted to listen to me. I remember calling her a "bitch" and she left. She went out my door (we were at my house). I believe that I also had some sort of confrontation with my mother during this dream. Later, I was on a large freeway. I was coming from somewhere and had to be in Winchester to work. There was a lot of traffic on the road and when I took an exit and came up to a toll booth, my husband pulled behind me. This was a pleasant surprise – he had followed me to make sure I was traveling o.k. He brought something up to me – it was like a round type of wall hanging with a pretty picture on it --- like birds or flowers which were brown and red. There was a number on it and it looked familiar (it was 1107 and several other numbers) and I recognized it as a number I had won in a raffle. The toll booth man confirmed this. I remember thinking that this man was very nice. We were on the border of Delaware and I remember thinking that it wouldn't be too far to home. But I was running short on time and I was trying to figure out where I could take a shower for work. My husband followed me. Where we were, there was a movie theater where you could see a movie for $16 a person, but that was too much money -- although we did stop there. I remember that there had been a nice hotel where I could have showered and not been noticed (I could go to a bathroom near the main lobby and slip in there).

But I had missed my chance and then couldn't make it back there. I think this happened in the sequence of dream before the tollbooth. I remember that other hotels in the dream charged you to go in and I couldn't afford that. I remember driving up the big hill on Millwood Avenue in Winchester toward work.

CHAPTER 10

As the Christmas season approached, it seemed very strange. I bought no presents for my family, with the exception of my grandparents and half-brother, Jesse. I was feeling anxiety knowing that I had originally hoped this would all be resolved before the holidays.

Dream Log: Friday, December 13th: I dreamt about ayoung woman at the woman's shelter. Her baby kept crying off and on (this really was occurring and I offered suggestions, but nothing worked). I also dreamt that Kathy's mother was walking up the hill in my backyard. She was coming to visit me.

Dream Log: Saturday, December 14th: Nadia and I had doll babies which were like real babies. We were being very gentle with them and were taking good care of them. Mark (we work with him) came over and patted the babies gently. We were sitting at a table. Nadia was sitting to my left. The table was square and wooden.

Dream Log: Sunday, December 15th: I was in the mall and I overheard my ex-sister-in-law Sarah with her daughter remark to another person about how she was doing. She was rather rude and remarked on the pressures of the daycare. I had my clients with me and I remember we were walking out of the mall (which was very spacious and bright) and sort of turning a corner and about to walk in a huge department store (which was a little darker but still bright). Sara was standing at the entrance with her daughter, off to the side. I seem to remember thinking that my job was harder and having an air of confidence as I got ready to walk past her.

Dream Log: Tuesday, December 17th: I remember receiving a letter that it was a sad day, but me and my staff would be laid off from our job from the Independent Living Center.

Dream Log: Thursday, December 19th: I had a dream that my friend Katie and I were in front of a house (my grandmother's) and there was a walkway made out of flat concrete squares (like I have in front of my house now). The one at the end (closest to the house) was covered in snow, but we were able to easily clear off the top layer of snow. We stooped down to do this with our hands, but I don't remember it being cold. We took an icepick and began chipping away the layer of ice. It started coming off in big jagged chunks. I remember Katie saying that it's been a long time since we've seen this (referring to the concrete underneath).

Dream Log: Friday, December 20th: I dreamt that I pulled apart my hair and my scalp was like sand and there were tiny black ants crawling on my scalp. I knew I didn't have lice -- that this was something different.

Dream Log: Saturday, December 21st: I had this incredible thirst and I kept guzzling all kinds of different drinks (i.e., soda, water, etc.), but I couldn't be satisfied. My stomach even began to hurt. I have dreamt about being thirsty before. When I woke up, I was thirsty.

Dream Log: Sunday, December 22nd: One of my former clients called me. She's deaf and hard to understand, so all I could make out is "Natalie (a staff)

went into the bathroom and said 'Oh No.'" So I went to
visit the client. My old work partner, Caroline, and my old
supervisor Jon were there. Jon was behind a counter and
there was a bag of onions on it. I talked with them and
thanked them for the Christmas cards. I also talked with
someone about one of the on-duty crisis people and said I
wouldn't want his job. I went out into an area that was like
a modern building. It was a hospital. My old friend Len
was very ill and he came a great distance on a bike. He
could barely walk into the hospital. The hospital resembled
an airport, with big windows from floor to ceiling and it
was very open and vacant in the entrance way. There were
no signs. The few personnel that showed up gave him the
wrong directions. Finally when someone did come with the
right instructions, Len had disappeared. We went out onto
a cement courtyard to find him. There was a ledge along
where there were a lot of people. I, an old friend Tom (who
had been with us) and a girl (I think it an old friend Louise)
got on the ledge. We all went along the ledge like snakes.
Tom was along the outside left, Louise in the middle, and I
on the outside right. I moved a little ahead of them because
I didn't think we could all fit too well along the ledge and
so I could hold both sides. When we reached the end of the
ledge, there was water with choppy waves. I could see
someone was down there in the dark and it looked like he
was in a plastic bag covering his body. Just then, a beam of
light illuminated him and it was Len. I reached out my hand
and I was able to lift him up out of the water. Then Tom
took him and told me that he was doing that so they could

swim and he knew I didn't swim well. Then we were able to get him help. I followed and kissed Len on the cheek. I remember thinking how I wasn't interested in us being a couple anymore. His hair was dark and his skin pale and he looked like he did before he had cancer. I noticed him looking at my breasts, but not with exceptional interest.

I also dreamt about one of my staff members, Tanya, sitting at our workplace smoking. I remember waking up feeling like a savior. I also remember in the dream my husband telling me how beautiful my hair was -- he was in the kitchenette and I was in the kitchen. I also remember during one part of the dream squeezing a thick white puss (like out of a pimple) out of my nipple (right breast). The left nipple had scabs on it and would only squeeze blood. I wondered if this meant I was producing milk in my breast (and maybe was pregnant) or was ill, like with cancer.

It had been an established tradition that everyone from both sides of our family would come to my house for dinner on Christmas Eve. My husband cooked the ham and I created everything else -pasta salad, rolls, vegetables, fruits, and lots of desserts. My grandparents would come in after attending Christmas Eve service at their church.

On Christmas Day, we spent time at Warren's parents' house in the mountains. Warren has 1 brother and 4 sisters. With his family, we had evolved over the years from buying everyone gifts, to buying all the children gifts, to picking names according to how many children you had.

It felt like Christmas was shrinking. As the family grew and expanded, they began to go different directions. As a result, it was less and less a priority for everyone to be there the entire day. Out of necessity, we stayed there until late in the day.

After we were sure it was safe, we went to my grandparents' house. In previous years, it had been a holiday tradition that after Thanksgiving feast, I would draw down the attic stairs and ascend to the attic, where a crawl space held a few boxes of very old decorations. I took great pleasure in putting up the silver metallic tree, arranging the oddly shaped and mismatched bulbs, and hanging stockings on the mantle just over the brick fireplace that was no longer used.

My role had significantly changed in the past year. Nanu had purchased a small tabletop artificial green tree with attached lights. All I had to do was carry it up from the basement before Christmas and plug it in. There were a few bulbs to hang, but most had been thrown away following assessments of crusty bubbles of mold and peeling paint.

Beneath the tree this year were gifts for my husband and me from my grandmother. And then I discovered two presents, one marked for Terry and one for Justin. The nametags displayed my mother's handwriting. There were also presents for us from my aunt.

"How did these get here?" I asked.

"Cathy brought them. I guess that your mother had already bought them and wanted to make sure the kids got them."

"We can't accept those. We can't accept gifts from people we aren't talking to."

"That's really weird," my husband said. "I don't know what to think that they wouldn't get us gifts, but would get my kids gifts."

My grandmother was upset, but we ignored the topic the rest of the evening and left the presents there as we departed for home.

Dream Log: Wednesday, December 25th: I was living in a small apartment. My friend Katie called me in the middle of the night (@2:30 a.m. -- I looked at my digital clock). The phone was full of static and I could barely hear her. She said she couldn't testify for me in court. I remember when I got off the phone, I believed it had been tapped. I wasn't sure if it were tapped by my stepfather or by the police. I was then in my bed sleeping and I heard something. Suddenly, there were several men breaking in -- but they were like FBI agents. I was very scared and I thought maybe they had tapped the phone. I saw a light in the hall before they came. I woke up terrified.

Dream Log: Thursday, December 26th: I was in a school and I had one of my former clients with me (Charlie). I was taking him to the bathroom and I turned my back on him for a moment and lost him -even though I knew he hadn't gone far. He was not in one of the classrooms. Someone spotted him at the top of the stairs on a platform (like they have in the malls, where there are two levels). I went up there. He spoke to me -- although I don't remember what he said. This was a non-verbal client (essentially). We tried to coax him down.

Dream Log: Friday, December 27ᵗʰ: My aunt and I were at my house. She asked me why I hadn't taken the gifts. I don't remember everything I said, but I remember telling her why and cussing at her -- telling her in the end "Fuck You, Fuck You." I did this in front of other people – I think one of whom was my grandmother. Afterwards, my aunt smiled and we began to resolve our issues.

Dream Log: Saturday, December 28ᵗʰ: I was with my first boyfriend, Danny. He was traveling by a canoe down the road (main road) which then turned toward my current house. I got in my own boat and followed him. I was moving very fast and thought we were going to the river. There was someone else with me and I was talking to them. They were not in my boat, but were traveling alongside. There were other people going in the same direction. There was one girl, Layla, who came up behind us. I talked very loudly and let her know that (without speaking directly to her) I didn't know why Danny and I were listed separately because we had been together. There was another boy I mentioned as well. She snickered as she passed us. (In real life, she had been interested in Danny and wanted to know why he was interested in me).

I remember it was very hard to steer my boat, I had to hold onto the sides and pull in one direction to get it to go in that direction. I was amazed that I was able to steer it straight and at such speed. We were supposed to be going down the river. Finally, we got to a classroom. My boyfriend had turned into Sam W. -- a boy with whom I

graduated. I didn't speak directly to him at first, but spoke
to his brother instead. I set my purse down in front of
another boy with whom I graduated -Sam L. Then I finished
my discussion. When I returned to the area to sit down, I
almost sat in the wrong seat. Sam L. pointed me to the right
seat and told me it was o.k. when I laughed and apologized.

I had on this velour skirt suit outfit which was snug,
but looked good. When I sat down, I noticed that two girls
at the other end of the room (against the wall) were talking
about me. They were commenting on theprospects of Sam
W. and I being together. I commented to the person next to
me (in a whisper voice, but I knew they could hear) that I
wasn't in the eight grade anymore and I would "bust their
ass." One of the girls was Jacqueline -- a black girl who
had been an acquaintance of mine in school. The teacher
came in. It was my first grade teacher, Mrs. Harold. She
was smiling and very friendly. Later, I had a dream that my
supervisor, Mickey, told Nadia and I that there was going
to be a board meeting. About an hour before the meeting,
we saw him in the hall and he asked me about the catering
set-up. I didn't know that I had to set this up. I knew that
the secretary at Hope House, Louisa, would have already
left to come to Winchester. I knew I had about $30 left in
my checking account and somehow I was able to purchase
a cake and other items for just under this ($26). I remember
thinking it might be more than $30 and I was going to
"float a check" until I got home to get the rest from my
husband, but this was not necessary.

The cake and other food were put in a big

conference room at the end of the hall. I went down the hall and ended up in a classroom. The room was full of students. In fact, the teacher was setting out wooden chairs because there weren't enough desks for everyone. One of my former boyfriends from Jr. High (again -- 8th grade) was sitting in the chair. The teacher gave him a laptop desk like I used to have when I was in school -- it is hard on one side with a clip for papers and a bean bag on the other side that fits your lap. I noticed that a leg broke off of one of the desks. I tried to put it back together, but couldn't. A black girl, Arlene, who was an acquaintance (distant) in school tried to put it back together for me. She lit a match and soldered it (even though it was wood). I remember being surprised that she burnt a match in the classroom. I realized that I missed the board meeting, but felt that it may have not occurred. The next day, I went in the conference room. Mickey (my supervisor) was there eating the cake. Other people were in there as well -- part of the cake had been eaten. Mickey said that the meeting had been cancelled.

    Dream Log: Monday, December 30th: I remember a client from the women's shelter leaving, but the reason she gave was not the truth. I and a group of other people followed her down a walkway. She turned right toward a house that was between two others. It was back from the walkway and you had to follow a wooden walkway to get to it. There were a lot of plants around. Although the style was not Japanese, something reminded me of a Japanese home – it was in a natural, sort of tropical setting. Then there was a counselor leading us. She was a sort of middle-aged woman with a "hippy"-like demeanor. We went in and sat down. I remember my cousin Randy Jr. was there -- he sat on another couch. My mother sat down on this huge cushioned chair (it was sort of old and was big enough to be a love seat). There was a black girl, Elsie, with whom I used to go to school. She was sitting next to my mother and her right arm was over the side of the chair and her right leg was toward the side of the chair as well. I sat down so that her arm and leg were wrapped around me. But this hurt her, so she moved her arm and leg from around me.

I told them that in family therapy, it is very important to the counselor where people sit. I remember thinking or saying that someone was between my mother and I (just like how we were sitting). I also thought they were going to do some physical scenes and I knew how the people would structure themselves. The room was very big and open with a very hippy-like atmosphere (the furniture was older, but comfortable, the floors were wooden, the room was slightly dirty, and there were some plants around). I went up to what was like a kitchen window in a cafeteria. They were serving cake -- strawberry or cherry. Manuel, a boy with whom I went to school, was there eating cake. I said hello to him and he reached out to hug me. I was surprised and hugged him very tightly back and kissed him on the cheek.

CHAPTER 11

In my family, it was tradition to celebrate New Year's Day with sauerkraut and pork roast. Once again, we waited until my aunt and her children had departed from my grandparents' house so that we could visit. Nanu tried again (without success) to get me to take the presents that had now been stored in her closet for a week.

Following the holidays, I received the results of my second pap smear. It reported as abnormal and I was going to require a biopsy.

Dream Log: Friday, January 3rd: Nadia and I went to Middleburg to go shopping/or the programs. We went in what was like an old mall (i.e. you would go in and there were little shops, not like the malls we have today). The floors were wooden and had an antique atmosphere. We went into one area and there were a lot of cookie jars. There was one area of all white cookie jars. They were originally priced at $46, but were 25% off, so I knew they'd be a little over $30. However, I didn't have any cash and was out of checks (true in real life). The saleslady told me I could come back -- the sale would be going on until Tuesday. I wanted to get a cookie jar for my grandmother in New York, who collects them. I was glad I could come back.

Dream Log: Tuesday, January 7th: I dreamt about my husband's ex-wife. She came to me and was asking me questions in a nice way and I responded to her in a nice manner. I no longer felt angry with her.

My husband took me to the doctor's office for the biopsy. As the doctor snipped at several parts of my cervix, I felt a rush of pain. My face became flushed with heat. I felt like I was losing control of my body. At the end, the doctor showed some kindness as he held his hand out to me to help me sit up and said, "That's a really rough thing to go through."

The results of the biopsy showed pre-cancerous cells. In a very dry, unemotional tone, the gynecologist informed me at the follow-up appointment that more than likely, my abnormal cells had been caused by Human Papilloma Virus (HPV). HPV commonly was the origin of genital warts. I was mortified.

I had only had sex with two people in my life. My first husband had reported to me that he had had sex 5 times before me (we had begun dating as teenagers). His first sexual experience was with a casual acquaintance at the beach. My current husband had many prior sexual partners and his first wife had had multiple sexual partners. The gynecologist suggested that my current husband could do a vinegar test -- where he could pour vinegar on his penis and observe if any white areas appeared (which would indicate the presence of abnormalities).

My husband did this and found nothing. I had no communication with my first husband and so couldn't ask him if he had had this. I began to have the disturbing thought that I may have contracted this as a child from my parents. My grandmother had a vague memory that my mother had undergone some sort of gynecological procedure similar to what they were now suggesting for me -- cryotherapy ("burning and freezing" of the abnormal cells). But since we weren't communicating with her, we wouldn't be finding out. Perhaps sharing a bathroom, shower stall, etc. had provided an avenue for transmission of the virus. Our home was not very clean.

And then I had more disturbing thoughts. My stepfather had had warts all over his fingers and hands -- had he somehow transmitted the disease when he molested me? Could it have lain dormant in my body all of this time and by speaking out about the abuse, my body somehow was reacting and "outing" the virus? I would never know. My therapist said she had heard of such things.

I was scared. Suddenly I felt the urgency of life. For so many years, I had felt hopeless and contemplated suicide -- and now, actually faced with the prospect that I had a condition that in the worst scenario could lead to death, I wanted to live.

Nanu was very supportive. We were talking about the upcoming cryotherapy one afternoon when my Aunt Cathy came in. I remained in the kitchen, out of sight. She knew I was there, but I was trying to avoid face-to- face contact with her. My grandmother, however, wanted us to connect. She brought up that I had had an abnormal pap smear and would have to have abnormal cells removed. My aunt responded with, "Oh, that's no big deal." Anger welled up inside of me. I couldn't speak to her. I could only shake my head at her stupidity. I went home and typed a letter to her.

January 8, 1997

Dear Aunt Cathy,

    I use these terms "Dear" and "Aunt" liberally. I am writing this in response to our confrontation at Grandma's this afternoon. I am sorry that Grandma had to inform you of my biopsy -- I'm sure she was indirectly trying to get you to respond in a caring, guilty, or apologetic manner to me. I was not surprised by your lack of empathy -it has been your pattern for as long as I have known you. I was surprised, however, that you chose to speak to me. I'm not sure whether or notyou really understand what is going on here.

    First of all, I want you to know that the gifts which you gave me for Christmas are in Grandma's closet. She put them there because she didn't know how to deal with them. I am sorry she is in the middle of this, but I believe that I had no other option but to leave the gifts. I have made a pact with myself to be as honest as possible and true to the situation. I cannot accept gifts from people who by their actions have shown me that they do not believe me, are in denial of the situation, or simply do not care enough about me to take the time to hear, understand, and respond in a positive manner to my side of the story. And I was especially offended that you so quickly called my parents to tip them off that I was filing charges of abuse, but you couldn't call me once to ask my side of the story. I guess you put in the effort when you want to do so and let things fall apart when you don't want to take control. I've seen you do this my entire life. I offered to bag the gifts with an attached note explaining this, but Grandma didn't want me to do this. I think she is still hoping for us all to find some sort of resolution that will make us a happy family again. I know that this will never happen because to me, we were never a happy family.

I'm not sure what your angle is. I know that you have rarely responded to me in a compassionate manner. I'm not sure whether you have been jealous of me because even though you had the first grandchild (whom you gave up -- yes, I know that nasty secret), I was able to take the first grandchild role and was given a lot as a result. Or perhaps you are resentful of me because I have been able to accomplish a lot, despite my situation. Or maybe you have had some sort of tragedy in your life which makes you incapable of accepting that anything happened to me. Who knows. And I really don't care anymore. It really doesn't matter what the excuses are. I know that you are a bitter lady and what some people have thought was strength in your personality, I see as weakness. You try to control everybody and everything around you because somewhere you must feel very out of control with the way your life has turned out.

I realize that throughout the years you have given me a lot of nice gifts. I would have traded them all for someone who spoke to me with respect, treated me like a person, and accepted the decisions I have made in my life. And of course, someone who would have withheld the criticisms and arguments in lieu of genuine concern and love.

I have chosen to come out and file the charges of abuse because I want to stop this person from ever doing it again. And there is no other reason. I waited until now because it took time for me to build up the courage to do this. You've already made it clear that you are not interested in hearing my story. That is your right. I hope that when you get to the end of your life and look back on your life, you are able to find something satisfying and honest about it. I am not perfect, but even if I screw up from now until the day I die, I will be able to look back on these times with the satisfaction that I changed my life for the better.

By your actions, you have chosen sides. As a result, it would be hypocritical for you to give me gifts during the holidays or even to make conversation with me when you see me. I must say that I didn't miss spending time with my family at the holidays. I hadn't enjoyed holidays for a long time. If I wasn't stressed out over being in the presence of Mickey, I was stressed out over the screaming matches you had with your children. I'm glad I don't have to subject myself to that anymore. And I hope that you are glad that now you will be able to save a little money at Christmas by marking a few people off of your list. I was very angry with myself that I couldn't confront you in person. But I am a much better writer than speaker, and by writing, I wouldn 'tleave anything out. You know, I tried to think of one time in my life whenyou were very nice to me. I could only remember one time – I think I was five or so and you were babysitting me. We were cruising around with a bunch of people and you spoke to me in a very kind, soft voice. That's the ONLY pleasant memory of which I could think. I could, however, recall many arguments about school, people, decisions, and of course, how you thought my house should look. I have a specific memory of you blasting in my apartment when Jackson and I lived on Viscose Avenue and Randy Jr. pulled weeds and threw them out into the yard. I was having company that evening and you set such a mood right before they came. I'm sure you probably don't remember that. And of course, my mind is selective. Perhaps you can remember a time when you were a different person other than this person who is out to prove to the whole world that they are stronger, smarter, bitchier, and more correct than anyone else. Unfortunately, I cannot remember such aperson. I know that at times you cared in your own way, but you didn't present it the way I've learned people can present their feelings. Presentation means a lot to me. If you are bitching at me, the message that you love me gets lost. And I can't trust anything you say if it's not consistent with the way you present it.

All of this doesn't mean that I don't love you and that writing this letter doesn't hurt me. However, I cannot expose myself to unhealthy situations in my life anymore and I certainly would never bring children into the world with my family the way it was. I wish no harm to you and your family. This letter officially severs all of our ties. Unless, of course, lightning should strike you and you

would say and do all of the right things needed to repair
our relationship. I won't wait for that day. God bless you
and good luck to you and yours. You'll need it.

Meredith A.
DeAngelo-Pearson

I shared a copy with my grandmother so that she
could read the letter before she was called about it. Just as I
had thought, within a few days, my aunt contacted her.

"I got a letter from Meredith today," she said.

"I know," answered my grandmother.

"You do?" My aunt was surprised.

They continued to converse about this subject only
briefly. Then my aunt asked if the presents were still there.
Nanu confirmed that they were and within a day, my aunt
picked them up. I was scared, but relieved. On a good day,
my aunt reminded me of Rizzo in Grease. She appeared
outspoken and bold, but had a buried soft underbelly. She
was someone who was good to have on your side and
dangerous to have as an enemy. I knew now that she would
be a force to be reckoned with.

I continued to attend therapy regularly. My therapist
validated me when I described to her my communication
with the gynecologist. She knew him personally and
acknowledged that his demeanor was rather blunt and dry.
She also told me that abnormal cells could be caused by
other things besides Human Papilloma Virus. She told me
that I really wrote well and was amazed by the letter I had
written to my aunt.

I went in for my "burning and freezing" procedure. As my legs rested high in the stirrups, the gynecologist delivered three rounds of the "freezing" procedure with brief intervals of rest. In my mind, I imagined that the interim period was a period where I was "thawing" and found this to be extremely painful with only brief moments of relief. My face grew very hot and the gynecologist surprisingly told me I was pale. Afterwards, I lay down in the seat of the car as my husband drove me home. Even though this had been a necessary and voluntary procedure, I felt invaded and tormented.

CHAPTER 12

Out of anger, I wrote my next poem.

A Sestina for My Mother

Free and warm streamed the sapid milk,
Cascading from your swollen breast
Saturating my yearning lips.
Calm against your throbbing heart,
I nestled in your soft, strong arms
And basked in a fresh mother's embrace.

Naiveties found comfort in your embrace.
Distractions sprang from cookies and milk
Your hair fell softly over my chubby arms
As you nuzzled me to your gentle breast
And assured me of your brimming heart.
"I love you" whispered from your vowing lips.

You suffered with your lonely lips,
Desiring for a man to embrace,
A man to share your fragmented heart,
A man to provide the honey and milk,
A man to lay a new babe to your breast
And to grip you in his soft, strong arms.

He slithered quietly into your arms.
His words flowed polished from his lips.
He spawned a new babe to your breast.
Familiar comforts of the small embrace
Disguised the life departing with the milk

And the growing snare over your heart.

Humble over the truth in my wounded heart,
I sought refuge in your chilled arms.
You fed my brother his bottled milk
And required me to seal my quivering lips.
You weaned me at the mercy of Hell's embrace,
Ripping from my mouth the comfort of your breast.

I have no children to hold to my lumpy breast.
I have no trust to hold in my bruised heart.
I have no mother to hold in my crippled embrace.
I struggle to hold back my craving arms.
I struggle to hold back my tortured lips.
I struggle to hold back my ache for milk

Mother, you have fed me sour milk,
Hoping I would ignore its paste on my lips.
I vomit with grief over our nippleless arms.

Nanu cried after reading the poem. I wasn't doing well with comforting others – I was very much caught up in my own emotional upheaval. I copied portions of "A Courage to Heal" for her and my husband to read. They wanted to be on my side, but this also was impacting their lives.

My therapist facilitated my reflection of the memories of my parents. I described to her that I could remember when I was little watching from my swing set as my mother and stepfather walked into my grandmother's house. They were just dating then -- I was about 3 years old -and I couldn't tell them apart. They each walked in with identical styles of t-shirts, hip high jeans, and wide belts. At that time, Mickey had hair just as long and straight as my mother.

Later, as Mickey cut his hair short and rounded out his image with thin-rimmed glasses, he looked like John Lennon to me. This was a startling revelation given that John was always my favorite Beatle. Because my mother was attractive and new in what was a very small town at that time, she had many young men interested in her, but for some reason, he captured her heart.

I found love letters that he wrote to her in purple ink, affirming that he wrote in that color because it was her favorite. Letters from other young men she dated at the time indicated their frustrations with her obvious growing interest in Mickey. She worked with him, took classes with him, and gradually revolved her life around him.

My mother was gone a lot during the time we lived with my grandparents. She obtained her G.E.D., went to work, and went on to obtain an associate's degree. But she occasionally took me on her dates and cruises around the town. For many years, teens and young persons in the town found amusement by waving to their friends as they drove the long circuit on the main bypasses of the 9 square mile town.

In the early 1970's, there was a hot spot called "The Comet" -a drive-in restaurant where youth were the primary patrons and loiterers. It was there that I heard the first song I remember hearing: "A Horse with No Name."

When I went to elementary school, I remember being so proud when my mother would pick me up. Her hair was at its longest, straight, and a beautiful sandy color. She was much younger than most of the other mothers. Other children would look at me with my short, straight dark hair and butch demeanor and ask, "That's *your* mother?"

She left me with Mickey a lot in the early days after they married -- she worked evenings and graveyard shifts at the local textile factory. He played games with me, took me out to eat, and took me to visit his friends. His friends were funny to me. They cussed often and then would say, "Pardon my French." He didn't always understand me, but in those days he was learning and he tried. On one occasion, he offered to make me breakfast and I emphatically told him I wanted a "dip" egg. He became frustrated and yelled, "I don't know what a 'dip' egg is!" But then he called my grandmother and found out that I wanted a 3-minute egg. When we moved into our new house in Hell Town, I would pick up Tiger, our cat, and carry her around. He told me, "Watch out - she'll shit on you." This was a lovely comment for a first grader.

One evening, he and I were eating in Kentucky Fried Chicken. He showed me a picture of Richard Nixon behind bars with the caption reading "I'm not a crook." I was lost. I was about 3 years old when Watergate occurred. While I was familiar with and remember some events of that era (for instance, the day it was announced that the last troops had departed from Vietnam), I certainly didn't have the wit at this age to understand the implications of the joke.

I remember him taking me to a place called "The Quarry" to swim. It had a nice beach and high rock walls where people climbed to dive into the clear water. My parents also took me canoeing there on occasion. It was quite a gathering place for the younger set and once I observed a naked young lady take her place on the beach after a dip in the water.

As I grew older, my mother didn't seem to cope well with my changing body. I was built differently than her and more like my aunt. I was heavier set and my breasts, which began growing in 3rd grade, were larger. One day I changed into a closely fitted red sleeveless shirt before my parents came to pick me up from my grandmothers. I did not yet have a bra and my breasts emerged in small cone shapes beneath the shirt. When my mother saw my breasts, she grabbed onto Mickey and laughed loudly at me.

By 6th grade, my body was maturing further. I went to the one county intermediate school with 4th and 5th graders. On one rainy day just before spring, I felt strong and accomplished as I climbed the rope in physical education class. This thick rope which suspended from the ceiling had been an obstacle for me. I was trying to slender and mature my chubby child figure. I had continuously studied and practiced the techniques that would help me to get to the top of that rope. Finally, I achieved my goal attired in a plaid tan skirt, pantyhose, and loafers. In those days, there was no emphasis on uniforms or other appropriate attire before junior high school.

Following P.E., I went to the bathroom and saw that my pantyhose had a long snag from rubbing against the rope. And I saw the blood on my underwear. Between sex education, a girl on my school bus who took the time to educate me, and some knowledge from other friends and my grandmother, I was well enough informed so that I wasn't taken by surprise with this onset of menstruation.

But I had a dilemma. That was the weekend I was staying with my friend, Cassie, in town. The entire weekend, I told no one (not even Cassie) that I had started my period and went without any supplies. I was too afraid that that would mean that I would have to go home. When I did return home and shared my news, my mother couldn't believe that I had kept this a secret. She soaked my bloody underwear in bleach in the bathroom sink. Soon after, we went to my grandmother's house, where I excitedly shared my news. My mother told made a point of letting me know that this event -- having my period -- did not make me a woman.

I wonder now if, because of the abuse, my mother purposely tried to make me unattractive and that was her attempt at protecting me from my step-father. In 7th grade, I was in Junior High and she wouldn't let me shave my legs. I would sneak and shave the top of my legs and try to cover the rest with knee high socks. In gym class, we were doing gymnastics and some of my friends would pull down my socks, finding humor in the display of dark curly hair growing on my legs.

My mother wouldn't buy deodorant for me and told me that I just needed to take showers. After gym, my body odor was terrible. I began to bring baby powder to use in an unsuccessful attempt to hide the odor. This also brought me ridicule and teasing from my classmates. I tried to go in the bathroom stall to hide my application of baby powder, but when I came out, I saw a small group of girls trying to look casual as they watched me and chuckled to each other. Eventually, I began to borrow the use of Katie's deodorant when I was at her house, or in the morning, use my step-father's deodorant, appropriately named "Brut".

It was during the teen years that the mental and emotional abuse escalated. My step-father seized opportunities to engage in inappropriate conversations and activities with me. When he knew I was having sex education in school, he would sit down with me and ask me specifics about what I was learning. As I grew older and liked to dance and exercise at home, he made a point of showing me the "correct" way to do push-ups -- having me extend my body he held his hands on my torso.

He liked to comment that I had a nice body and that he would like to date me. When I was 13, he gave me a very nice card and had written my name in calligraphy -- as if I were very special. As we would ride down the road together alone, he would make a point of blatantly looking at and commenting on women walking on the street. Then he would tell me that at his age, it was o.k.to be attracted to young women. What was interesting was that if he heard of a pedophile on T.V., he would make a point of saying how "sick" they were. Once we were watching a movie about a girl who had been abused by her stepfather and hated him. He commented, "That's how Meredith feels about me." My mother smirked and I did not comment.

It seems like I finally got a hiatus from the abuse through 11th and 12th grade, when I had a regular boyfriend and spent much of my time away from home either by working, going to school, or participating in extracurricular activities. By my senior year, I had my own car and freedom began. I also began to understand the impact of abuse. I remember seeing the movie "Nuts" with Barbra Streisand who portrayed an incest victim. I remember thinking: *You can go crazy from stuff like this.* It was almost liberating to realize that there were other ways to cope other than trying to be perfect.

A final source of denial came when I graduated. I had been talking to my grandmother about moving in with her and my mother disapproved. She was very angry and said that Nanu didn't need me to move in. I just began slowly moving my items in carloads to my grandparents' house. Then one day while I was at work, my mother called me and told me that they (*i.e.,* my stepfather and her) were loading up the truck with my stuff and taking it to my grandparents' house.

Even though I was ready to move in there and ultimately this was a help to me, I felt betrayed and abandoned. Later, I discovered that my mother had confiscated nearly all of the music that I listened to -- many were her albums, but had been in my room for years. I felt hurt. We argued over the "Sgt.Pepper's" album. It was the first album I bought with my own money ($7). I bought it because my step-father had said that my mother would like it. I listened to that album over and over -as I did all of my Beatles' albums. That music and the radio had been my constant comfort – especially during the period when I had no access to anything outside of my room during my 8 months of seclusion. I won the argument and walked away with the record, but again felt that somehow my mother was betraying me.

Your parents are the first people with whom you establish a relationship and learn about relationships. When incest occurs, your biggest lesson is in betrayal and it is a monumental task to build trust and relationships with other people. It took me forever in life to realize that life is about relationships – a person needs to maintain healthy relationships with other people. An additional difficulty is that in most families with incest, there is love and there are some good memories -- and you are heartbroken that your family cannot be all that it should be for you.

"I'm almost glad the abuse happened, because it has made me who I am today," I told the therapist.

"How do you think it has made you different?" she asked.

I stumbled. I was at a loss. I tried to think about the young girl I was before the abuse. In thinking about it, I had some very positive qualities that had diminished after the abuse. I remember myself as being more confident -- especially with people.

As a young child, when we visited my great-grandmother at her retirement complex, I remember my grandmother telling me, "Now Meredith, don't go in there telling all those ladies about your dog. They don't want to hear about it." We would enter the large congregational area for food and activities and I saw an instant audience. I talked to them about everything. My grandmother would laugh at me. I was so much more extroverted.

I remember playing outdoors all the time as a child. As an adult, I rarely participated in any outdoors activities. The most time I spent outside was when I would take an evening walk with my grandmother. I'm not sure if eventually I became so introverted and "home-bound" out of comfort (as an adult, I found it more pleasant to be inside where there were no bugs, allergens, or crowds) or out of habit after I had been secluded in my room so much as a teenager.

The only answer to the therapist that even seemed remotely correct was that because of the abuse, I had worked hard to achieve all that I had in the way of education and career – both more interior and introverted pursuits in my case. Perhaps I wouldn't have been so focused on those if had had a more rewarding home life.

CHAPTER 13

My grandmother was suffering. I tried to encourage her to go to counseling.

"I have you to talk to. That's all I need. I don't understand how it works anyway -- you just talk to a person and I can do that with you."

She wrote a letter to my mother, telling her some of the things I had shared with her about the abuse, and asking her to contact her. It was met with no response.

My problems were compounding in every facet of life. At work, it appeared that my program was not going to be fiscally viable. My organization had not adequately identified the appropriate clientele for the program so that Medicaid would support the program. Without Medicaid, the program wouldn't be able to last. I was going to have to change positions or seek employment elsewhere.

My husband's ex-wife was deteriorating in her alcoholism and a myriad of issues were constantly presenting themselves. I was still recovering from my cryotherapy, still having nightmares, and still trying to cope with the impending case. I hadn't heard any news in a long time and calls to Otis were not being returned.

Dream Log: Saturday, January 11th (during a nap): I dreamt that I took down the Christmas decorations and it was very dusty on top of my entertainment center, so I had to clean it. I also dreamt that I was outside of this old house. I don't know whose house it was but my husband's ex-wife, Dana, and another young woman were there

*(standing behind Dana). I was angry at her for drinking
again and when the other girl moved away from her, I put
my hand against Dana's throat and held her to the wall. I
was getting ready to tell her that if she didn't straighten up,
she was going to lose the children (i.e., I would take them).*

*Dream Log: Saturday night: I was supposed to meet
Terri, an old high school friend. It was New Year's Eve and
we were having a sort of reunion. It was nighttime and I
got to our meeting place, but Terri had already left. At first,
I couldn't remember where the party was, but then I
remembered it was at a place called the "Sundance." We
were in the city -New York and I had a cab driver take me
there.*

*There was a big room and it was very bright. There
were a lot of people with whom I went to high school. My
ex-husband was there and we danced a waltz-like dance
together. We danced well, but it didn't feel right to me. At
first, I was confused and I kept thinking I shouldn't be with
him and didn't want to be with him. Finally, I realized I was
married to Warren and I felt relieved. My first boyfriend
(3rd grade) Alex was there and he was sitting very close to
me. We watched a video from school. I was in a fashion
show with my friend Kathy and I was modeling a bathing
suit. I realized that I looked good, but I wasn't much
smaller than I am now. The bathing suit was a pink and
green bikini I used to have. Alex gave me a very long kiss.*

*Dream Log: Sunday, January 12th: I dreamt that
my husband and I made love and he was very gentle with
me and sex didn't hurt at all. I was worried it would hurt*

after my procedure. I also dreamt that I went to my supervisor regarding several issues and he listened to me.

Dream Log: Monday, January 13th: I dreamt it was New Year's Day. My husband and I were celebrating and we were in this brightly lit room and there was a sort of loft with a bed and a table with champagne glasses on it.

Dream Log: Tuesday, January 14th: I dreamt that my husband and I were supposed to go on a trip by airplane. I had gotten my paycheck cashed and put the money in a long gift box which I put in my pocket. I was walking down the street and I was in a bad area. There were two men following me. I believed they were going to mug me and take the money and then I wouldn't be able to go on the trip. I ran into a worse neighborhood, but then I turned and saw where the good neighborhood was. I thought that they had gotten the money, but they hadn't. And I ran towards the good neighborhood. For some reason, I was a little nervous going on the plane, but we took off o.k. and I believed that if I could just get through the trip, everything would be o.k.

Dream Log: Wednesday, January 15th: I dreamt that my Great-Aunt Maggie (my grandmother's sister) and Great-Uncle Don and -Aunt Peg (grandfather's side) had come to visit. I think they knew about the molestation, or at least that there was a family conflict. They were in my livingroom. It was sunny and neat. Then we were at my mother's house. It was very dirty and chaotic. She had a buffet there and I looked on the ledge. There was a cup there where my mother had put her jewelry. I found a ring *in there that belonged to me --a small ring with an emerald and diamonds which I wear on my pinky. My husband gave it to me at Niagara Falls for our anniversary last year.*

I knew that my stepfather had taken it from me and put it there. I took it back. Then I was traveling with an old friend, Len. We were headed toward the mountains. We came upon this old mine shaft. There was Len, me, and another female. There were two trains on the tracks ready to go into the mines. Len was sitting on the ground refusing to go. I was already in the car and the machine clicked a couple of times (indicating the train was ready to go) but I wouldn't let it go until he finally got in the train car with me. Then I looked over and on the side of the mountain opening were four TV screens showing simple comedy things (cartoons, 3 Stooges, Marx Brothers). Then I realized that this was actually an amusement ride.

I was with my husband then and my brother-in-law Matt and sister-in-law Jenny. We were all on vacation together and having a good time. We rode into the mine cave and there were all sorts of people trying to touch us to scare us (like they were our fans). There was one black-haired man with a beard who was rather large (big-bellied). He seemed to be in charge and commented that no one had said "hello" passing through. I spoke up loudly and said that some people were shy. He came up to me and said that (because I spoke up) I could have 4 tickets to come back tonight. We were very happy and I remember that Jenny and Matt had taken the week off to go on vacation and I had several days off from work.

Dream Log: Thursday, January 16th: I dreamt that it was New Year's Eve. I was with another lady and we went into one area where dinner was being served, but at a much cheaper price than the other area -- even though the quality was the same. Again, there were a lot of classmates and people I knew there. Then I went into another section where there was dancing.

Dream Log: Friday, January 17th: I was in the car with my mother and we were discussing our relationship and I told her that as long as she was with Mickey, we couldn't have a relationship.

I had been waiting anxiously for return phone calls from the sheriff's department. Finally, I was contacted by Captain Benjamin Logan. He was in charge of the investigations department and apologized that they had not been in touch. He set up an appointment for me to come in the next week.

Dream Log: Sunday, January 19th: I went in my parents' house. It was pretty dirty. There was a kitten in the kitchen and my parents had put up a blockade to keep it in there. But I allowed it to escape. My mother told me to keep the cat in the kitchen. So I tried to set the blockade up. But no matter how much I tried to set things up, the kitten was faster and made it through the weak points. Then I was near a swimming pool. I wanted to swim (which would be pretty unusual in real life). My husband told me I could borrow his shirt to swim in -- it was a blue and white striped shirt. But first I had to go inside a school building. I went in the one classroom -- my 7th grade classroom where a teacher with whom I was very close taught. They were serving pizza and I sat down and ate a piece very quickly -- then I regretted it because they had actually had little sample pieces. I was going to go back out to swim, but the buses were going to come in 10 minutes and I wasn't sure that I would have time.

Once again, I entered the brown building and let the dispatchers know who I was and that I needed to meet with Capt. Logan. A well-built short man with silver hair came into the lobby. He had a kind voice and kinder blue-gray eyes.

"Meredith? I'm Captain Benjamin Logan. Please call me Ben. Why don't you come on back with me?"

I followed him to his office, which was more of a closet with a desk and a bulletin board cluttered with wanted posters, handwritten notes, newspaper clippings, and pictures of various officers and evidence. I sat down in a wooden chair facing his desk.

"Thank you for coming. I want to apologize to you again that this has gone on so long. Apparently Otis had developed a problem with pain medication and things got out of hand before I realized it. I have been going through all of his cases trying to catch up and I came upon yours. What I would like to do is go ahead and meet your friends in person -- the ones who submitted written statements -and then get this stuff over to the Commonwealth Attorneys' office as soon as possible." I told him that I would arrange to get my friends here.

Dream log: January 21st: I dreamt that I was in my grandmother's house and I had been talking on the phone to Katie, my friend who I've had since childhood (the first person I told about the abuse). I realized that I had run up the phone bill ($16 for one call), but I was going to offer to pay for this. My total bills were @$50 (I saw the bill), but there was also a charge for $50/a month which would be recurring which my grandparents would probably pay for me because it was to trace phone calls (especially prank phone calls from my stepfather). I think their phone bill was about $1,000. Then I dreamt that Mrs. Foster (the first adult to know about the abuse) was sitting in her livingroom with me. We were waiting for someone to arrive -- perhaps Katie. She began telling me about an incident where she had felt she was being watched and she had gone out to the truck, but it wouldn't start and she knew it had been tampered with. So she ran back inside and called Stan (my former neighbor). She believed it had been my stepfather. I asked her why she had never told me this. Then I asked her if she wanted to see my house. By then, Katie was there. I told them to excuse the dirt, even though the house looked pretty clean. Then we went outside to look at the 5 acres, but the outside actually looked like my parents' yard.

Dream Log: January 24th: *I was up by my mailbox. I was going to leave note for the mail lady letting her know that we would be fixing the driveway as soon as we could (i.e., the mud). A couple was in the neighborhood looking at homes, and they saw mine and asked if it was for sale. I told them no, and that I could not sell my house. But if the price was right, I might consider selling. I offered to give them a tour. The house was sort of like it is in real life, but a lot bigger. There were more rooms and the layout was so big. Some rooms I was renovating, but they loved it all and it all looked so new.*

Later, I was on a boat talking to realtors. They had estimated the house price as $245,000 (actually about $100,000 more than in real life). We only owed @$218,000 and the couple offered $300,000. I was very excited. I remember thinking that we could probably pay off most of our bills and have a nice down payment for a new house.

The next weekend, Katie came up and visited with Captain Logan. She remembered him -- she had been friends with his daughter when they were young children. She once again advocated for me. Katie's stepfather had worked for the sheriff's department for several years before moving out of town and through Katie, had encouraged me to press charges and see Otis. My sister-in-law Jenny also met with Captain Logan. She didn't remember a lot of what I had told her when we were friends in college, but she also spoke on behalf of my character. I met with Captain Logan briefly following their visits.

"Your friends are really something. They spoke very highly of you and your character. And that Jenny... she was really something. You tell her she made quite an impression on this old man." He told me to expect a call from the Commonwealth Attorney in the next couple of weeks.

Dream Log: Sunday, January 26th: I remember that there were a few people in my house. Lena, a staff person, was there and I had taken off my shirt to change and she asked me what my bra size was. I don't remember what I answered, but I remember that my breasts looked very full and nice. Lena took off her shirt and changed into a nightgown. It was beautiful velour, deep red with very bright white lace falling on top of it -- covering the entire gown.

Dream Log: Monday, January 27th: I dreamt that I was graduating from high school. There were a lot of people I knew there. At one point, I went into a livingroom area and three very nice looking men came in. One of them was Kevin Bacon -- the actor. They all had their shirts off and they were very tanned and muscular and they wanted to spend time with me. Kevin hugged me. I felt very good. For some reason, I was dressed in red, white, and blue.

Dream Log: Tuesday, January 28th: I dreamt that something happened to make me realize that my husband had been married before even his first wife. I called this woman on thephone and she made a comment that she thought I was a waitress or maid. I told her, no, that I had a master's in psychology. Then she began speaking to me very respectfully and I learned that Dana had been in contact with her and Dana had influenced this woman to make passes at my husband. I was in a very grand old

mansion when I was making this call. I asked my husband
why he had divorced this first woman and said that she was
very nice. He said that he couldn't see himself with anyone
over 17 years. Then the math didn't add up (i.e. his age and
the length of time with each woman). I also dreamt that I
went to the gynecologist to have my freezing surgery done.
It did not hurt. The nurse was very nice and gave me a new
pad to put underneath me —- fresh from the pack. I felt
moist and she examined me and told me that there would
be bleeding, but I didn't see any blood at all.

    Dream Log: Thursday, January 30th: I dreamt that
there was a celebrity wedding outdoors, although I didn't
really know the couple getting married. My husband and I
were best man and matron of honor and we were more
dressed up than the couple getting married. In fact, I had
on the white wedding dress from my first marriage. It was
very pretty with lots of ruffles. Attending the wedding made
me late for work. However, I only had to run up the street a
block or two to get to my work. I actually ran past it and
had to turn around and run back. Nadia and Alison
(another co-worker) were waiting for me -- we had a
meeting. But I wasn't that late and they were happy to see
me. All of this action occurred on the road that leads to my
house (the main road before you head out of town).

    Dream Log: Friday, January 31st: I dreamt that
because of a bill my neighbors didn't pay (neighbors being
the neighbors I had as a child -- I believe the same
neighbors who first knew about the abuse), the Mafia was
"collecting" by punishing everyone else. I was on a train

and a whole group of people were being held and killed one by one. I was the last person left and when I saw an opening between the two male captors, I ran to escape. I kept running and I came to my parents' house. I went into my old bedroom. At first, it was filled with water, like an indoor swimming pool. There also was a water bed in the room. I had heard that to be a lifeguard, you had to tread water for two minutes and then swim two lengths of the pool.

I tried treading water on my back but there wasn't enough water. So my mother told me to turn over onto my stomach and I did until the water ran out. I was very worried about my neighbors and wanted to call them - especially my first real boyfriend. My stepfather was sitting on the couch in the family room. To his right were his mother and my mother. He made a comment to the effect that all I was worried about or who I listened to was my boyfriend. When his mother questioned him, he said he was concerned or worried about this because I didn't listen to him. That's when I spoke up and said that that was because he was abusive. I remember "telling him off" calmly and my mother was supportive of me and didn't deny what I was saying. I found opportunity to call my boyfriend, but didn't because I wasn't sure how his family would react to me asking for him. I ended up seeing the family anyway. My friend's father was in the dream (he's dead now) and he told me he'd take care of the situation.

Dream Log: Saturday, February 1st (the last dream log during therapy): For my last session in counseling,

Miranda had set my appointment at 10:15 a.m. and I was trying to figure out how I was going to take off work to make the appointment.

Week after week I had been faithfully meeting with Miranda Marco. She had helped calm my irrational fears, validated my feelings, examine my experience, analyze my dreams, and look toward the future. I noticed subtle changes within myself. I was more confident in the decision I had made to press charges and felt good about the decisions I was making in my life. I was more assertive at home and at work. Often I talked about my struggles with the program at work and Miranda praised me -- saying that the organization was lucky to have hired survivors who knew how to navigate through obstacles. As we approached our last meeting, Miranda told me that she doubted that the case would ever go to court -- that it was rare that they ever did. I was surprised. As we parted, Miranda told me that I was welcome to come back to her if I ever needed support.

CHAPTER 14

Meanwhile, I learned that at the women's shelter where I was working, the position of Executive Director was still vacant. The previous Executive Director had been fired and for the past 6 months, we had been operating sans leadership. Two interviewees fell through and given that the future of my current position at my full-time employment was sketchy, I decided to interview.

Three agency board members interviewed me. I was confident and energetic, and was offered the job the next day. I put in my notice at my other employment. After I put in notice, another day went by and I received a phone call from the Board President. "Meredith, I have something to tell you. Madeline (the former director) is suing us for sexual harassment. I hope this won't impact your acceptance of the job." I knew that Madeline had issues and that whatever issues presented themselves, I could try to handle.

"No, it will be o.k. I'll still be there on the 17th."

A week later, the headlines in the regional paper read that the former Executive Director was suing the agency for several hundred thousand dollars. I was mortified. And I began to realize that publicity went hand-in-hand with the agency and the position I was about to hold. I then received the call I had been waiting for. The voice over the phone was soft, but confident.

"Hello, Meredith? This is Rachel Waters, Assistant Commonwealth Attorney. Could you stop by my office this week to discuss your case?"

We scheduled a meeting for the following Thursday. Rachel's office was adjacent to the looming historic brick courthouse -- a little white brick building with uneven wooden floors and the musty smell that embeds old buildings. I parked across the street next to the bank and walked past the tattoo parlor. A few people were standing at the front of the courthouse smoking. They were obviously on break from a court case and barely noticed as I walked past them.

I opened the screen door and met the receptionist, who invited me to take a seat until Rachel was ready. When the intercom beckoned, I ascended a cramped staircase into a relatively small office with beige carpet and a cherry wood desk. Rachel was an attractive woman, but very thin. She had large dark eyes and very dark, short hair that fell tapered at her neck. She held out a very long, white, soft hand that would appear to belong to a 19th century maiden more than a prosecuting attorney. We shook hands firmly.

From behind the door, another figure rose in stark contrast to Rachel. A rather gruff looking heavy set man in his 60's with short white hair stood up.

"Mrs. Pearson, I'm Robert Graystone. I'm from Victim/Witness. If you don't mind, Rachel asked me if I could sit in while she interviews you. Think of me like a brother-in-law -- someone that knows you well and can be your friend in the courtroom. I can offer you accompaniment if this goes to court."

I nodded my head to allow his presence. Rachel proceeded to ask me a number of questions -- most of which I had already answered in my statement. She wrote down my answers as I spoke. She held her hand against her forehead and appeared to be heavily concentrating. The afternoon sun made the room warm and stifling. After about 45 minutes, the stream of questions ended.

"What happens now?" I asked.

"I have to review all of the information and call you after that."

"I've accepted the position as Executive Director of the shelter. Is there a way to keep my name out of the paper if this goes forward?"

"We do make it a priority to try to keep victims' names out of the press. However, there is nothing to deter the newspaper from researching the issue through court documents -- which are public -- and printing your name."

"Well, the former Executive Director is suing the agency and I just wouldn't want anyone to see my name and affiliation and think 'there's another wacky director.'"

Mr. Graystone eagerly spoke up. "Well, I can't promise you they won't think that. But we'll do what we can. Here's my card. Please call me if you need anything." He was trying to be friendly, but I didn't find him supportive. He walked me out, talking about people he knew at the women's shelter and his views on the organization.

Before I started my first day of work, Rachel contacted me.

"Meredith, I wanted to tell you that I have reviewed all of the evidence and I don't think that we have enough to move forward."

"What does this mean? What are my options now?" I truly didn't comprehend what she was saying.

"We have to have a certain amount of evidence to move forward in order to increase the likelihood that we would have a successful outcome. If you would like, you can still pursue this as a civil matter."

"I don't understand."

"You could still go to the magistrate and pursue charges yourself."

"I don't think I want to do that, but thanks for your time. Also, can I get my journals back now?"

"I don't have your journals – I reviewed everything at the sheriff's department. You'll have to contact them."

I called and spoke to Captain Logan.

"I'm calling because I met with Rachel, but they aren't going to be prosecuting my case. They said there isn't enough evidence.

"Oh, I'm sorry, Meredith" He seemed genuinely upset that they weren't going to try the case. He expressed that he liked attorneys who went out on a limb and tried to go forward with whatever they had. But the reality I came to accept is that it would have done no one any good to put in a lot of time and effort, only to find that it wasn't enough for the court to find a verdict. He was surprised when I asked for my journals.

"We don't have those -- we gave all of that stuff to the Commonwealth Attorney's office."

Over the next couple of weeks, I called back and

forth between the Commonwealth Attorney's office and the Sheriff's Department. The journals were nowhere to be found. I had this vision of a few young men standing in the evidence room reading my private thoughts and feelings -- laughing and commenting about how crazy I was. But there was nothing I could do about it. The case was over, my family was broken, and I had nothing to show for all of this.

CHAPTER 15

I delved deep into my job. The first weeks and months put me back in touch with all of the players in my case. We facilitated a community council addressing the needs of sexual and domestic violence victims. The meetings were held at the sheriff's department -- where I had to walk past Otis's office (Otis was back at work now) and then sit in a meeting with Captain Logan, Robert Graystone, and Rachel Waters. On occasion, they all contacted me or my staff through various cases we were working together. Every time I saw them, I immediately thought about their roles in my case.

On my way to my new work, I had to drive down the main by-passes of the town. For the past several years, my jobs had taken me to Winchester, Berryville, and New Market. I could travel to work from my home through beautiful, tree-canopied back roads and the western state highways to completely avoid travel through Front Royal. My previous job at the women's shelter kept an evening schedule, so travel through Front Royal had frequently been during the dark. But now, I was in the thick of town. And frequently I would pass a brown service truck with a very familiar driver -my mother. She looked straight ahead, chomping gum, seeming ambivalent to anyone around her (even her only daughter).

Occasionally, casual interactions at work brought reminders of my family front and center. When I first began work at the shelter as a part-timer, the person who hired me was one of Aunt Cathy's sister-in-laws. At first, she thought Cathy was my mother and I had to clarify that she was not. In addition, my Aunt Cathy had taken a pottery class facilitated by one of my board members. When this board member first met me, she also asked me if I was Cathy's daughter. Apparently, my aunt must have watched me quite a bit when I was younger –- on more than these occasions acquaintances confused me as her daughter.

In addition, a few years into my realm as Executive Director, I received word that Aunt Cathy's mother-in-law had slipped and fell in our thrift store. Knowing her personality, I worried that somehow this incident would turn into a larger issue. Fortunately, it did not.

Shortly after Easter, I wrote a letter cutting myself off from the Catholic Church. I had attended the Presbyterian Church with my grandparents as a child, the Methodist Church with my parents, and the Catholic Church with my first husband. I had been baptized Catholic and as I returned to the church after my divorce, I began to work through the steps necessary to prepare for the first communion. I attended mass every week. I gave a first confession to a very nice Irish priest with a thick lilt in his voice. I took my first communion on Easter. Following the service, the main priest approached me. He took my hand.

"Were you married before?" he asked.

"Yes," I said.

"Then you can't take communion."

I was very upset. I was sure that perhaps one of my ex-husband's family members had seen me in church and had complained about me. Later, I realized that it was possible that the priest finally remembered me and my name from the premarital counseling that my first husband and I had undergone -- the counseling that I now partially blamed for making me feel a little too committed to the relationship which should have ended before marriage. In pain, I wrote to the church and told them that I would no longer be attending the church and wished for them to remove me from the membership roster. My current in-laws were now joking that they never wanted to receive a letter in the mail from me.

As summer approached, I was meeting frequently with a small group of ladies with whom I had graduated high school. We were planning the 10th year reunion. I hadn't attended the 5th year reunion -- I didn't feel that I was "together" enough to be able to speak articulately about who I was, where I had been, and where I was going. If I had been mature enough, I would have realized that this is typical for 23-year-olds. Then word spread that the 5th year reunion had been a flop and the former officers had no money or willingness to orchestrate the new reunion. I had been the student government president and felt some sort of obligation to step in and rescue the situation.

Between my new job, raising my step-children off and on as their mother was still having difficulties with alcoholism, and planning for the class reunion, I kept busy. It helped to keep me from focusing on my shattered family.

I entered a weight loss program. Weight, food, and body image had been issues for me for many years. My image issues started early. In 3rd grade as my body was evolving, my mother bought me clothes that were labeled "chubby." I was embarrassed.

I remember that my stepfather had certain items that he communicated were "his." So I engaged in secretive eating at a very young age. While he was in the shower, I would take bread and spread it with butter and sugar to have a snack. I relished the times when my parents weren't at home so that I could eat what I wanted.

Katie and I were fully influenced by Flashdance and all of the other dance crazes of the 1980's. She bought an aerobics album and I went to her house every night to dance or do aerobics. In Junior High, we frequently went on diets. At that time, Karen Carpenter had just died and Anorexia was getting a lot of press. I became very interested in the issue and in I0th grade, practiced it.

That year, I ate less and less and exercised more and more -- being extremely active during physical education class and doing hundreds of sit-ups and dance moves at night. My extremism culminated during one week at Virginia Tech during 4-H Congress, where I went an entire week with eating just one or two meals. But I looked great and was getting a lot of attention and comments from everyone about my body and looks.

The year I began dating the boy who became my first husband, I packed on 30 pounds. Fast food, lack of physical education, and replacing sit-ups at home with dates outside the home all contributed to a fast weight gain for a body that had been starving.

I remember visiting my mother at her work and

talking with her about getting a job. She suggested going to work for UPS and I said that was physical labor. She told me that I could use some physical labor. Little comments about weight always penetrated deep into my emotions and memories. Mickey's mother was notorious for commenting on any noticed weight gain. She would pat my rear and say, "You are putting on a few pounds aren't you?" Even Nanu had her moments. She would say I had a nice fat face and then change her words to say I had a round face.

I yo-yo dieted for several years and then successfully dropped a good portion of the weight before my first wedding two summers after high school ended. Weight came back on again with the stress of the marriage. As our relationship deteriorated, Jackson would lash out that he didn't want to have sex with me because I was a fat bitch who was just like her mother. At that time, I weighed 150 pounds. Meanwhile, I was trapped in that common cycle of depression, guilt, and overeating. I could control food, but I also let it control me. I tried bulimia for a while -- taking laxatives to rid my body of what I was putting into it. This brought me only marginal weight loss success.

When I left my first husband and began dating my second husband, I lost a significant amount of weight again. I've heard that when you fall in love, your brain releases endorphins similar to the high you can experience with exercise or drugs. It certainly worked that way with me. But then as the stress of the relationship increased, so did my weight again. After our wedding, we began to experience ongoing issues with custody of his children. I developed a stomach issue where I felt like I was going to throw up and was prescribed steroids. My weight went to an all-time high. Later, it went even higher.

So although I lost weight prior to my reunion, I was still much heavier than I had been in high school. However, the personal work I had been doing helped me to feel better about my body image. What I wasn't feeling better about was my family. I knew that my step-cousin Joshua could be at the reunion. I was relieved when I found out he would be attending a NASCAR event the weekend of the reunion. I was nervous as my name and number went out over the radio as contact information for the reunion. I kept telling myself that it would be o.k.

I took a bottle of tequila to the reunion. Tequila gives me a fast intoxication and it helped me to lessen my anxiety. I didn't know how to comfortably be the person I was now -- I felt like I was expected to be that old flirtatious girl I was in high school. Although, in reality, most people were already forgetting what others were like in high school. Joshua skipped the NASCAR event and came to the reunion -- he and I talked briefly and he was surprisingly friendly. We didn't acknowledge any of the family issues that were occurring.

At the reunion, I spent some time conversing with an old friend, David. For years, I had had dreams about him. I think they signified my connection with my old life. At the reunion, I asked him how he had been and told him that I had had dreams about him. He, in turn, told me about some struggles he had been having. I gave him one too many hugs and the mood of my waiting husband shifted significantly. By the end of the reunion, he was very upset and as we drove home, we argued. But by the time we got home, we had made up and although he had no idea, I felt strongly that I had moved on and was letting go of my old life. After the reunion, I felt a stronger connection than ever to him.

CHAPTER 16

I was ready to have a baby. In some ways, I had always planned it this way -- thinking that I would want to have a baby after 5 years of marriage, after my high school reunion, and before the millennium (so that if my child lived to be over 100, they could touch three centuries). I talked with my grandmother and asked her if she would be willing to baby-sit for me while I worked. She agreed and we began trying. I had already removed myself from birth control pills the year before - condoms had worked well in preventing pregnancy. I thought that after over 8 years of using birth control pills, I would have some difficulty getting pregnant. But I didn't.

Within days of conception, I knew I was pregnant. I was bloating significantly after eating, my breasts hurt, and I was very tired. I dreamt that my husband's grandmother (deceased) came to me in a dream and was giving me vitamins to eat. I hadn't even missed a period yet when my husband and I drove up to the Urgent Care in Winchester for a blood test.

It was night and the waiting room was nearly empty. They drew blood and within minutes, handed me back a little plastic square device upon which a little pink "+" shown in the display area. We were very excited. We drove back to my grandparents' house and then called my mother-in-law. I notified my Board President immediately the next day, somewhat nervous because of the situation with the former Executive Director (whose problems had amplified with her pregnancy and post-partum behavior).

I set up an appointment with the doctor, who performed a pap smear. My husband went with me. This was the same physician who had performed my cryosurgery and in the same dry and nonchalant tone, he told me that I had a red line on my cervix. He told me that it was most likely nothing, but in the worst case scenario, it could be cancer and I might have to consider aborting the baby if I needed treatment. We were horrified. I went home dazed and worried until the results of my pap smear returned normal. I was adamant that my husband attend every appointment with me. I ultimately regretted this.

"I don't know where you were with your first three children, but you just act like you have never been around a pregnant woman before," I told him (frequently). He worried over everything -- sometimes with good reason and sometimes not. It was a difficult year for us -- we were going through custody battles with his ex-wife, who served time in prison and re-hab during this year. During the court proceedings, I noticed that Otis was now a bailiff. He congratulated me on my pregnancy when he saw me outside of the courtroom. The hope of a new child carried us through. Ultimately, the children were returned to her and we were devastated.

We were fortunate in that early-on we were able to have ultrasounds. I was able to watch the creation of life unfold and while I was excited, I was more caught up in myself than the child I was carrying. My husband made a visit to my mother at her work. She allowed him in the office.

"I just wanted to let you know that Meredith is pregnant -- before you heard it from someone else," he said.

"Thank you," she replied.

He also took this opportunity to tell her to visit my grandmother and that I had pressed charges because I had thought she would want to leave.

"I've been married over 20 years and have a lot invested in the relationship. What do you think she would do if something like this happened between you and her?"

"I would hope and expect that she would leave me!" My husband answered. He tried to get a commitment from her to visit my grandmother, but she wouldn't make one.

We returned for my 20-week exam. During this visit, they test for Spina Bifida, Neural Tube Defect, and Down's syndrome. When I received the first phone call from the office, I was told that the test results had shown an abnormality. In my pre-natal education, I had learned that Neural Tube Defect meant that the baby could be born essentially without a brain. Spina Bifida was potentially significantly handicapping, but there had been great strides made regarding its prognosis. And I knew Down's syndrome. I was afraid. Knowing that I had had extensive experience with the mentally retarded, I hoped that God wouldn't give me a child with Down's syndrome just because He knew I could handle it. My husband and I were both overwhelmed.

"Maybe you should have an abortion -- we can try

again," he said. He had little experience with children with severe handicaps and was not able to comprehend the thought that he may have produced a child with me that could potentially have any of these problems. I spent the entire weekend in tears. I told him that I couldn't have an abortion.

On Monday, I received clarification from the doctor's office. The Spina Bifida and Neural Tube Defect portions of the test had been fine -- it was the Down's syndrome that had fallen outside of the "normal" range. And according to my results, it was still a 183:1 chance that the baby would have Down's syndrome. Anything under 295:1 was marked for a call from the doctor. I still elected to have genetic counseling and an amniocentesis. I knew that it would be important to know for peace of mind and preparation.

We went to the specialist's office, where we watched a film about Down's syndrome and the test that had been done. The specialist spent some time outlining our families. We watched the health histories of our two families unfold on paper. On my side stood schizophrenia, drug and alcohol problems, and depression (father), narcolepsy (maternal grandfather), high blood pressure (maternal grandmother), diabetes (maternal grandfather and paternal grandmother), cancer (maternal great-grandmother), heart attack (paternal grandfather), and others. On my husband's side stood anxiety (mother), heart problems (maternal grandmother and grandfather), cancer (paternal grandmother), and mental retardation (paternal aunt). For a few minutes, I was a bit overwhelmed and thought that perhaps we shouldn't have chosen to have a child. But apparently, there wasn't strong evidence that we had genetically-facilitated diseases.

We went into a large and brightly lit white room that was very cold. I put on a hospital gown and lied on the table. The specialist applied the cold jelly to the sonogram and began to slide the sensor all around my stomach, carefully observing the positioning of the infant. She said that she thought the physical features indicated a normal baby -- although only the amniocentesis would confirm this.

The risk factor for miscarrying was about the same as the risk of having a baby with Down's syndrome. I felt that it was important for us to know for certain so that we could have time to prepare and adjust. Then they applied liquid to sterilize the area of insertion and prepared the largest needle I had ever seen in my life. She carefully explained that the needle would be inserted and she would draw out the needed amount of amniotic fluid which would be tested. The anticipation was more intimidating than the actual procedure.

She carefully warned me about midway through the procedure, "You will begin to feel a cramp right about now." And I did, and before I knew it, the procedure was over.

"Would you like to know what sex your child is?" She asked.

"You can tell?"

"Yes, the test will confirm for 100%, but I am 90% sure right now."

"O.K."

"It's a boy."

She walked out of the room and my husband and I just grinned at each other. When trying to conceive, I had positioned myself during sex to be on top -- which I had heard would influence the conception of a girl (the male sperm supposedly aren't strong swimmers). My husband had already had three sons -- it was statistically time for a girl. We had picked out a girl's name already - Olivia (my husband's middle name was Oliver and the name was Italian which spoke to my heritage). I was going to have to reposition my whole attitude and thinking.

I had already bought a name book boasting access to 8000 names. Gerald Alessio was the name we agreed upon. Gerald could be considered Irish (my husband's heritage) and Alessio was Italian. The name meant "brave spearman, defender of mankind." I also had wanted the name to spell initials. "GAP" to me meant that the baby would fill a "gap" in my heart.

The results later confirmed that the baby did not have Down's syndrome. The rest of the pregnancy progressed quite well. By Easter, I felt as if something plucked me from the inside of my stomach -- the first movements of the baby. I was excited for the baby growing inside me, but also struggling with an 80 pound weight gain. I looked like I was going to burst from all of the fluid I was retaining and my wedding ring cut deep into my finger.

Worse yet, the baby was due in August -- August 21st (my anniversary) - and the summer proved to be a hot one. I chose to cancel my annual trip to the U.S. Congress for the National Alliance to End Homelessness conference. This proved to be a blessing -- two congressional guards were killed during the days I would have been there.

In early August, a rather strange event brought some amusement to me. I was pouring myself a bowl of fruit loops when something hard dropped out into my bowl. It was blue, but clearly not a food item. It appeared to be a button. I contacted the food company, who had me read the bar code and other information on the box. From this information, they were able to identify the state and factory where the cereal was produced and the likely shift. There had been no report of a missing button, but they were confident they would be able to determine the worker who was missing a button.

I found it all a little eerie, but also thought that perhaps it could result in several months of free cereal. I received an apology letter with detailed instructions on how to return the item. The letter was accompanied by coupons that afforded me 6 boxes of free cereal. Not quite the exciting outcome I had hoped for.

My in-laws graciously held a baby shower for me at the end of July at the local Moose Lodge. We had sent an invitation to my mother, but she didn't come. My grandparents came, as well as my Uncle Don and Aunt Peg. But that was the extent of my relatives. I had a handful of friends there and the rest of the attendees were from my husband's family. They were all very generous and it was an exciting time.

We bought dark cherry nursery furniture – a crib, changing table, and dresser. My mother-in-law painted the nursery bright white before we posted large decals of Elmo and his friends on the walls. Our nursery theme was "Sesame Street". I had learned in psychology that "Sesame Street" was one of the greatest influences on my generation and I still believe it is one of the best shows on T.V. I did not allow certain items in the nursery. There were no mobiles hanging over the crib and no playpens. I had learned there was some evidence that suggested that these items could lead to learned helplessness.

I fully intended on working until I went into labor -I could see no point in spending any time at home "wasting" my vacation and sick leave without a baby there. I went in on the Thursday before I was due. I had had a few stress tests, but with no real concerning results. At this visit, the doctor asked me if I was still working. When I told him "Yes," he replied, "Well, I think it's time that you quit. I want you to take it easy and spend most of your time in bed. If you don't have the baby this weekend, you are going to be pretty miserable. But we don't have to deliver for two weeks."

I went back to work for one more day -- quickly tying up all of the loose ends in preparation for my absence. At about 7 p.m., my husband and I decided to have dinner out for our anniversary. We went to the local Melting Pot, renowned amongst many locals and visitors. The square-cut pizza is cooked with a sweet cream butter crust.

I had an insatiable appetite. I ate a half of a pizza and a full meatball sub. I looked around the crowded restaurant and thought, *If my water breaks here, I'll never be able to fit past the crowd and into the bathroom.* Following the gorging of Italian food, I felt I needed ice cream. We drove through the local Tastee Freeze and I ordered a large Heath blizzard. I now felt fully satisfied.

But as I was going home, I felt like I was discharging something. When we arrived home, I went to the bathroom and a small rush of liquid came out and then stopped. I rushed out of the bathroom.

"I think my water broke,"I told my husband.

"What? You're kidding! We just got home! What do you mean you *think* your water broke?"

"I *know* it broke. Come on, we've got to go."

"I've got to brush my teeth." He went to the bathroom. When he came out, I said, "Let's go!"

"Wait, I have to get some clothes." He rifled through the closet.

I already had my bag packed and directed him to take it to the car. We drove to Winchester. I had arranged to have the baby there, thinking I would have better care than in Front Royal. While on the road, Warren called his mother.

"We're on our way to the hospital. Meredith *thinks* her water broke," he told her.

"We're on our way," she said.

In the car, I began to have contractions. There was no doubt I was in labor. I reminded my husband that it was my due date. Upon my arrival at the hospital, I found that my doctor was on duty. He had me undress from the waste down so that he could check my cervix. He found that I wasn't dilated, but decided to finish breaking my water.

"It's time to have this baby,"he said.

My husband picked up my red stretch maternity pants and held them high so the doctor could inspect them.

"Did her water really break? I mean, look at these pants -- they are hardly even wet," he said.

My humor with his denial and panic overcame my embarrassment. The doctor covered well.

"Sometimes the water doesn't break all of the way, or the baby's body blocks the full stream. We're going to go ahead and make sure that the water is broken." He inserted some sort of device into me that finished breaking the sac and expelled the water. I fully disrobed into a hospital gown and he took my weight.

"Gee," he said, looking at my chart. "You gained a lot of weight with this pregnancy. Were you just eating a lot or what do you think caused it?"

"Well, I'm retaining fluid, also," I offered. I didn't offer some of the other facts. His chart indicated a weight gain of 60 pounds. I had really gained 20 pounds before the first time I saw him -- making a total weight gain of 80 pounds. And it was doubtful that "fluid" made up a significant amount of the weight. Up until this time, I had made most of my appointments in the practice with him.

Maternity patients were expected to rotate visits with the doctors in the practice, but I tried to go to him most often because he was one of the few who didn't mention my weight. So I was a little surprised that he was mentioning it now. I somehow squeezed into the wheel chair and was taken into the labor and delivery area. The room was private with nice cherry wood furniture. It gave the illusion of a hotel room. My mother-in-law and sister-in-law soon arrived. I began to feel nauseous.

"I feel sick,"I told the nurse. "Can you find me something in case I have to throw up?" She tried handing me one of those little pink trays. To this day, I do not know what purpose they are supposed to serve.

"That's not big enough!" I said and grabbed a trash can just in time. I was relieved that I had thrown up -I wasn't looking forward to seeing how all of that pizza and ice cream came out during labor. I went into the bathroom and sat on the toilet. My mother-in-law very kindly came to the door and told me, "Honey, I don't think it's a good idea for you to just sit on the toilet in there."

I was not feeling very sociable and starting to get aggravated with my guests. I came out of the bathroom. It was nearing midnight. The nurse asked me if I would like something for the pain, which was starting to become more intense. During all of my pregnancy planning, I had wanted to do a "natural" birth.

My husband and I had taken the Lamaze classes, where we learned all about visualizing and relaxation techniques. I knew that there might be a problem when we were practicing our "counting" in class. My husband got very close to my ear and was counting in a soft voice, "1, 2, 3." I would burst out laughing at this odd voice and tell him that he sounded like a serial killer. Now I had only been in the hospital a little less than 2 hours and I was happily accepting the offer of narcotics.

"I thought you didn't want anything? You know it could harm the baby," my husband said.

"I'm sorry I'm not Wonderwoman," I snapped at him.

My husband, mother-in-law, and sister-in-law all found comfortable chairs and attempted to sleep. The narcotics began to take effect and I dozed off.

CHAPTER 17

I woke around 7 a.m. with the early morning sun just coming through plastic mini-blinds that were covering the windows. Nearly every mother who gives birth seems to have a special self-interest in their own birth story. But I experienced a small set of events that I think are pretty unique as far as the birthing experience goes.

I was given the typical Pitocin combined with an epidural to speed my labor in the least painful manner possible. Several hours went by with no significant progress and then we noticed the small puddle on the floor. At some point, the IV had not been reconnected to the appropriate tubing and my Pitocin was running onto the floor. This delayed the birthing process significantly.

Fortunately, the epidural had enhanced my good mood and I played my Beatles C.D. along with a classical music lullaby C.D. and held onto my little Buddha (which was supposed to be my focal point). Finally, in the early evening, I was allowed to push. The nurse tried to encourage me by saying "push like you are taking a big poop." This made me resistant. Jenny and my husband also tried to coach me. For an hour, I tried unsuccessfully to push the baby out, but he decided to back up into the uterus. It was then that I was given the opportunity to undergo a Caesarean Section. By that time - nearly 24 hours after I went into labor -all of the medical personnel had changed shifts. A short pear-shaped physician, Doctor Fester, was now leading the process.

I was wheeled into the operating room. A painful

shot in my arm sent numbness throughout my body. A huge drape was put over my head. My husband sat on a stool near my head. He was attired in full blue hospital attire. I began to smell something burning.

"What is that burning smell?" I asked.

"It's like an electric knife, but you don't want to think about that too much right now," the anesthesiologist replied. It was only later that I realized that the smell was from the medical personnel sawing through my flesh. I was aware of items being put on the drape above me. The exhaustion and medication had altered my thinking and I was quite sure at the time that my internal organs were up there and were going to be put back later.

After nearly mounting the operating table to reach into my stomach, Doctor Fester delivered my son. I could hear crying and crying, but couldn't see the baby because they whisked him to the table and my view was blocked. My husband couldn't get up for a few moments and then decided to go with the baby to the nursery. There had been reports of a baby switch at UVA hospital and we worried this could happen with our baby. Finally, they brought the baby back for a picture with us and then took him off to the nursery again. I threw up again and then spent about an hour in recovery.

A crowd of my husband's family eagerly rushed to see the first glances of the baby and then scattered to go home. Everyone was exhausted. The baby was swaddled and quiet when it was returned to us that evening. After a couple of hours, we called the nursery and had them take the baby there so that we could get some rest. I was overwhelmed as long as the baby was present in the room and felt that I needed to have him taken to the nursery in order to have complete relief.

The days in the hospital went by rather quickly. My grandparents came to visit, as did members of Warren's family. Warren stayed in the hospital the entire visit - sleeping on the couch. The hospital provides luxuries that can mislead a new parent. Whenever the baby was taken to the nursery and then returned, he was neatly swaddled in a colorful white and blue blanket, with a hand-knitted cap covering his head and a pacifier planted securely between his tiny lips. I held the baby all of the time and tried to breastfeed him often, although he still seemed hungry. I gave him some of the bottles the medical personnel had given us and he gobbled these up.

There were some issues with the nursing staff. While the first couple were attentive (one had gone to high school with me), others seemed to lose track of me. I had been told to call a nurse for assistance when I needed to go to the bathroom for the first time after the removal of my catheter. I was expected to go to the bathroom in a 5 hour period. In the late evening, I buzzed for the nurse after I went to the bathroom. She came in and asked me what I needed.

"I went to the bathroom," I said. She held her hands out and shook her head -- giving a non-verbal reply of "so what." I had to explain why I had contacted her about this. She left and said she would be back, but never came.

A blood drain had been attached to my stomach and had to be drained by the medical personnel. Two nurses came in at one time.

"This makes me sick," remarked one of them. Later, at 2 a.m., two different nurses came in my room to remove the blood drain.

"Why are you doing this now," I asked drowsily.

"The hospital goes on all night," a nurse replied.

The next day, the doctor came in and told me I could probably go home.

"I'm going to remove your staples," said the doctor. He proceeded with a rather painless procedure.

"Ow!" my husband yelled out. "One just hit me." Both the doctor and I laughed, thinking that he was kidding. Then Warren held out his hand, revealing the small metallic staple that had popped him.

Before I left the hospital, I was supposed to get up and walk around. This would facilitate my healing. Unfortunately, no one coached me through this process and I lacked the motivation to take the initiative myself. I did manage to waddle to the scales, where I found that I had already dropped 40 pounds with the birth of my 8 pound baby.

When we got home, Gerald cried and cried. I tried to breastfeed, but my breasts remained soft and it was apparent that no milk was coming in. The baby didn't appear to be going to the bathroom at all. I had been given instructions to breastfeed often and on demand -and definitely not to give the baby any bottles.

Gerald would only sleep for short stints of time on my chest while I laid in the recliner. I was overwhelmed out of fear and frustration, but in love with this little chubby face that was looking to me for resolution. We took the baby back to the doctor after two days. His weight had dropped by 8 oz. and the doctor suggested Pedialyte and told me to continue to try to breastfeed.

That night at 3 a.m., I was in the livingroom feeding Gerald and felt something wet on my abdomen. I looked down and there was blood all over me. I thought that my stitches had burst. We went to the local hospital, where I was told that my incision was draining. They changed my dressing. When we got back into the car, I began to cry and I told Warren that I couldn't take it anymore. I wasn't going to breastfeed.

The next 6 weeks were a blur of diapers, feedings, and visitors. I checked in at the office after 2 weeks. While I went in, Warren took Gerald to my mother's office. She held the baby for a moment and said, "You all will be confusing him by giving him an Irish and Italian name." She thanked Warren for bringing him.

Before I returned to work, we took a long vacation. We went to Canton, Ohio to see the Football Hall of Fame, Cleveland, Ohio to the Rock and Roll Hall of Fame, Niagara Falls, Canada, and Cooperstown, New York to the Baseball Hall of Fame. Not interested in the sports museums or the casinos, I spent a lot of alone time with Gerald. Somehow in all the movement we found a way to bond and form a routine. I felt satisfaction, ease, and love with my new baby. The fresh northern air appealed to his temperament and I felt renewed. To finish up our vacation, we stopped in Danbury, Connecticut. We were going to visit my family in New York.

CHAPTER 18

I have no memories from my childhood of my father or his parents. My mother had arrived in Virginia when I was nearly 2 years old. My father had attempted to visit her a few times and she called the police and had him arrested. During one of his "visits" I was playing on my grandparents' front porch. I found my own ways to deal with his absence. As I was a small child, the people next door were having a wake for one of their relatives who had died. I carried gravel from the driveway to the sidewalk and built a small mound of dirt and gravel, pretending it was where my father was buried. Then I had my own funeral for my father. I presumed he was dead.

Later, in high school, I found a bag of letters at my grandmother's house that he had written to my mother after she had left him. Some of the letters gave a return address of Bellevue. When watching "Miracle on 34th Street" at Christmas, a scene revealed that Bellevue was a mental hospital in New York.

Adapting the Jimi Hendrix song "Hey Joe" he wrote "Take me down, Little Christy, Take me down. Because you are the Queen of the Underground." The song goes on to describe a man who is going to "kill his old lady" because he found her messing around with another man. To accompany the letter, he enclosed a picture of himself holding a gun faced toward the camera.

During high school I saw the movie "Less than Zero"and was struck at how one of the characters repeatedly left and returned home during his times of heavy drug usage. It reminded me of behavior I had been told about my father. I pressed my grandmother for information.

"Did my father use drugs? Just tell me."

"Yes!" she replied. It was so hard for her to reveal any information to me. But it was the first clue I had to his behavior.

When I graduated from college, my grandmother told me that my grandfather had sent the newspaper articles highlighting the graduation announcements to Brewster, New York for publication. Brewster was where I had lived the first two years of my life with my parents. My curiosity was piqued, but I didn't pursue the search for him.

I had names of family members from a genogram project I had completed in college -- information my mother had reluctantly given me. Warren called information and found a number to my grandmother's house in New York and called for me. A young girl answered the phone.

"Hello?" she said.

"Is Leo there?" he said.

He could hear the little girl put down the phone and run off. Far away from the telephone, we could hear her excited voice exclaim, "It's someone asking for Uncle Leo!"

An older voice with a thick New York accent came on the telephone.

"Hello?"

"Is Leo there?" Warren asked.

"No, he's in the hospital. Who is this?"

"My name is Warren. I'm a friend from Florida."
We knew from the letters that it had been a habit of my
father to migrate to Florida whenever he was ill. He did not
offer any further information and ended the conversation.

After Warren and I were married, we reviewed the
video of our ceremony with my sister-in-law Susan. She
asked me what I knew about my father. I had little
information to give. I expressed to Warren that I would like
to find him, but didn't know how to do it. Following an
insignificant argument we had a few weeks later, I received
a call at work from Warren.

"I called your grandmother in New York," he said.

"You did what? Why?" I was shocked.

"Because you had said it had been bothering you
that you were going to turn 25 and didn't know your
father."

"What did she say?"

"At first she was very suspicious, but then she
warmed up. She's going to call you tonight."

Through a series of calls, she gave me information
on the family. My father had been diagnosed with
schizophrenia many years ago and had been rotating
through hospitals, group homes, and occasional trips to
Florida. He had just returned home after being gone on one
such trip. He had three sisters. Isabella was the oldest and a
teacher. She had been married for many years and had a
daughter. Teresa was the middle daughter. She had been
divorced for many years and was heavily involved in
corporate work. She also had a daughter. Maria was a

hairdresser who owned her own beauty shop. She was married to an African American man. My grandmother felt it important to convey this to me early-on -- probably out of fear that my Virginia influences had made me prejudiced against interracial relationships. I think it was probably one of several misconceptions that she had about me.

As we continued through a series of phone calls, we planned for my visit. I was going to visit near my birthday in March. She told me she was going to make it a surprise for my father, but on one Sunday night, he called.

"Meredith, it's your father." He had a pleasant tone with a New York accent. He told me how excited he was that I was going to visit and that he had always thought of me. I was excited to talk to him -- I felt an excitement and a sense of closure for the first time in my life. I also felt compelled to tell my mother. I called her at my grandmother's beckoning.

"I need to tell you that I'm going to visit my father in New York."

"You are?" she responded in a purposely non-chalant tone.

"Yes and I felt like you needed to know."

"Just be careful," she said.

"He was diagnosed with schizophrenia. Did you know that?"

"No, I didn't. He had a problem with drugs when I was with him. I've never seen anyone do drugs like he did -- just anything and everything. And it seemed like it started when his grandfather died. I didn't think anyone would be affected like that from a grandparent dying, but he was. He used to look in the mirror and see his grandfather's face. He would go off for days at a time and no one would know where he was. It makes sense, though. I think his mother had those tendencies -she was always taking diet pills. His father was very nice to me, though."

"I had told her not to tell my father that I was visiting, but she did anyway and he called the other night," I said. "He seemed nice."

"Just be careful what you tell them and how much information you give them. Just like you telling her not to tell him -- she did anyway. You know, they always knew where you were. It wasn't any big secret. And they didn't come to you."

My mother had given me some things to think about. Perhaps she was indirectly talking about the abuse when she was asking me to be careful about what I told the family. Perhaps she was trying to discourage me in her own way by letting me know that they had lacked taking any efforts to find me. Perhaps her life with him had been very terrible -- more terrible than I would ever know. And perhaps I was an everyday reminder of him.

At that time, I was working as a secretary for a subcontractor for a large computer corporation. One snowy afternoon, I was in the office since the subcontractors were not afforded the luxury of flexible leave time. I received a call through the 800 number.

"Hello, Meredith. This is Maria, your aunt from New York."

"Oh my gosh. Thanks for calling," I said.

"I hope it is o.k. to call you at work. I just wanted to hear your voice. I am so excited that you are going to visit us." She proceeded to tell me some things about the family in her charming voice. She explained that she was very close to my father, but that he was sick and it was sad. She had worried that she would never see him again when he disappeared this last time.

Before I visited, I imagined what my family would look like. I pictured my grandmother as a large, dark-haired Italian woman, with the three daughters following in her image. Finally, the time of the trip arrived. We drove to New York on the long path through Pennsylvania, where the snow seemed to increase with the distance on our journey. We found the Sleepy Hollow motel in the middle of the small town that looked very much like Front Royal. My grandmother had paid for the room and checked it out before we visited to make sure that "no welfare people were living there."

She met us there the next day with my father and we went to breakfast. Over the next couple of days, we spent time visiting at her house and my aunts' houses. My grandmother's home was a large home that gave the illusion of a cottage from the front view. It was backed by a large yard leading to the reservoir. It was warm and inviting, but also somewhat dirty as she had apparently spent more time at Bingo and other activities since my grandfather died of a heart attack. My grandmother looked nothing like I had imagined. She was short and overweight with blonde hair and glasses that came to points at the ends. The daughters were all very thin -- Isabella had short blonde hair and the other two had dark hair styled in fashionable short styles.

My father was well-groomed (which apparently took a great deal of coaxing by his sister, Maria, who cut his hair when possible) and sported a tuff of salt-and-pepper hair. He had great stories of visiting Haight Ashbury, traveling, and smoking pot with Timothy Leary. While his mother constantly said that "he gets along with everyone,"the reality was somewhat different. He did have some violent tendencies and admitted to me that on one occasion, when having an episode, he threw a brick at someone.

He was obsessive about smoking, his music, his medications, and his treatments. It seemed that he had traded some compulsions for others. He appreciated that I had made him a photo album that captured pictures of me at several different life stages. At that time, he lived in a group home with nearly a dozen other people. When we took him home the final night, we were startled by the wild appearances of some of the people who resided with him. Many had disheveled hair and eyes made wide from anxiety and psychotropic medications.

As time progressed, I tried to visit a few times a year. Once we were even able to take Terry and Justin with us to visit. In the early days, the trips were generally very enjoyable and lively, with the family coming together around our visits. I continued to mail pictures and occasional letters. He had occasional relapses with alcohol that were followed by regular visits to AA and NA. His collection of 90-day sobriety chips was extensive.

Over time, the pleasure of the visits changed. Because I didn't live there, it was difficult to tell if family members were just busy or if family dynamics were playing out. But unless there was a scheduled event, it seemed that we couldn't get all of the family there at one time. My grandmother made excuses for all of them.

For a long time, my father dated a girl over 20 years younger than himself, whose mental illness was much more severe than my father's. My grandmother sarcastically called her a "Jewish princess" and felt that she was not a good influence on my father. Warren and I took the couple out for a large "pie" (i.e., pizza). The princess reached into the pizza and pulled a hunk of cheese directly off of the top, leaving the pizza basically unfit for consumption by anyone else.

I could sense that my grandmother held some resentment for my mother leaving. Even if she was not the cause of his downfall, the stress of the situation didn't help. And she seemed to hold resentment against my grandparents. Shortly after my mother had become pregnant, my grandparents had accepted my grandfather's job transfer to Virginia. Although both parties said that they parted "amicably,"they both resented what had happened. My mother's parents wished they had never moved to New York, where they had watched both their daughters fall into bad relationships. And my father's parents apparently took my parents in to live with them during the time leading to my birth and shortly following. My grandmother in New York felt that my other grandparents had abandoned the situation.

I realized that too much time had passed to be able to recapture everything that had been lost by our separation. Often it seemed like we just weren't connecting in the way that I wished that we could. We tried to keep contact through occasional phone calls and holiday letters, but conversations were sometimes difficult. But I had received a lot of support when I told her that I was going to press charges against my stepfather and I knew that it would be important for us to visit her with our new baby.

It had been a hard trip of creating make-shift baby beds with hotel chairs and couches, washing out bottles in sinks, and adjusting to so many different environments in so many days. Getting to a home was a welcome relief. My grandmother bragged about how good Gerald was, but also was beginning to show signs of her age with aggravation and grumpiness. Warren asked if we could order something to eat.

"What do you have, a tapeworm?" she responded. We laughed at her, but felt offended. At my aunt's house later, she told me that my degrees didn't mean anything as far as knowing about my father. My father didn't accompany us on the trip to my aunt's house -- his visits with us were getting shorter and shorter each time we went. His memory also was not good and he kept forgetting to refrain from smoking around the baby. By the time the trip was over, I was ready to go home.

CHAPTER 19

The week after vacation, I was manic. I stayed up until the early morning hours to "Fall clean". I wanted everything done before I returned to work. We fell back in a home routine. The leaves were beginning to change into their bright reds, yellows, and browns, and the air turned crisp.

One afternoon, I fixed a large mound of leftover spaghetti for lunch. A few hours later, I broke out into a sweat and started having chest pains and stomach cramps. I stripped off all of my clothes in the livingroom. I ran to put Gerald in his crib. He was crying. Warren was taking a bath.

"Get the baby! I'm sick!" I yelled. I lied down on the bed. Then I got up, threw up, and instantly felt better. I thought this was a fluke. But a week later, I had the same sort of attack -- this time after eating a dinner of ham and baked potato. A few doctor appointments and an ultrasound later, I was diagnosed with gall bladder disease and elevated liver enzymes.

"You're choc full of gall stones," the doctor told me. Surgery would be in November -- soon after I was to return to work. The next few weeks were hard as I adjusted to going back to work, leaving Gerald with my grandmother, and keeping up with visiting family. After a trip to the mall to get Gerald's first Halloween costume (Elmo) and a birthday party, we came home to find a message from Julietta, my cousin in New York, asking me to call. I called her right away. My Aunt Teresa answered.

"Meredith, it's Teresa. Your father and Gram were in an accident. Your dad is o.k., but Gram didn't make it." Gram had won her small 4-door sedan at the Indian reservation Bingo. She was well known for her fast speed and erratic steering as she zipped through Brewster. The need to speed was one of the few genetic traits I likely inherited from her.

As we learned more, it appeared that the accident may not have been what killed her, but the actual lack of attention and care she received at the hospital. When she entered the hospital, she apparently had internal bleeding that went undetected. We returned to New York for the second time that month.

The funeral home had been converted from an old large Victorian home. During our prior holiday visits, we always marveled at the elaborately lighted life-size manger scene displayed on the front lawn. As the years progressed, the plaster Baby Jesus was noticeably absent due to theft. On this night, the home loomed over a dark lawn.

Gram was laid in a coffin in a very small room that was crowded with people attending the viewing. I looked briefly at her and memories triggered in my mind.

"Opas would want you to kiss him. Why don't you kiss him?" Mickey suggested. He was holding my young 14-year-old arm. I was still wheezing from my non-stop crying. Opas body was cold and bluish.

"You can do it. You can kiss him," he continued to coaxed. Finally I bent down and pressed my lips against that dead flaxen cheek.

Later, when Katie's father died, I also kissed his cheek. But I was alone and I did it out of choice -- thinking that it was a sign of respect. Today, my grandmother didn't get a kiss. I knew it wasn't necessary.

The viewing and the funeral mass were surreal. I didn't sit with the rest of the family and felt somewhat like an outsider. But I did learn that my grandmother was well-respected in the community. She had served on the board of my father's mental health organization for several years, had been active in the church, and had many friends. I wished I had been able to really get to know that good side of her -- the side that you can only learn about someone with closeness and time. I had been afforded neither opportunity.

After the post-funeral dinner with my relatives at the Middlebranch, an upscale restaurant in Brewster, we started the long trip back. I put Gerald snuggly in his car seat and sat up front next to Warren to view the string of lighted cities we would pass as we navigated through various highways and toll booths. Suddenly, Gerald got an air bubble in his stomach. He began screaming and Warren lost his cool.

"You should have been in the back with him! You are a selfish bitch!" he screamed.

"That's real good, Warren, right after my grandmother just died."

We didn't speak from Baltimore to Alexandria, where I left him to spend the night with friends so that he could get up early and go to work. He was working as a delivery driver for a donut chain -- he had recently switched jobs. He had owned his own ceramic tile business for 10 years, and then became a delivery driver for a bread chain before switching to donuts. Although he was not completely happy with the switch from self-employment, he stayed in delivery driving during my pregnancy to provide me with the needed health insurance and steady income.

I cried as I drove home in the dark rain with my new baby. When I got home, I received a call from Warren, who was checking to see if I had made it home safely. He offered a sincere apology, which was enough for my forgiveness. Somehow, I could always forgive him and he could always forgive me.

I had my gall bladder surgery in November. It was a rather quick outpatient laparoscopic procedure, but I was asked not to do any lifting for several weeks. My grandmother came to stay with us for several days. It was good to be able to be at home and share the baby with her.

One day I was feeding Gerald in the livingroom. I heard a woman's voice come out of the vent. The baby monitor lit up. Nanu also heard a woman's voice at a separate time. The baby would often look up at the ceiling as if he saw something. I began to wonder if there was an unseen entity living with us.

Warren had been with me for most of my maternity leave as he recovered from his own surgery. Over the past year, he had knee surgery and a hernia operation. His scars matched those I obtained from my c-section and gall bladder surgeries. All of the time and income he missed from work, combined with the increased expenses from having a baby, began a snowball of mounting bills. I had not anticipated the cost of formula as I had planned to successfully breastfeed. We were struggling financially.

Warren switched jobs again to work for a national airline. He began to feel very good about himself as he completed a grueling training and increased his computer literacy. But the wages did not reward the long commute. We continued to struggle.

I received a notice from a New York law firm that my grandmother in New York had left me $2,000 from her will. We were surprised that she had left me anything at all, although it was less than the grandchildren who lived close to her. I first borrowed from Nanu against the money due to come in from the will, and then we borrowed from Warren's father against the will. Both of them eventually forgave the loans, which helped us significantly as we tried to hold on to our house and get the mortgage payments out of arrears.

We were an endless cycle of working, tending to our new baby, having Terry and Justin stay with us on regular visitations, and just living life. And in the midst of it all, we were getting regular phone calls from bill collectors. They tried every tactic.

"Meredith, pick up," an unknown voice eagerly coaxed through my answering machine. Another voice behind that one whispered, "Say it again."

"Meredith, pick up," the first voice repeated. I

figured out it was a bill collector and didn't pick up.

Soon after that, I received a surprising phone call from my neighbor. Within our neighborhood, houses were separated by 5 acre lots. I had only spoken briefly to our neighbors in the three years we lived there. When at home, I tended to be reclusive.

"Meredith, this is Josie Riley, your neighbor. I wanted to call you because you need to know that there is a bill collector who has called me, as well as Lenora Dalton, who lives on the other side of you."

I was as astonished as I was embarrassed. "Oh, I am so sorry," I told her.

"Well, that's o.k. Lenora called me and told me she had had a call and wondered about what was going on with you. I told her that it could be anything. I know with my daughter, her ex-husband ruined her credit through a divorce."

I was honest with her. "Well, I would like to be able to blame it on someone else, but I can't. We just incurred too much debt and with the new baby, it has been difficult catching up."

"I have handled collections for many years and I am appalled by their behavior. I will be writing a letter to them and I will send you a copy."

The copy of my letter arrived in early March 1999, addressed to the president of the Park Avenue Bank.

Dear Sir,

I am writing this letter to register a complaint about some methods of collection that your bank has recently used. Last week I received a call from "Mr. Johnson" of your bank, who, after introducing himself, asked me if my neighbor was Ms. Meredith Pearson. I told him that she was and he stated that he had been trying to get in touch with her but had been unsuccessful. He then asked me if I would "put a note on her door" giving his name and phone number and asking her to please call him. I asked him where he had gotten my name and phone number and he stated that his company's computers had that information. I told him that if that was the case, why didn't he have Ms. Pearson's place of employment. He stated the last place of employment that he had. I then told him that I did not want to get involved in this and he stated that he could "assure" me that "there is no problem", but that he was "from her bank" and "needed to speak to her as soon as possible." I told him that I would not deliver his message. After I said this, I received a dial tone, not "thank you for your time", or anything else.

Please keep in mind that I live in a rural area and the distance between my house and Ms. Pearson's house is about the equivalent of 3 to 4 city blocks!

Last Friday, 5 March, my neighbor Ms. Lenora Dalton (who lives on the other side of Ms. Pearson), received a message on her answering machine which disturbed her. The message was from a Mr. Larry Johnson, who identified himself as being the "Collection Manager from the Park Avenue Bank". Ms. Dalton called me and played the message for me to listen to and then I told her of my similar phone call from Mr. Johnson the previous week

(I also recognized his voice). On Ms. Dalton's answering machine, Mr. Johnson spoke as if he were speaking to the answering machine of Ms. Pearson (even though Ms. Dalton's machine answered by stating that it was the "Dalton" residence). Mr. Johnson stated (on Ms. Dalton's answering machine) that "Your account is being passed to the legal department today. Please be courteous and return my call. It is very urgent. Please call me immediately ... I have some options for you. It is your final chance."

I realize that your company may have collection problems, but this is inexcusable, to say the least! I consider this an invasion of privacy. It is definitely inappropriate to call neighbors of your customers and advise them of the credit problems you may be having with them.

I would appreciate a response to this letter. If you have any questions, you may contact me at my home number. Thank You.

Sincerely, Josie Riley.

Not knowing my neighbors, I worried that the gossip of my financial troubles would soon spread throughout the small town. I was in a public position with a lot of financial responsibility -- I didn't want people to think that I couldn't manage funds. I had contacted Consumer Credit Counseling and began to work with them. I received a large raise that year from the board of directors, but it was too late to make any significant immediate improvements in my situation.

Unfortunately, we continued to sink financially and in June of that year, filed for bankruptcy. The attorney advised us that we should give up our house, but I demanded that we keep it. The same day that we returned home from the attorney's office, I received a call from a co-worker.

"Meredith, a man was here with a tow truck asking questions about where you were. I told him you weren't here and I didn't know where you were." Someone was trying to repossess our cars. I drove nervously the next couple of days and then one evening, the tow truck came to our house. A large man in his 50's came to our door.

"Are you the Pearsons?"

"Yes," my husband answered.

"I'm here from Autofinance. We are repossessing your vehicles."

Warren eagerly told him, "You can't do that. We've filed for bankruptcy and are protected under that."

"Well, I drove all the way from Richmond twice now."

"You can take a copy of the papers back with you. Here they are."

The driver left, obviously angry and on the verge of an altercation with my husband. When he left, we scrambled to clean out my car and park it in the garage. There wasn't room for the truck in the garage and we left it out.

When we awoke in the morning the truck was gone. It was disturbing that neither of us had heard anything to indicate that one of our vehicles had been towed away. Warren got on the telephone immediately. His tools had been in the truck and he needed them for his work. After much haggling, Autofinance agreed to let him pick up the tools. They would not return the truck.

CHAPTER 20

In early May, the annual Chamber of Commerce dinner and awards banquet was held. I made arrangements with Jenny so that she could watch Gerald while I went. Nanu begged me to leave him with her, but I wanted to give her the night off.

I looked forward to this event ever year. It was a time to dress up, enjoy a nice evening at the country club, and pretend that I was on the luxury liner of life instead of the sinking ship. I was to meet my co-worker, Jane, at the event so that we could sit together.

I walked in the building on the polished hardwood floors and began to browse through the silent auction items. I happened to look up and through the crowd, I saw my mother. She was carefully perusing the auction items and did not see me. I could feel my heart racing. I was panicking. *I've got to get out of here. I've got to get out of here.* I was flustered and felt trapped. Frantic, I walked quickly outside. Just as I walked out, Jane pulled up in her car.

"Meredith, your babysitter called the hotline. She left a message that you need to call her immediately. Here, use my phone." Still dazed by the other situation, I was now confusingly dialing my sister-in-law's number.

"Jenny, what's wrong?"

"It's Gerald. Things were going just fine. I was singing to him and then I sang the ABC song to him. It was like he suddenly realized that I wasn't you and he burst into tears. He's been crying for a half an hour and I can't get him to calm down."

"I'm coming now." I told Jane that my son was sick and that I had to leave. I raced through the back country roads that led from the country club to the mountain compound owned by my in-laws. I rushed into Jenny's house. She was holding Gerald and trying to soothe him. He was gasping for air, shaking, and crying hysterically. I immediately took him from her and tried to calm him down. I started crying myself and kept saying to him softly "I'm sorry, I'm sorry."

Finally, after quite a few minutes, he began to calm. He stopped crying, but continued to shake for several more minutes. Finally, when he was completely calm, I sat on the floor and held him. I told Jenny that the situation had actually saved me and provided an escape for me from my mother at the Chamber dinner. I realized that in all of my haste, I had missed dinner for the evening and had a little bite to eat there. Later, I called Jane and apologized to her.

Work had been going very well when I returned from maternity leave. I had acquired several new grants and new funding led to increased staffing. As we grew, there were lots of opportunities for career growth. Jane turned out to be one of my first serious career blunders. I had unwittingly promoted her to a position for which she was not appropriate and she became overwhelmed by the position. She offered to resign for the summer and at first, I told her that perhaps she was just burned out and needed to take a break. Then I found out that she had been engaging in a lot of erratic behaviors with fellow staff members and clients and what I had seen, I had somehow overlooked or ignored.

"Meredith, there's a certain inappropriateness about Jane. And I see you when you look at her. It's like a blank look comes over your face," said Kamila, who was the first one to break through to me about concerns. Others had hinted or come to me, but Kamila somehow broke through by addressing my own dissociation. I went back to Jane and told her that I was accepting her resignation. At first she seemed o.k. with this, but then it became obvious that she was very angry.

I felt totally betrayed by Jane, who had carried on a much different persona in my presence. After she departed that afternoon, her husband came to visit me. He was a small man, with curly light brown hair, glasses, and a soft voice. As he spoke to me, it was almost as if he were speaking through his teeth he was so wound tight with anger.

"Jane told me what happened. We just might talk to a lawyer about this."

"O.K.," I said. I was panicked. The impact of the other lawsuit was nearly over. The former director couldn't find any witnesses to support her side of the story. Apparently some of the incidents she claimed were sexual harassment had occurred, but she had been a willing participant (according to witnesses). She was apparently mad because the former board president had been her friend and did offer her the loyalty she expected when he found out that she was not operating the agency appropriately. The sexual harassment claims appeared to be out of retaliation.

But the last thing we needed at the agency was another lawsuit or the threat of one. I received a lot of support from other staff members, who told me that they didn't want to tell me about the situation because they didn't want to bother me with it. I worked harder at being more open and accessible to staff after that. Later, Kamila confronted me with another issue.

"Let me ask you something. Are you Christy Williams's daughter?" She already knew the answer as I acknowledged it.

"Yes, why?"

"Someone just told me and I didn't believe it at first." "Why?"

"Because you are so different."

"Different how?"

"I don't know how to describe it. I guess you are just so down-to-earth."

"Who told you?"

"I'd rather not say."

"Someone from the police department?" Kamila had worked at the police department for several years before working for us.

"What do you think?" she smiled. She had obviously been told by someone at the police department, but she didn't indicate specifics.

"What did you hear?" I asked.

"Just that you two had some issues and didn't have

a close relationship."

"Well, my mother and I aren't close. She is married to someone who was abusive to me." I didn't share all of the details of the situation.

"I had heard that you all did not get along," Kamila offered.

I felt uncomfortable knowing that people were out there talking about us, but also good because Kamila acknowledged in vague terms that she saw a certain air of phoniness about my mother. My mother had very kind qualities, but as long as the abuse issues remained hidden, she would always emit a certain level of phoniness.

Following the bankruptcy, my husband and I operated for a time with one vehicle. Most days he would drop me off at work and then pick me up in our new used blue Ford minivan. For meetings in town, I generally walked or got a ride with a co-worker. One spring day, I had a staff member drop me off at the local restaurant where our community health council met.

I walked in and sat down. And so did Jane, the staff member who had quit a few weeks earlier. I couldn't breathe. I was having another panic attack. Once again, my mind was totally consumed with the thought that I was trapped and focused on how to escape. Jane introduced herself as the "council volunteer." I was overcome with confusion. I thought, *Why is she here? She must be crazy - what is wrong with her?*

I made it for about a half an hour and then left the restaurant. I began walking. I walked from the restaurant back to my office -- approximately 2 miles -- stomping all of the way down the sidewalks of the town.

When I returned to the office, threw my calendar and papers on the floor, and raced to the bathroom, where my colon vomited. Having what I viewed to be a sort of traumatic event over lunch ruins my digestive system. I talked with staff members about the situation and then received advice from some other volunteers in the field. I was going to try my typical technique -- I was going to avoid her and delegate staff to go to the meetings.

Jane sent a letter to the Board of Directors complaining about me. They called a personnel committee meeting and diffused the situation, but I felt threatened for a long time. It took her some time to secure other employment -- she continued to give me as a reference as she applied for human services jobs and I was careful to be as honest as I could and helpful when considering what jobs for which she was applying. Finally, she applied for a job in a group home and I was able to provide a reference that was helpful to her (in consideration of what they asked me and the type of job she would be performing). When she got that other job, it became apparent that she let go. I saw her at a local department store and she spoke kindly to me -- time eventually healed the situation for both of us.

I was beginning to become more and more confident in my disclosure of being a "survivor." I went to a hearing for the family violence commission and openly said that I was a survivor -- although at the time, I didn't mention what type of survivor. After I sat down, I noticed the TV cameras and had to do a lot of self-talk: *Don't worry, this is Richmond. No one will see it that knows you.* I also was still expressing myself through poetry -but my poetry was getting better. I began to include more of my writing in the newsletters we would distribute through my agency.

One Woman's War

My nightmares relive
The dark desert of an unarmed child,
The hunts, the screams, the hostility,
The cries for reprieve not heard.
The enemy camped in my home –
This enemy I pushed out of my life.
The enemy I never defeated -
This enemy invades my dreams.

My mind grips the memory
Of deliberate attacks on my dignity,
The loss, the anger, the running away;
The sadness, the wounds, the hiding away.
The enemy seizes you in your home.
He raids your family.
He assaults your friends.
And he plots your collapse.

My life progresses
Into agony of reckless intimacy,

The loss, the anger, the fuming away,
The sadness, the wounds, the hiding away.
You surrender this enemy into your home.
He butchers your family.
He tortures your friends.
And he maneuvers your withdrawal.

My survival begins.
Anger, loss, wisdom
Move you to collect your army.
You find your provisions.
You build your fortress.
You compile your strength.
Time ceases your fires.
Battle scars survive.

A woman battles within her country,
Her home, her family, her work.
Against enemies who weapons are mental and flesh,
Against enemies whose tactics are intimate.
Against enemies who reject defeat.
Her wars proceed.
It's Veteran's Day.
Where's my flag?

As I grew stronger and closer with my staff, I
shared my story with some of them. One of them, Sandy,
had worked with my mother and had always pressed me to
tell her why I didn't have a relationship with her. One day,

she asked me enough questions and I rolled through the story. When I was done, I felt relieved, but my skin was completely flushed.

Sandy offered, "I feel good about this. I can see that you love your mother and that you care about her. I'm glad to know that you didn't just cut her off without any feeling."

CHAPTER 21

Maybe I had cut her off with no feeling. I had long ago developed a survival skill that most days buried memories, thoughts, and feelings about my mother. There was so much negativity, but what was even more painful were the thoughts of happiness. Remembering her sweet voice, her long beautiful light brown hair, and the way that she could always make me laugh if she tried.

I remember her in a big fluffy robe with one of those old time hairdryers -- the kind with a long tube that led from a plastic bonnet covering her head into a small machine that whirred with air. Sometimes she would disconnect the hose or put the bonnet on me to give me an exciting blast of warm air.

I remember sleeping with her at night when I was a preschooler. Sometimes I wet the bed because I didn't want to get up and wake her. She never complained to me about this. I remember being excited when her hippy friends from New York and out-of-state relatives came to visit -- how they gave me so much attention and sometimes brought guitars and sang songs to me.

I remember her tucking me into bed as late as Junior High. I remember as a teenager shopping with her on day-long excursions through outlets in West Virginia and Maryland. Before she went back to work and had money again, she had a knack for convincing me that Levis looked like designer jeans and that outlet clothes were more unique than what you could find in a regular store. At that time, the outlets we went to stocked irregular or slightly damaged clothing.

After she had money, she tried to make sure that she bought me what she could. Unfortunately, as I got older, I began to wonder if the money was paying for my silence. We took aerobics together, bowled together, and shared similar political views. She was pretty good with staying up to speed with music and we liked many of the same songs.

But we didn't acknowledge the snowy morning when she broke down crying because Mickey asked her not to talk on the phone so long to her mother. There was no school that day. While he departing for work, we would be isolated and unable to travel. We didn't talk about why she cried for such a long time after she slipped and fell just outside our door. Above all, we couldn't address the abuse that was tearing us apart.

Once we had been at a holiday gathering and I shared that I had scored very high on a mini test in college that assessed how "dissociative" you were. My aunt walked out of the room and my mother just shook her head and ignored what I was saying. I knew that she wanted to believe that because I was sustaining success with my education and my developing career, I had not been impacted from the abuse.

That ability to dissociate had sustained me through my first marriage. I met Jackson when he dated a friend of mine. She met him briefly and targeted him to date in order to secure an invitation to the prom. He was a senior when we were sophomores. Then I began a friendship with him by prank calling him and pretending to be Dr. Ruth Westheimer. I could imitate her voice very well and enjoyed the fun of prank phone calling. With another boy, I had pretended to be a cousin of my friend Katie and notoriously named myself "Gloria Vanderbilt". I sustained a phone and written relationship with him for a long time under this alias.

Jackson eventually discovered my identity and set me up with Alex, a boy that I had targeted for a prom date. Just before Jackson's graduation, his older sister died. She was a young woman, who died as a result of a contaminated blood transfusion in the pre-AIDS period when blood was not as scrutinized as it is today. During this time, I became very attached to him and wanted to comfort him during his loss.

My friend broke up with him after the prom. He briefly dated another friend before developing a summer romance with still another one of my friends. I remained his friend through all of this, often talking to him on the phone, accompanying him and my friends to the movies or other events, and even occasionally going on double dates with them.

Alex, my prom target, had only lasted two weeks in a relationship with me. He was a very nice looking boy, but the entire time we spent together revolved around making out in an acquaintance's trailer. In actuality, Alex was more like a vampire than a kisser -- focusing his time on leaving large hickies to the point where it appeared that I had been beaten around my neck.

My 1st love returned home on a brief leave from the Navy and I knew I needed to break it off with Alex. When my navy boy went out of town, I was free to date others. Several weeks after the break-up with Alex, I met him outside the pizza delivery where he worked. It was a slow night and he and I tossed a football back and forth and flirted. When he finished his shift, he drove back to my friend's house with me. I told him that I couldn't get back with him and kept telling him to leave. Finally, he walked out the door. And then he said, "Meredith". I looked over and he had taken his long penis out of his pants in an apparent attempt to show me what I was giving up. I screamed at him to leave.

By the end of the summer, Jackson and I were getting closer. For the poor rural teen, Friday Night Videos (which aired between 12:30 and 2 a.m.) was the only available substitute for MTV. Many times, my mother would join me to watch Michael Jackson, the Police, Duran Duran, and the other break-through performers of the day. When watching alone, I would close off the family room door and call Jackson. My parents, to my knowledge, didn't know I was talking to anyone -- I was careful to dial quietly and whisper. On his end, he would wait by the phone and typically answer after one ring so his parents did not wake.

One night, I confided in him that I wasn't sure if I could ever have children.

"Why?" he asked.

"Because I have heard that people who were abused sometimes abuse their kids."

"What are you telling me, Meredith?" he asked. "I don't want to hear this." His speech was slurring and I could hear him gulping his beer. In those days, the drinking age for him was 18 and his parents allowed him to cart in as much beer as he wanted to purchase. He frequently brought in a couple of packs of 6 or 12 beers to drink for his weekend.

He was still dating my friend, but Jenny (my future sister-in-law and friend at the time) was trying to convince us to date each other. She worked with Jackson at the time. I called him over one night to walk with me.

"If I come over there, you are going to do something," he told me. He knew that I liked to tease. I promised him that I would do something. When he arrived, we took a walk up to the cemetery. It was one of my favorite destinations. We sat by a headstone and talked. I was stalling and broke into the story about my abuse.

"I can still see his face." I shared with Jackson the story, which included description of Mickey's grimace as he was putting his hand on my leg to molest me.

Jackson told me that this was really killing the mood. And finally, I said, "O.K. Let's just do it." I leaned over and put my mouth over his. This first kiss was terrible -- awkward, wet, and totally out of sync.

"What was that?!" He exclaimed. We laughed and quickly agreed that perhaps we were better off being friends. I didn't tell him that two of my friends he had dated had complained about his kisses.

Despite this failed first attempt, we later decided to

date. He told my other friend that he was going to date me. At that time, he smoked marijuana recreationally. I told him that I would not put up with any drug use and he vowed to quit.

Our relationship quickly progressed to include heavy petting. I would meet him at a local park-n-ride, where we would spend a significant amount of time together. The first week we dated, he asked me to give him oral sex and when I wouldn't, he slammed his hand down on the dash.

"God damn it!" he yelled at me. I had begun to trust him with my body and his outburst made me feel betrayed.

"I want to go home," I said.

The next day, he apologized. He told me that he had to get used to me holding off on sex. For a brief time, he worked at the bowling alley with me until he got a technological job in Northern Virginia. He began long commutes to Northern Virginia, where he worked the night shift. I would meet him at the local park-n-rides following my shift at the bowling alley. I would typically leave the bowling alley at 10 p.m. or 11 p.m. and sleep in my car until he arrived.

On school nights, I was often getting home well after midnight or 1:00 p.m. One night, Katie's stepfather was patrolling the parking lot and shown the light in my car.

"Meredith? What are you doing?"

"I'm o.k.; I'm just meeting my boyfriend here to talk about homecoming," I answered.

My grades began to slip and at one point, I had three D's. My mother began to restrict my weekday travel and my grades rose again. One afternoon, Jackson picked me up from play practice. When he walked into the auditorium, I waved at him. My friend Ethan whispered to me, "Who is that?"

"That's my boyfriend, Jackson," I answered.

"Oh, Meredith. An ugly redhead?" Ethan and I had a close relationship and while I valued his opinion, I shushed him and hurried offstage.

Jackson had apparently observed our exchange. He glared at Ethan as I approached him.

"What did he say to you?"

"Nothing."

"What did he say?"

"Nothing, come on." I didn't tell him.

On another occasion, Jackson and I went to the movies at the Apple Blossom Mall. A new boy from my government class, Troy Zebulan, approached us. He held his hand out to me and I reached for it, barely touching him before Jackson intervened and moved Troy's hand back from mine.

"We're just friends, man," Troy said.

Our dates frequently consisted of going to the mall and the movies, hanging out at his house, and going out for fast food. My weight began to rise and Jackson frequently commented on it. He was very tall and thin, a stark contrast to my more buxom figure. Just before my 18th birthday, I lost my virginity to him. We used saran wrap as contraception. Later, we had sex during my menstrual cycle or utilized withdrawal as forms of birth control. Usually, we had sex either in the car or in his parents' basement. We typically had sex only a few times a month -- which probably lent to the effectiveness of the faulty birth control methods we were using.

Even though my weekday travel had been restricted, my curfew was 12:30 a.m. on the weekends and I stayed gone from home as much as possible. The sexual abuse at home seemed to halt during this period. Staying gone from home seemed to be the most successful deterrent. I continued to suffer the effects, though. I was having regular headaches, nightmares, and terrible insecurity.

Jackson liked to "kid" that I was "fat." He liked to argue with me and criticize me to offset his own insecurities. He took body enhancement pills from the health food store and worked out faithfully in an attempt to turn his rather lanky body into a more muscular and stocky structure. He called me a "nympho" when I asked for sex. And on one occasion, he burned cigarettes on his arm to show me how tough he was. He continued to drink, but because I went home every evening, I didn't realize the extent of his problem.

I chose to go to college near my home -- Jackson didn't believe that our relationship would last if I went away. He was right. I continued to flirt with boys at school. Following graduation, my friend Len came with a friend to bowl at the alley. At that time, I had advanced in my career to be able to work not only the snack bar, but also at the front desk. This meant that I supervised the entire alley and often, had to perform simple maintenance.

I had to go to the rear of the alley behind the lanes to fix pin jams. When I went to restore Len's pins, he followed me into the maintenance area and kissed me. His tongue went deep into my mouth and left me feeling astounded. Before he left, he kissed me again.

Eventually, I told Jackson. At first, he told me it was not a big deal, but then he became irate. In a subconscious way, I believe I was looking for him to break up with me, but he didn't and his hurt drew me further toward him.

I moved in with my grandmother following graduation because I knew I didn't want to marry as an escape from my parents. Jackson and I began to prepare for a Catholic wedding. Our preliminary relationship tests indicated that we might have some difficulties with compatibility. We also attended a "Marriage Encounter" weekend.

The more we attended the pre-marital counseling, the more I felt obligated to follow through with the marriage. And as with most things, I wanted to be successful and finish what I had started, even though there were warning signs everywhere. A few months before the wedding, I chose to change the date and found that the Catholic Church wasn't available on that date. We had been told that the Church could bless our union in another church, but when Jackson approached the priest, the priest asked him, "So you want to commit a sin and have me cover up for you?"

We decided to get married in my grandparents' church. To avoid any problems, I decided to walk up the aisle with Jackson rather than have Mickey give me away. We completed three sessions of premarital counseling with the Presbyterian Church and planned for the ceremony. A few months before the wedding, we rented a duplex from Jenny, who was moving out of town. Jackson moved in and we began to prepare for the wedding.

Jackson's family gave me a surprise shower on Mother's Day. I woke up late that day. The house was quiet and I thought that there was no rush given I was going to a family function. When I arrived, I found a large crowd of my family, Jackson's family, and a few friends. Everything went relatively well. Jenny's family also gave me a lingerie shower.

The wedding itself had several blunders. As we began to walk down the aisle, we realized that we were on the wrong sides and switched midway. Throughout the ceremony, I cried often -- mostly from exhaustion and realized anticipation. I also found opportunity to laugh as the Unity Candle wouldn't light. The minister pulled his pocketknife out and carved up the wick so that it would light. And at the end of the ceremony, the minister said, "Now I would like to introduce you to Mr. and Mrs....." He stopped and looked at us with a blank stare. He had forgotten our names. Jackson cued him and everyone laughed.

At the reception, we danced once with each other

and the rest of the time with everyone else. I told everyone how happy I was and flitted around like the belle of the ball. My energy seemed to be coming from endless glasses of champagne and the excitement of an incredible party.

Finally, we left for our honeymoon. We were renting a condo in Myrtle Beach for the week, but had no specific reservations for the night of the wedding. We gained great pleasure from the honks and beeps of the other cars amused by our "Just Married" decorations that highlighted my electric blue compact car.

In North Carolina, we found a budget hotel alongside the interstate and decided to stop. I saw a roach climb the wall and decided to leave the light on. I prepared for bed and lay down. I waited for Jackson to make an advance. Nothing happened. I rolled over and waited. I was determined that for one night, I was not going to be the one to make the first move. As the wait continued, I began to cry.

When Jackson asked what was wrong and I told him, he told me that he thought I was missing my grandmother. We then had sex. As the honeymoon progressed, the situation didn't get easier. Every night, it seemed we fell into a pattern where Jackson needed to drink, we would fight, I would cry, and then later we might have sex.

During the day, we found plenty to do. We played tennis, went to the beach, played miniature golf, and enjoyed fabulous buffets every night. We enjoyed each other's company and laughed a lot. The condo was new compared to the apartment we had rented. The simple amenities of an on-site washer, dryer, and dishwasher combined with the tropical décor and spacious layout was a new experience for me. We put all of our cash from the reception into the refrigerator and felt rich as we spent our "cold cash".

But at night, he felt overwhelmed and pressured to perform. I was dealing with my own emotional issues, which ebbed and flowed constantly during the week. I found myself triggered by the release of a new Aerosmith video "Janie's Got a Gun", where an incest victim shoots her father. In those days, the videos played over and over throughout the day and each time it came on, I stopped what I was doing to view it with my full attention.

As our honeymoon came to a close, Jackson communicated that he thought things would be better when we returned home. But they were not. For the first time, I began to realize how much he was drinking. He would sleepwalk and on one occasion, he went into the bathroom and urinated on top of the closed toilet lid. We were having sex less and less. He would call me from work on his lunch break and tell me, "Please don't pressure me to have sex tonight." I returned to school and was working part-time. Money was tight. Cigarettes and beer were a daily necessity and I had to spend money on those before groceries. I frequently went to the grocery store and bought 2 packs of cigarettes and three 12-packs of beer and spent the remainder (usually about $20) on the groceries that would last us until the next paycheck.

On one occasion, the cashier -- who just happened to be the fired former bus driver from Linden -- commented that it looked like I was having a party that night. I thought about it more as a realistic long-term plan to obtain freedom from the relationship -- if he continued to drink and smoke at this rate, perhaps he would be dead by age 40 and I could move on.

We traded in my new electric blue Sprint so that he could have a fully loaded red sports car. When his commuter car broke down with a "cracked head" during the summer, we were unable to replace it. I had to walk to work. We argued all of the time. "You are just like your mother," he would tell me. I began to think that if I ever left him, he might try to use my abuse against me and bring it out into the open.

"You are a fat bitch," he would frequently call me. I would go into the bathroom and sit on the floor in the dark, crying. I wanted to end my life, but couldn't gather the courage. I was bulimic -- taking laxatives in a halfway attempt to lose weight. I would spend my evenings in this desperate cycle of arguing and crying and then return to school in the morning, pretending everything was fine.

And then he began requesting strange things from me. He frequently listened to Howard Stern, who was now being broadcast from New York on one of the local stations. The broadcast topic often turned to anal sex and Jackson become interested in trying it. He badgered me until I submitted. And this became his preferred mode of sex.

He didn't like affection. "You are like a fly," he would tell me when I tried to give him unsolicited affection or foreplay. On one occasion, he had me dress up in a leather skirt to turn him on. At Christmas, he gave me a vibrator. And I was willing to take whatever I could get -- for a while. He increasingly spent more and more with his friend, Dan, who lived in Northern Virginia. I became more and more distant, and stayed away from the apartment as much as possible.

When I disclosed to friends what was happening in our relationship, they told me it wasn't right. I was alone a lot. He would tell me that he expected that I would cheat on him. A song Heart became popular. The song, "All I want to do is make love to you" was about a woman who meets a stranger and has a casual sexual interlude that later results in a baby. When Jackson heard the song, he gave me his interpretation -- that the woman's husband was a good guy, but he had something wrong with him and she was unfairly cheating on him.

Shortly after our one year anniversary, we went on vacation with Jenny and Matt. We returned to the condos in Myrtle Beach where Jackson and I had honeymooned. On the trip down, Jackson continually criticized me and I broke down at dinner. Matt and Jenny were embarrassed for me.

Once at the condos, I chose to give Jenny and Matt the room with the double bed -- I felt that Jackson and I could sleep separately in the bedroom with the twin beds. Jackson caught a cold and told me that the best way for him to heal was to chase NyQuil with beer and stay in bed. This is how he spent most of his time during this week.

Jenny, Matt, and I spent most of our time together enjoying the beach. At one point, Jenny and Matt took some alone time and Jackson came out of his room. Jackson asked where Jenny and Matt were and when I told him, he told me that we needed to have sex. I didn't want to at that point -- I was done with him. The last time we had sex, he had coerced me with guilt, saying "Do it for the marriage." I imagined he was someone else in order to get through it.

My imaginary lover that day was Warren, Jenny's older brother. I had been working with Warren for several months and we had become good friends. And while I tried to deny it, I had fallen in love with him. He and I discussed the prospect of having an affair -- but nothing had transpired. I wasn't sure that anything was ever going to happen. Warren loved his wife and wanted to stay with her until his children were grown.

As we waded in the warm waters at Myrtle Beach, Jenny, Matt, and I deeply discussed the problems I had in my marriage. Jenny and Matt had dated since the age of 13, and I always admired the closeness of their relationship. The tall and handsome Matt was always attentive -- especially sexually -- to the beautiful and fair-haired Jenny. They enjoyed spending time together, and seemed to find ways to work through any issues that arose. We had double dated with the couple on many occasions, including to the proms of my Junior and Senior year. Although they could see the fault lines running, they indicated they were sad at the prospect of my marriage ending.

Again as we left Myrtle Beach, Jackson tried to assure me that things would be better when we returned home, where he wouldn't be sick and we could be alone and return to our routine. Jackson was trying to get me to move to Maryland, where we would be closer to a new job he would be taking after vacation. I fantasized that I would live with my grandmother during the week, continue with my schooling and employment, and start an affair with Warren.

The same day that Jackson and I returned from vacation, Warren and his 1st wife Dana had a major altercation. I knew that I was coming into a critical opportunity and I made the decision to leave Jackson. I did what I could to walk out of the marriage quickly and conveniently. I took all of the kitchen and personal items and left Jackson the rest. I moved in with my grandparents, who were happy for my return.

At first, I took the mutual credit cards, thinking that I would have difficulty as a woman in my position getting credit cards on my own. And then I found myself unable to pay for the credit cards with my part-time salary. Jackson demanded them back. He was devastated over the break-up. His family members appeared sad and then angry, over the situation.

Once, during the Festival of Leaves, I walked down the street and saw Jackson's older sister walking toward me with her two children. I smiled at her and she gathered her children up as if I were going to hurt them. On another occasion, I saw a different sister in a restaurant and smiled at her as I passed her. "Don't you smile at me," was her response. Other interactions with his family were uneventful.

The timing of my leaving was terrible for Jackson. He was very depressed and looked horrible when I went back to get some things from our apartment. Clothes were strewn about and the bathroom was dirty. It was Jackson's first week at the new job in Maryland. I thought he would go ahead and make the move to the apartment we had secured in Maryland, but he moved back in with his parents. I worried he would never recover. But a few years later, a very public announcement emerged in the local paper. Jackson was engaged to marry a very attractive and slender woman with long blonde hair. He had moved on.

CHAPTER 22

As the next year's Chamber of Commerce dinner approached, I debated on whether or not I should attend. I knew that it would be important to overcome my fears and to continue attending whether or not I expected my parents to be there. I was dressed beautifully and had the support of four of my co-workers as we walked into the country club.

After we sat down, I saw that the table held for Shenandoah Quarry was near us. At first, I hoped that my mother wouldn't come this year -- she hadn't been there the first year that I had attended.

But suddenly Mickey and my mother appeared. It could have been possible for us to avoid seeing each other, but the microphone and speakers were set up behind my table -- which meant that throughout entertainment, announcements, and awards, my mother and stepfather had to face my table and look directly over my head to see the speakers. For two hours, I put on a show, ignoring that they were there, smiling and interacting with my co-workers, and acting as if I were completely engrossed in the event. After we got in the car to leave, my assistant Sandy summed it up best: "Well that was strange."

That May, I felt inspired to write to three teachers who had been inspirational in my life. I wrote the same basic letter to Mrs. Geoffreys, Ms. Capp, and Mrs. Orchard. I began with: *I'm writing this letter because I know that it can never be too late to express gratitude toward someone.* Then for each, I reflected upon a few memories I had of them. I then added:

I know that many people in Front Royal/Warren County do not have a great respect for the education provided to its students. However, I believe that I received a very good education. The education that I received in Warren County eventually enabled me to complete a graduate degree.

Without going into detail, I would like to disclose to you that for many years I was an abused child at home. People would have never believed this because on the outside, I looked happy and successful. School was my escape -- a place where I found hope. Because of teachers like you, as well as some close friends and supportive family members, I have been able to survive, move on, and overcome some of the obstacles laid before me in this life. I want you to know this because as you continue out there in the world, I want you to remember that you can never know the positive impact that you can have on another person.

I know this letter must seem a little weird. What can I say but that I'm in my 30's now and this seems to be the time for emotional cleansing. (Ha! Ha!) Take care. Thank You!

One of them visited me at my work, one of them responded with a card, and one of them I didn't hear from until years later. But I knew that each of them was special and that they would want to know how much of an impact they had had on me -- merely by serving as role models and encouraging me and supporting me in my schooling during some of the most difficult years of my life.

For my family, I had continued to send occasional

cards at Christmas. I heard nothing from my mother. But near Christmas, I heard from my brother. He wanted to visit with his new wife. I arranged to have a dinner for Jesse, his wife, his wife's parents, my grandparents, Warren and myself. I bought them a wedding gift and they brought gifts for Warren and I, and also Gerald.

At first the conversation was awkward and then it flowed more freely. During our conversations with them, we discovered that Jesse had wanted to invite my grandparents to his wedding, but Mickey had told him that would create too many problems. And because Mickey paid for the rehearsal dinner and a honeymoon to the islands, Jesse's silence was bought.

Jules, the mother of Kathy (my friend from high school) had waited tables for a time at the posh restaurant in town. Several months ago, I saw her and she told me that she was waiting tables the night the rehearsal dinner for my brother was held at that restaurant. She had made it a point to ask the wedding party, "Where is Meredith?" but was conveniently ignored by my parents.

Jesse shared his wedding photos with us. My Grandmother was highly upset that she had been excluded from the wedding, but we made it a point to avoid talking negatively about my parents. Jesse's new in-laws, however, let it slip that they were feeling conflict over the situation. We parted congenially and they left with promises to keep in touch.

Warren attempted to take Gerald for another visit to my mother's work. This time, my mother met him at the door and shook her head. Warren was hurt and angry, but left. Nanu continued to voice her despair over the situation. My grandfather had a medical procedure and my mother didn't visit him in the hospital. Nanu increasingly said she didn't know how this would ever work out and she fantasized about the day we would all be reunited.

"Mimi cry all day," Gerald told me one day. Her depression seemed to be getting worse. One morning, I walked in to bring Gerald and she was still in bed. She got up, but I thought it was very strange. Following a visit to the beauty parlor, she became overly angry that they had misplaced her hearing aids and told her that they couldn't find them. Eventually, they called and told her that they found her hearing aids, but she remained distressed about it. And suddenly, she was becoming forgetful. We would walk around Kmart and she would ask me the same thing several times. Then she would laugh and say, "I'm getting old."

It wasn't a matter of age. Something was wrong. She suddenly had no short term memory. One evening, I was picking Gerald up from her house and noticed he had a long red burn streak across his stomach.

"How did this happen?" I asked.

"I don't know. He must have burned himself, but I don't remember."

Another morning, I brought Gerald in and she burst into tears. I knew that I couldn't leave him with her. I became hysterical, went to work briefly to cancel my attendance at a conference and clear my schedule, and then gathered myself enough to call the doctor. I had been encouraging my grandfather to take Nanu to the doctor, but he was going to wait until her regular appointment (several weeks away). I called the doctor and explained her symptoms. They agreed to call my grandparents and set up an appointment under the guise that it *was* time for her regular appointment.

Warren was skeptical. He thought that my grandmother *was* now overwhelmed with babysitting and didn't know how to get out of the obligation. I kept trying to convince him that something was wrong, but he couldn't believe it. I made arrangements for Warren's sister Susan to watch Gerald for a couple of days. He managed to struggle through it.

I called Warren's sister, Jenny, who was now at home following the birth of her second child. She agreed to try to baby-sit for me until we could figure out an alternative. Gerald had terrible separation anxiety and I had to leave him crying, every day. I decided it was time to call my mother at her work.

"Hello, it's Meredith. Don't hang up," I said quickly.   "O.K."

"I wanted to let you know that there's something wrong with Nanu." I proceeded to tell her about the symptoms she was having and that I had called the doctor.

"Mm hmm," she said. I could tell from her voice she had a mix of frustrated feelings.

"She may be having some mini strokes or something like that," my mother offered. I told her that I thought she should visit my grandmother. We ended our conversation with no commitment for the future.

When I knew a doctor's visit had occurred, I called my grandfather. He told me that Aunt Cathy had gone with them to the appointment.

"The news is real bad," he said. I was outside on the cordless phone pacing the sidewalk to concentrate on the conversation. He continued to convey the information.

"She has a brain tumor that is inoperable and she has 3 or 4 months to live. They could treat the tumor with radiation, but that would only prolong her life maybe a year."

I was stunned and couldn't digest the information. For years, I had fully expected that my grandfather would be the first to go -- he was the one with narcolepsy, diabetes, prostate issues, and other problems. Now I recalled that when my grandmother and I would discuss death, she would often remind me that she might not outlive Grandpa. *How silly of me*, I thought. Her father was dead at a fairly young age and her mother died of colon cancer when she was still in her 70's. However, my grandfather's mother and aunt lived until their 90's and some of his older brothers were still alive. Longevity was present in his family, not hers. It was so strange, though.

She was the one who didn't drink alcohol, didn't smoke, had carefully prepared nutritious meals every day, and drank water constantly. Her only vice was coffee. In the morning, she fixed a pot and throughout the day, sipped on several cups seasoned only with non-dairy creamer.

From one minute to the next, all Nanu could say about the situation was "I just don't know what is going to happen to me." She would forget exactly what was wrong, but was adamant that she didn't want any treatment. She came to my house with Grandpa for a visit and kept saying, "Don't let her have another baby, Warren. She doesn't need another baby."

My feelings were hurt, but I guessed that she was worried that she couldn't care for another baby who might come along. Deep down, she seemed to know she was going to die. She had watched her mother suffer through cancer. She made it clear early on that no second opinion was desired or obtained, and no treatment was necessary. I went with my grandparents to the next doctor's appointment just for my own information. At the appointment, my grandmother confided in Dr.Easterly about my stepfather. She kept saying, "He won't change, will he?" She wanted to be relieved of this mental burden that she had been carrying for 4 years now.

I asked the doctor about hospice. He told me that they typically come in to support the family after a diagnosis is made that the person won't live more than 6 months. He said he would arrange it. I felt like I was losing my grip -- it seemed like I was losing control in all facets of my life. I took my anger out on Warren and he called me on it.

"Meredith, I know that you arejust willing to give up everything because your grandmother is dying. But I'm not going to let you," he told me. It was the reality check I needed to continue to move forward. I began to remind myself of the words my Grandmother had taught me, "This too will pass."

In August, we celebrated Gerald's second birthday. My grandmother walked slowly in, her feet beginning to shuffle. She still interacted jovially with the crowd. Her memory issues were apparent -- she held Jenny's baby and kept asking whose baby it was.

She had become fixated on my grandfather's brother. His brother and second wife had visited us several years ago when they got married. Nanu had it in her mind that they were coming to visit again and she didn't want them to come. She talked about this often.

Her demeanor began changing. One day we returned from the department store and she tried to adjust her hearing aids. As she would put her hand up to her ear, the hearing aid would whistle very loudly. She would continue to try to adjust it, but seemed to be turning it the wrong way. "Damn it,"she said and flung herself back on the bed. Gerald was with me and later, he mimicked her behavior to his father when we returned home.

I called later that night and began to make it a regular ritual to talk with my grandfather during that time of night. He told me that he had come out of his bedroom one morning to find her completely naked at the front door -- this from a woman who was overly concerned about what other people thought. She had also asked when Hanukah was. I wondered at the significance of this for a long time, since we were not Jewish. I validated him that he couldn't do this (*i.e.,* take care of her alone). He needed help.

"Guess who came by today?" he asked me.

"Who?"

"Your mother," he said.

"What did she say after all of this time?" I asked.

"Hello," he told me.

"Was she with anyone?" I asked.

"She came in with Cathy," he said.

He also told me that Nanu's sister was coming to visit. I had great hope. Maggie was Nanu's younger sister -- my great-aunt from Ohio who had moved to Florida in her retirement. They had been very close sharing their lives together in their youth and young adulthood -- being married, raising children, and suffering through the deaths of their parents. I presumed that she would come to stay for the duration of this episode. She came with her daughter and stayed for a weekend. I came to visit a few days after her arrival to visit. Grandpa was the only one there.

"Where's Aunt Maggie?" I asked.

"At the hotel, I guess," he said.

"When is she coming back?"

"She's not. As far as I know, she's on her way home." "What?" I was confused.

"She was really tore up," he said. "They were very close when they were young." He went on to say that he didn't know if Cathy said something to her or not, but they just decided to go home."

I began to feel hopeless and wonder who was going

to help us. My grandmother walk was now a complete system of shuffles. She was barely getting around. Within a few weeks that seemed an eternity, hospice began to come in. They delivered a hospital bed. I went to visit by myself and sat down in her bedroom with some reading materials. As soon as she saw me there, she said my name and began to cry. Then she got up.

"Where are you going?" I asked.

"I don't know," she answered and got back in bed. It was hard to keep her in bed.

I began to visit every couple of days, carefully riding at the top of the road that led to my grandmother's house so that I could get a view of the house and make sure they didn't have other company -- particularly my aunt or my mother -- when I wanted to visit.

Sunday mornings seemed to be safest and eventually, I chose that as my main visiting day. Increasingly, though, instead of socially visiting with my grandparents, I used the time to clean their house. I took Gerald in to visit a few times with me. I would hold him down to her to kiss her. Once, my mother was there and we chose to come in anyway. She remained in the kitchen reading the newspaper. Gerald went out to the kitchen and said hi to her, not realizing that she was his grandmother.

In the grocery store, I saw an old acquaintance of my grandmother's. I told her of my grandmother's condition. She had no idea of what was happening and within a few days, delivered a casserole to my grandmother's house.

Nanu was losing her ability to speak. But at one point, I took her to the bathroom and tried to help her, but we bumped heads. "Meredith," she said in an aggravated voice. For a time, she could still say my name. But then she got to the point where she would just look at me and nod, as if to say "I know who you are."

Cathy and Christy were taking over the finances. My grandmother had always been diligent in balancing her checkbook and keeping the bills paid, but apparently had begun deteriorating with these tasks for a couple of months before being diagnosed with the brain tumor. According to my grandfather, they spent hours mulling over the checkbook, sorting out the entries and establishing an understanding of the financial statements.

One day, my mother-in-law and Jenny came and met me at my grandparents' house so they could visit. I went downstairs with my grandfather for a brief time and when we came back up, my mother-in-law conveyed to me that the hospice worker had left and passed on the instructions that the worker had left with her.

When I got home, I received a phone call. The caller i.d. gave me a second's warning that it was Aunt Cathy. She was angry.

"You put my mother's life in danger," she told me.

"What are you talking about? I asked.

"You had no business bringing Bessie Pearson to the house. Mom didn't want everyone to know her business or to see her like this. And the hospice worker should have never given her information about her medications. I mean,

Christy and I are the ones taking care of her and we are the only people who should have that information. I don't mind you coming to visit with Gerald, but you should have never brought Bessie to the house. And she should have had sense enough to come and get Daddy to give him the information. She shouldn't have even been there -- she didn't even know Mom."

"She did know Nanu. I'm sorry that she took that information, but she did that because no one else was around."

"I don't care. That put her life in danger and she had no business taking that information. She should have had better sense and I'm sick of hearing about her."

Wonder what she's talking about, I thought. How could she be sick of my mother-in-law? For a brief moment, I recalled that Warren's sister had briefly dated someone from Uncle Randy's family -- perhaps somehow the resentment had developed from that.

"And another thing," she said. "I went down to the police department and I found out about Richard Monroe. I talked to him and he doesn't even know what you were talking about or Warren."

My heart increased its pounding.

"Warren did a tile job for him," I said. I knew that much -- I had been in Richard's house when Warren was doing the job.

"Well, he doesn't know what you were talking about," she said.

"So you don't believe anything happened," I said.

"Well, I believe something happened, but it wasn't a big deal. You are just a tattletale. And I think that your husband is behind a lot of this."

"What?" I had no idea what she was talking about. While Warren had supported me throughout this journey, it had been a long and difficult path for him, also -- and one he would never have convinced me to embark upon. In fact, at times, he was afraid of what was going to happen to the family as a result of pressing charges.

"You think he is behind this?" I asked, my voice conveying my surprise.

"Yes, I do."

"Well, whatever," I said. I didn't know what else to say to this ignorance.

"Whatever," she said and we ended our conversation.

I became hysterical. Gerald was with me and I couldn't function. I called my mother-in-law and asked her if she could come and see me. She drove out to my house. By the time she arrived, I had worked through some of my feelings, but she helped me process through the situation. I remained amazed that Cathy thought Warren was behind this -- she presumed that because I was with him at the time I pressed charges, he had somehow been an influence in it. The only "influence" he had provided me was the safety net to be myself and to take the risks I needed to take.

Although Warren had been skeptical in the beginning about my Grandmother's prognosis, he had later confided to me that he just couldn't believe that God would let someone as good as my Grandmother die. He wasn't perfect, but our good times had far outnumbered our bad times and we had grown together into a fairly healthy and enjoyable relationship. My aunt couldn't believe that the girl who was once such a victim had grown out of that role. And I was amazed that she had likened my disclosure of abuse to "tattletaling."

I called my grandfather and talked to him about the situation. He was angry that Cathy had acted that way and said he was going to say something to her. I asked him not to -- that she already thought I was a tattletale and that would just play into that persona. I also called my mother to further mend fences. I conveyed to her a little about the misunderstanding with Cathy, but decided to reframe the situation and focus on other issues.

"I know this must be really hard on you. I know what I am feeling like and I can't imagine what you are feeling like since you are the ones taking care of her."

"Well, it's not so bad. We are taking shifts and just encouraging her. Like the other day, she had to go to the bathroom and we set her on that thing in her bedroom and talked her into going."

I also told her that now that I had children, I would like her to be a part of our lives.

"Well, let's just all get through this, first," she said. I also spoke to the hospice worker and apologized to her.

"We have some family issues," I told her.

She smiled at me and said she understood. Then my grandfather told her what I did for a living. She acknowledged that it was tough work and I, in turn, acknowledged that what she did was tough. She told me that they were going to give my grandmother a sponge bath later and that she really seemed to enjoy those. That was interesting.

One Christmas long ago, my aunt and mother laughed as they asked me, "Have you ever seen your grandmother take a bath?" By doing that, they drew attention to what I had observed my entire life -- no I hadn't. She was always clean, but completely washed off with soap, a washcloth, and water from the sink. She never took a shower or a bath. She told me that she was afraid of the water. She had been thrown in the water to learn to swim and refrained from it since then. But she would add that she was careful to never instill that fear in her children.

At some point, I began to notice that my grandfather was including "Mickey" inconversations. I began to suspect that Mickey was coming to visit my grandmother with my mother. I continued to be careful about my visiting times. My suspicions were confirmed when my grandfather showed me pictures he had taken of Nanu -- in one of them Mickey stood comfortably with Cathy, my mother, Nanu, and Cathy's children.

I couldn't believe that Mickey had slipped back into their lives so easily -- what a snake. And my grandfather was too weak -- he needed help for the situation and could not stand up to any of them. The pictures he showed me looked like a family portrait with all the family members gathered around my grandmother's bed. And my absence spoke to an important point -- I was no longer a part of this family.

CHAPTER 23

Warren was mowing the lawn with his small red tractor on that 11th day of October. The sky was sunny and clear. The air was crisp and again the leaves were at their peak of color. I hadn't been to my grandmother's house in a few days, but planned to get there before the weekend. I answered the phone after several rings. Nanu had always taught me that it was polite to wait 2 or 3 rings, so that you didn't appear too eager to answer the phone and a caller to hang up if they changed their mind about the call.

"Grandma died this afternoon. She went peacefully," Grandpa said. I ran outside and let Warren know and he dropped his head.

"I want to go," I said. Can you watch Gerald?"

He nodded and I drove as fast as I could down the winding road to town. When I arrived, I noticed my mother's and my aunt's cars in the driveway. I went through the door, turned the corner, and walked down the hall to my grandmother's bedroom. My aunt saw me and shook her head, letting out an aggravated sigh that apparently was her natural reaction to seeing me.

My grandmother was propped up in the hospital cot with her head turned limply to one side and her hair misshaped from lying in bed so long. Standing beside her was my mother. She was holding my grandmother's hand and stroking it. I sat down in the chair by the bed.

My mother began to talk.

"She went very peacefully. Her heart rate started to go down about noon and it got slower and slower. I asked

Elsie (*i.e.,* the hospice worker) if this is what it is like when someone dies." I gasped a shudder, beginning to cry.

"Meredith, you don't have to be here -- really." I didn't move at first. There was a male hospice worker there. I told him that they had done a very good job. He told me that it was nice to work with a family such as ours.

"You all are obviously close. You'll get through this." I wondered what in the world made him think that we were a close family. My mother convinced me to go in the other room. I went to the kitchen, where I found my grandfather. I hugged him.

"I just want you to know that I love you both -- you all have done so much for me and I appreciate it."

He said, "I love you too," and then skipped a step away as he choked back a tear. The coroner arrived. It was Seth -- a boy who had been a year above me in school.

"Hi, Seth. You went to school with my niece Melanie Fincham," said Aunt Cathy, speaking about her niece through her marriage with Randy Sr. I quickly spoke up behind her to tell Seth hi. In a very short moment, Seth and his associates had unfolded a gurney and took it back to my grandmother's room. A few minutes later, the gurney was being wheeled out with Nanu's body zipped up in the large black body bag.

My aunt watched the gurney exit through the door and my mother stood behind her, laying her head over Cathy's shoulder. Before I left, I felt compelled to speak to my aunt. I hugged her and said, "I'm sorry."

"O.K.," she said. "You need to tell your mother

that." I was implying that I was sorry for her loss, but she seemed to be interpreting that I was apologizing for the trouble that she perceived I created. I also chose to approach my mother with a hug and conveyed "I'm sorry" to her also.

When I left, it was late and dark. The stars were bright in the sky and I sobbed and screamed in the privacy of my car as I drove home. "Where are you?" was all I could think in the desperateness of the moment. I had no answers that could console myself. I went home and stayed up until the wee hours of the morning writing a poem.

Where You Are

Where are you now?
My heart aches and
My mind discovers you
In our children.
Many little ones
Rocked in your arms
To made-up songs,
Solaced by your
Tender-turned voice.
Playing bounce-ball,
Baking mud pies,
Gaming for hours --
Motherhood was your bliss.

Where are you now?

My heart aches and
My mind discovers you
In our teenagers.
Confused souls who
Found calm purpose,
Cheered by your aid
Fostering faith,
Expecting growth,
Marketing morals –
Guidance was your skill.

Where are you now?
My heart aches and
My mind discovers you
In our adults.
So many lives relished in
Kitchen-table chats,
Coffee-pot socials,
Grocery tête-à-têtes, --
Hostessing all
Was your talent.

We yearn for your lap
Where comfort always sat.
We seek for your hands
That once wiped away tears.
We chase your stock words
Hoping "This too shall pass."

Where are you now?
My heart aches, but
Angels have discovered you --
Our Nanu, our Mom,
Our Grandma, our Mimi.
And your love will warm us
Reaching from Heaven now.

I called my mother-in-law when I got home and asked her if she would go shopping with me. I was going to need clothes for the funeral. I called my office to let them know that my grandmother had died.

The next day, I stopped by my office and got my paycheck and then met my mother-in-law for the drive to Winchester. We went to Sears and Kohl's and I bought a Navy short-sleeve pant suit and a black long-sleeve pin-striped pant suit. My mother-in-law complimented me on how I looked and offered to pay for one of the suits. I thought it was ironic that my whole life, my grandmother scrutinized my wardrobe to influence me to dress professionally and conservatively in a way that would flatter my figure. It took her death for me to buy an outfit she would have liked.

After we came back to Front Royal and I returned my mother-in-law to her car, I drove to Grandpa's. My mother's car was there, but I didn't have time to let that deter me. I went to the T.V. room. There was Mickey sitting on the recliner watching T.V.

"Where's Grandpa?" I asked. "Downstairs, I think,"

he answered.

I went through the kitchen and descended the stairs to the basement. As a child, I had been scared of the basement -- always running up the stairs very quickly to avoid the ghosts that I dreamed resided there. Some of my fear may have originated in a fall that I don't remember. I apparently fell down the stairs as a toddler and my grandfather caught me before I hit the floor. The only evidence of the fall was the scar above my eye and overprotectiveness of my grandparents, who installed a lock and became panicky whenever a small child approached the basement door.

The three large rooms in the basement had now become family storage with stuff from nearly everyone. Grandpa also had an "office" set up with his own hoard of clutter. I found him there.

"I wrote a poem and I was wondering if perhaps it could be read at the funeral." I said.

He took it out and began to read it aloud. And then he stopped as he choked back a sob. He carefully folded the paper and put it in the front pocket of his shirt.

"Yes, that's really nice. I'll give it to the minister."

Unfortunately, I had to go to the bathroom before I left his house. I walked quickly past the T.V. room and into the bathroom, where need overcame my paranoia that I was being heard as I urinated. When I left the bathroom, I said a quick "goodbye" out of politeness as I crossed the T.V.room.

Before the viewing, I received phone calls, cards,

and visits from friends and Warren's family. One of my acquaintances through work sent flowers specifically addressed to me and my family to my grandparents' house. It was during this time that I realized the obvious -- working in my field had helped me to surround myself in an environment that was generally safe. Although working with victims of domestic violence has inherent risks, most of the people working in the field try to improve themselves mentally and emotionally. Abuse isn't tolerated or accepted. And by creating that environment, I had slowly moved into a place where I had minimized opportunities for other people to victimize me. Distance had not made my heart grow fonder of those whom I had cut off. Distance had given me perspective and understanding that I could never go back.

CHAPTER 24

The next day, my visit to my grandfather's house further prepared me for what was to come.

"Christy, Cathy, and I went to the funeral home to see Grandma earlier. And she looked really pretty. The funeral home really did a good job with her."

Viewing night arrived. I left Gerald with my mother-in-law. As Warren and I approached the funeral home, I saw my brother standing outside. He was smoking a cigarette. He gave me a hug and I asked him if his father was inside.

"Yes," he said.

"Well, we're going to go in," I said.

As we entered the room, Grandpa came up to us. He looked like he was in his element -- socializing with everyone. We settled in a place closer to the back of the line of pews. Three of Warren's sisters, his brother, one brother-in-law, and a sister-in-law sat down in the aisles around us. I stood and began to say hi to the people I knew. I was surprised by some of the people in the crowd. My old neighbors who had lived next to my parents approached.

"Meredith, we don't see you visit very much," they noted. I leaned forward toward them and said in a low voice, "No. I really tried to escape from there."

"We understand," was their response. I wondered what they knew and what they had seen in the years they had lived next door. I saw Mickey's sister-in-law across the room. I said hi and she nudged her husband to come over to me. We spoke for the first time in at least 7 years. I hugged

Mickey's brother. He and I had always gotten along well, but I perceived hesitancy from him as he hugged me. I wondered if he feared that I might somehow turn a hug into an incident to press charges over. After all, I'm sure that I was given some sort of reputation within Mickey's family.

Mickey's sister and brother-in-law (Joshua's parents) also took time to interact with me and I perceived much of the same friendliness mixed with hesitancy. Mickey's mother walked back fast from the casket and pushed through the crowd, going right past me. My grandmother had seen her more than once in town and had been ignored by her following my allegations of abuse. I was shocked that after her blatant snubbing of my grandmother, she had the nerve to attend the viewing.

A few friends from work came to show their support for me. Most knew some of the background and recognized the difficulty of the situation. One of my board members did not. She worked for the Tourism Association and as she approached me, she casually indicated my mother and asked, "Who is that woman?" I told her that it was my mother and where my mother worked -- she knew her from interactions through town events. I leaned forward and told her that I had a little bit of a dysfunctional family. She nodded in support and understanding.

Jenny offered to walk up to the casket with me. I patted the arm of my cousin, Rachel, and said "Hello" as I passed by her and walked up the aisle.

Grandpa had been right. My grandmother looked herself again -- her hair was neatly teased against her perfectly made-up face. Her cheeks looked naturally flushed and her face looked calm and attractive -- not grey, pale, or dead. Inside the coffin were pictures of Rachel's children. Out of the corner of my eye, I could see Mickey.

Mickey sat facing front in the first aisle catty-corner to the left of the casket. I had passed him as I walked up, but had focused my sights on the coffin. As I turned slightly, I could make out his features. He was aging now. He had always had thin hair, but now large streaks of scalp were showing at the top of his head. He had grown his hair longer and it looked stringy. It's funny that as a child he had seemed so huge and threatening to me. Now I could see that he was just a little man whose body was bearing the aura of guilt, fear, and insecurity.

My mother and aunt seemed to be guarding the casket, but moved away slightly as I took my time there. As we were done, Jenny acknowledged Cathy and said "goodbye" and then as she said "goodbye"to my mother, my mother reached out and hugged her.

To our right, I saw my Uncle Don and Aunt Peg and several of their children. I hadn't seen these second cousins in years and we were excited as we saw each other. We chatted about what we were doing and I introduced them to Warren. They obviously knew nothing about any of our family dynamics. As we spoke about my grandmother, they shared with me a story that I had not heard. Apparently when my grandmother first started having symptoms, she drove to get Chinese food, but remained in the parking lot near Kmart for several hours -- not remembering why she was there or what she was doing.

Warren and I went back to our place near the back of the room for a few minutes longer.

"Don't they all put up a good act?" my husband asked of his sisters. They nodded and smiled as I laughed. I didn't feel like I was hiding anything, though. I felt like I was doing my own sort of challenge by standing tall, looking good, and meeting them at their own game.

Before we left, we gave Grandpa a picture of Gerald to put in the casket. The absence of his picture in the casket was a blatant disregard of my family and one I could quickly combat. I found out later that following the viewing, most of the family returned to my grandfather's house. We were not invited and apparently not missed. I continued to vent through poetry.

Triumph

I dashed to the scene,
Face drawn in pain
From backed-up sinuses,
Eyes blurry from floods of tears.
"Is she still here?"
And she was.
Arms long and bony,
Face so thin yet puffy,
Hands spidery blue at the tips,
Cold, white, wrinkled,
Hair too short and straight,

Flat on one side
From lying in bed too long.
It was not her.
Yet it was.
I waited for her chest to rise and fall.
Yet it did not.
"It's so quick."
And it was.
3 months before watching
A fussy toddler who adored her,
Taking too long walks,
Obsessing over nutrition.
Then the depression hit,
Anger at the two daughters,
A 3-hour trip to pick up Chinese
She never found,
And a 5-minute memory.
"Well, the news is real bad,"
He said to me that day.
Brain tumor and three to four months to live
And now the daughters are back
And visits are planned
And people are coming
With food and help and hospice and more food
Strangers making her bed, changing her diaper,
Giving her a bath with White Shoulders.
She's never been so clean.
I watched my son.
"Mimi's sleeping" as he stroked her hair.

"She's looking at you, mommy" with
A blank stare going through you, sometimes
With tears and early on with "goodbyes".
I had watched them roll her out
In a zipped up bag on a hospital cot.
One sister hung back behind the other --
The private behind the commander.
One could not cry.
One could not stop --
She had been stroking that hand
In anguish over lost years.
I thought we had time but
I smoothed waters early thank god
Because there were the daughters again
With their mates circling in
And I joked to myself
About grandma rolling over in her grave
If she saw the people who were there.
But she lied still in her mother's dress,
Melon chiffon against a green-grey coffin.
They really did a first-rate job.
She hadn't looked that good in months.
And now the story would be buried.
Tears and hugs for display,
Apologies and goodbyes.
Again I waited for her chest to rise
And fall against those hands
Now restored to natural color.
Yet it did not.

And as I welcomed those prodigals
And their relatives,
I found pleasure
Because I know Karma --
She forces a good game of civility
And in that there is triumph.

The next morning, my sister-in-law Susan, her husband, and my father-in-law came to my house to stay with Gerald. Warren and I drove to the funeral home. As we pulled in, there were a few people over there. I asked the usher where I should park and told him I was a granddaughter. He asked me my name and when I told him, he told me that my name hadn't been given for one of the cars to line up in the family part of the procession.

I walked up to the coffin. Katie arrived at the funeral home and put her arm around my shoulders.

"I'm so sorry," she said. We stood there for a minute and then stepped back. Aunt Cathy was approaching the coffin and seemed to have a brief look of disgust on her face as she passed me. She had her arm around my Great Aunt Maggie.

Warren and I walked back to the rear of the funeral home, where my Grandfather was gathering with the family. Jenny saw me and was about to come in the area and I shook my head to indicate not to come in. The officiant was coming to say a prayer specifically for the family. We all bowed our heads and when he was done, Aunt Cathy made a point to barrel ahead to help lead the line. I felt like I was on display as I entered the sanctuary. I halted for a minute -- feeling somewhat dizzy, but more halting out of wanting to just stop for a moment. As I entered, I saw two women take notice of me. I wasn't sure who they were.

I sat in the last of the family rows. My brother made a point to sit near me. The minister began to say a few words and then offered his wife to read my poem aloud. As they mentioned that I was the author of the poem, Rachel's son turned around and looked at me. Everyone else stared straight ahead. My aunt had a small purse with the strap crossing her body. She had brought her husband, Randy Sr. He was wearing a white shirt and jeans. I wondered how she had convinced him to come. I could hear Jenny's baby in the background and was aggravated -- I wanted silence all around me.

Following the end of the ceremony, we went to get in our cars. Since I was not part of the processional, we watched as it began to move. When my brother's car approached, he waved at me to pull out in front of him. I was grateful for his small displays of kindness.

We drove out the long hilly highway to my grandparents' church, where she would be buried in the small cemetery. This was the church of my early childhood, with a beautiful cobblestone entry and a small, old-fashioned lay-out. This was also the church of my first wedding. A tent had been set up within the cemetery. Once again, Aunt Cathy barreled ahead to ensure that she sat on the front row with Great-Aunt Maggie. She was directing others to sit. I stood in the rear.

Following the brief words and adjournment, Jesse's mother-in-law approached me. She hugged me and I told her that I was sorry we hadn't been able to get to know each other better. Someone else approached me. It was Dana, a former co-worker of my grandmother's.

"Meredith, I don't know if you know who I am or not, but I'm Dana and I used to work with your grandmother." I hugged her.

"Yes, I know you."

"Well, I just want you to know that she talked about you all of the time. She was so proud of you. I told her when all of this happened that I would see her on the other side."

"Something funny I want to tell you," I said. "You know, they often say that when people are dying, they hang on until a special event or holiday. But the only one coming up was Halloween and she hated that, so I knew she wouldn't live until then."

Dana laughed. "You're right. Every year, she would always say to me that she was going to cut her lights out and pretend she wasn't home!" We talked for a brief minute more. I noticed that Jesse had apparently broken down and his wife and mother-in-law were consoling him.

The crowd began to gather in the bottom of the church, but I had already arranged to have my own "wake" at my house. When my mother-in-law had asked if there was anything she could do for me, I had told her that I would appreciate it if we could gather at my house. I knew that I would not be comfortable with what was to be the "official" family gathering. As we began to leave the church, my grandfather came to talk with my mother-in-law and sister-in-law. He was being friendly.

Aunt Cathy was still under the tent and as she came out of it, she began to yell, "Daddy, Daddy!" It took a few minutes for him to hear her and respond to her, but when he did, she indicated that they were going in the church. It appeared to the rest of us that she was more aggravated that he was spending time, laughing, and smiling with us.

At my house, we all enjoyed nice conversation. Katie and Jenny shared a bottle of wine with me. Katie talked about some issues with her in-laws and we joked about her leaving her children while she flitted around to funerals. We laughed over my Aunt Cathy's behavior. Warren commented that the officiant's wife hadn't read the poem properly. I'm not sure how Warren had heard it in his head when he had read it the first time. His sister had talked to him afterward and he had shared that the poem made him cry.

As everyone left, I felt the surreal loss begin. Over the next couple of days, I dreamed of my grandmother a few times. The first time, she was feeding me and my Grandfather food. When I told him about this dream, he shared that he had also had a similar dream. The second time I dreamed of her, she wasn't saying anything, but silently waved goodbye.

CHAPTER 25

We began to feel my grandmother's loss in small ways. I tried to visit my grandfather every week or two with Gerald. I would spend the time cleaning the bathroom and the kitchen, where dirt seemed to pile up. Grandpa told me that the girls -- meaning Christy and Cathy -- came by about everyday. They usually took him out to dinner, to the grocery, and to appointments. I wondered why they couldn't see the filth that was building up. I became resentful as I imagined that they were viewing me as the maid.

But then I remembered that my mother wasn't the best cleaner of her own house. It was common for us to have a crusty build-up of food on the glass table in our family room (where we frequently ate), clothes piled up throughout the hallway, several days worth of dishes piled up in and around the kitchen sink, and a nest of hair and grime along the back of the toilet. She liked to stay gone from home and shopped compulsively, often collecting a small wardrobe of clothing for which she never even removed the tags and wore. I knew now that this was probably how her depression had displayed itself. I reminded myself that I needed to contribute something to my grandfather's care -- and this was one of the few avenues that I had.

I also knew from my knowledge of community resources that I could link him with at least one group that would greatly help him maintain his independence. I called the Aging Society, a group that provided community services such as "Meals on Wheels,"and other in-home supports. They met with Grandpa and assessed his needs. They set him up for daily meal delivery and cleaning service several times a week.

I was still feeling the need to stalk his house to ensure the coast was clear before I pursued visits with my grandfather. I tried to keep the conversations short as it was typical for my grandfather to talk about the other members of the family -- including Mickey, my mother, and Aunt Cathy. I only found solace in my idea that if he were talking about them to me, he was probably talking about me to them. Occasionally, he also told me stories I found humorous.

"Aunt Cathy fell down the stairs - slipped and fell on her butt."

"Was she o.k.?" I asked.

"I guess so. She has a lot of padding back there."

For as long as I could remember, my grandparents had maintained their own separate bedrooms. This allowed them private space and my grandmother a reprieve from my grandfather's erratic sleeping and snoring. After Nanu died, my grandfather eventually began to use my grandmother's bedroom as his office. He set up a desk with a computer and began to use the Internet. He didn't touch her clothes or personal items, though, and the room appeared very cluttered.

He was going back and forth to appointments at the Veteran's Hospital, but his health was in decline. His teeth were deteriorating. He was obtaining frequent bruises from falls caused by dizziness. And his medications seemed to be creating havoc instead of healing.

I had my own methods of coping with my grandmother's death. Near the end of November, Warren, Gerald, and I took off for a vacation. When we got in the car, we had not yet agreed upon what our destination would be. So we started heading west and began our vacation in Memphis. After a visit to Graceland, we headed south to Biloxi, Mississippi, enjoyed some time in New Orleans, drove through Montgomery, Alabama, stopped near Atlanta, and finally nestled in Pigeon Forge.

We spent one evening in Dollywood. They had a little church set up there that was decorated for Christmas. As they prepared for a little service, I could hear music starting as the glow of candles lit the interior. I wanted to go in, but the tears began to well up in my eyes. Everything was reminding me of my grandmother.

When we returned from vacation, we began to prepare for Christmas. Before we left on vacation, Jenny had expressed to me that she couldn't care for Gerald anymore. He spent much of the day crying and she was overwhelmed in caring for him and her newborn. I was disappointed and felt angry for the predicament we were all in, but appreciated her honesty. Warren took over watching Gerald during the day and I began to alter my schedule to work weekends to ensure that I pulled my 40 hours. Then I would go home and switch with Warren if he had a tile job.

I decided to deliver cards to the people who had taken time to converse with me at the funeral -- Jesse's

mother-in-law and Dana, who used to work with my
grandmother. I decided to hand-deliver my thank-you card
to Dana when I went grocery shopping. As I neared the deli
counter, I saw Dana walk back to the rear. I asked the girl
at the front if I could speak to Dana. When Dana was
retrieved, I told her that I wanted to bring her a card.

"Meredith, how are you?"

It seemed that somehow those words penetrated
through my facade and I couldn't speak. Finally, I mustered
an "o.k." and tried to minimize my tears as I walked
through the check-out. I was steadily wiping my tears when
I saw Dana approach me.

"I just had to hug you," she said. I held her tight as
she gave me words of comfort. My tears remained with me
as I walked to my car in the parking lot -- trying to avoid
eye contact with anyone who might know me. I was
grateful that on that day I had experienced her caring,
though. It was nice for someone to ask me how I was -- and
for someone to recognize the significant loss that had
occurred in my life.

For Christmas Eve, I had my in-laws bring Grandpa
to my house to partake of our typical reception. He seemed
to enjoy the company. At Christmas, he offered us an
unwrapped set of knives. He seemed to lack knowledge as
to how to manage the finances. He had always been on
such a tight leash with my grandmother. From the moment
he got up, she set his life scene for the day. She laid out his
clothes, which she had washed and ironed most of the time.
She prepared all of his meals according to his nutritional

needs. She frequently drove them both wherever they needed to go since he had narcolepsy. She managed the checkbook and the bills and allotted him a certain amount of cash to spend. She was the final say on most major purchases. She tracked and dispensed his medications. But because he had been the family income provider for so many years, he did have a lot of freedom with activities and was highly involved with several civic groups. And of course, he had the freedom to vote for Democrats in contrast to her votes for Republicans.

With the lifestyle he was now living, he was gaining weight. His physical appearance was deteriorating. I walked in after Christmas and he said he felt bad and couldn't even get out of the chair. Later, he was diagnosed with depression, which had become so severe that it had nearly crippled him emotionally. He was prescribed an antidepressant. His pills increased and he was now using an elaborate system to track his medications. One day I came over and heard sounds in the basement.

"What's that?" I asked my grandfather.

"Probably Jesse," he answered.

"Jesse? What's he doing in the basement?"

"Well, he's living there. I don't know what's going on. He had a fight with his wife and they are splitting up. From the stuff he brought in here, it just looks like he liked to buy and buy. I told him that he needs to grow up."

I found myself wondering how "fight" was defined -- had there been abuse or domestic violence? Grandpa didn't offer any more details, but did offer his dismay over the situation. He seemed quite annoyed at the music, the dog, and the late night hours that Jesse had brought to his home. I continued to offer that Grandpa could live with me, but he conveyed that he didn't want to be a burden.

I became obsessed with the idea of moving out of town and surfed the Internet each night in search of employment. I particularly was looking for out-of-state employment. I wanted to leave Virginia and I wanted to leave my field -- I had had enough of domestic violence and sexual assault. I poured over each edition of the *Chronicle of Philanthropy* and other non-profit magazines and continued elaborate Internet searches. I began to see a pattern emerge -if I applied for anything remotely related to the field of domestic violence or sexual assault, or to residential shelter, I was immediately contacted by the search committee. I felt trapped in my life.

The first exciting prospect was a job in Alaska -- in a location far beyond the limited road system. We would only be able to get there by plane. In the winter, the river froze to provide a highway for ground vehicles. The dramatic landscape, archaic residential systems, and dark remoteness all appealed to me. Warren was playing cards at the local Moose Lodge when I called him and told him that the Alaska job had called.

"Let's go," he said. "I'm sick of it here, too."

I interviewed well (over the phone) and Warren and I began to have discussions about what would be feasible economically to make the move -- including disposing of all of our belongings. My mother-in-law was upset over the prospect of us moving, but the worry was all in vain. I received feedback that my references were not strong enough. I had wanted my job search to remain low key and therefore hadn't submitted strong references from the field.

My next big interview was with a Catholic-oriented group in the bay area of California. I also interviewed well and the search committee told me that they were considering hiring me. Warren and I put our house on the market. We decided that even if I did not get the job, the move would provide us with a fresh start. I continued interviewing -- Texas, Ohio, Minnesota, California, Alaska, Oklahoma, Myrtle Beach. Myrtle Beach would have been a good job, but they wanted me to start in two weeks and I knew that I couldn't leave my agency with such short notice. We also were in the middle of a building project, and I had mixed feelings about leaving them prior to the completion of the project. In some cases, I was offered jobs and the salary wouldn't support the move. In others, such as a job in New Jersey, my lack of strong references again proved to be an issue. The original job in California fell through -the agency changed priests and was going to hold off on the new hiring.

A certain faction of my husband's family began dying off from a rare form of cancer. It seemed that through that winter and spring, we were attending funeral after funeral. As each person died, we both became more desperate to change our lives. I took it upon myself to repaint our living room, kitchen, and hallway. I spent my weekends engaged in yet another obsessive activity that would help me zone out of my life. I had never painted inside a house before and painted everything white -- desiring the look of purity and cleanliness.

When I told my grandfather about selling the house and mentioned that it might help us to have some money, he replied, "Well, you know you've got to get out of this borrowing money from people all of the time." I was upset and offended.

"Grandpa, we haven't borrowed money from anyone in years," I said. He quickly changed the subject and I wondered what had sparked this obvious attitude toward our finances. The house wasn't selling. It had been priced too high and we dropped the price twice.

After many weeks of showings, a disabled gentleman with a walker came to look at our house. His realtor was less than warm to him from my observations and the prospective buyer didn't even look at all of the rooms. But his one visit led him to fall in love with the house and make an offer, which we countered. Finally, we were provided with an offer we could accept.

At that time, we had two Chou dogs that I spontaneously acquired while my grandmother was dying. We hadn't cared for them well -- they were big dogs and we kept them outside most of the time in all sorts of elements. I knew that we could not keep them given the uncertainties of our move and I connected with a woman at work who was able to facilitate their movement into animal foster care. In college, I had acquired two gerbils in a similar rash decision and also had given them to the animal shelter when I was getting married. I knew that I had to try to break this pattern of taking on the care for lives that I couldn't properly manage.

CHAPTER 26

After 5 years, we were going to leave the house that we had grown to love. I held two yard sales and sold a few carloads of items at the local flea market. We tried to sell as much as we could -- partially to avoid the pain of moving it. At closing, one of the realtors asked me if we were relocating out of town. I told her that we had considered it, but not at this time.

"That's good," she said. "Because you are really good at what you do."

Yes, I was. As much as my personal life had been a constant string of ups and downs, I had always ensured that I put enough energy into my education and career to provide me with stability, normalcy, and hope. But part of why I had been so successful was that I had been able to create an environment that was supportive, challenging, and inspiring.

I didn't have to deal with sexual harassment in the all-female environment. It was an expected norm that our environment lives up to the standard of being healthy, respectful, and safe. And because I was Executive Director, I had a lot of power and control over sustaining this -- which ultimately brought peace to both my personal and my professional life. I was beginning to feel like a "survivor" and no longer a victim. I continued to write to express my transformation.

Survivor's Sestina
We are the any raced, cashed, faithed women

Born to the any preformed others,
Learning from our brothers how to be sisters,
Learning from our husbands how to be wives –
Not recognizing we are survivors
Stumbling through the early years as children.

Dreaming of our arms heaped with children,
We imagine us as super women,
Blocking our pain as abuse survivors,
Glorifying our roles as mothers,
Accepting our travails as right for wives,
Sharing our epics with friends and sisters.

We learn our commonality as sisters:
We are the beaten, molested children
Who became baited, raped, broken wives,
Who became detached from fellow women,
Who became overwhelmed with being mothers
As we faced agony as survivors.

We are the any raced, cashed, faithed survivors
Whose families preferred brothers, not sisters,
Whose families valued anything but children,
Who weren't protected by downtrodden mothers,
Whose societies never valued women,
Whose cheating mates killed trust in fellow wives.

We are the escaping -through-affairs wives.
We are the escaping-through-drugs survivors.

We are defy-as-much-as-we-can women.
We are cutting-off-our-families sisters.
We are petted-to-glass ceilings children.
We are struggle-to-take-care-of-you mothers.

We seek counselors to replace our mothers.
We hunt men to return to being wives.
We move, lie, cheat, steal to keep our children.
We wallow in chaos as survivors.
We borrow past our ·welcome from sisters.
We are the easy-to-blame as women.

We need time to heal as survivors.
We need time to band back with our sisters.
We need to live free, happy, safe as women.

The Chamber dinner was uneventful this year -- I attended but my parents did not. Typically near the end of summer, our organization held an annual meeting, inviting all staff, board members, and volunteers of the organization. This year, we held the meeting in the basement meeting room of a local church. As I was setting up our display board, I happened to look at the entry as people began to arrive.

Jackson's mother was coming in with one of our thrift store staff. I did a double-take. It was her -- a few years older than the last time I had seen her, but as usual groomed and dressed with Nancy Reagan style in a peach ladies' business dress suit and heels. She had been a larger woman when we met, but the death of her daughter, stress, and old age (she was in the same age range as my grandparents) had reduced her to a petite size 6. I turned to Sandy.

"See that woman back there? Look casually," I said. Sandy turned her head casually and then returned her eyes to me.

"Yes," she said.

"That's my ex-mother-in-law," I said.

"Well, don't panic," she said.

The dinner tables were set up in long rows with chairs facing both sides. Jackson's mother sat near the front. She was sitting with the person she had come with, as well as one of my board members -- who had employed Jackson's father and Jackson for a time. I took a few deep breaths and tried to not be paranoid that my relationship with Jackson was being discussed over the glazed chicken and mixed vegetables.

I facilitated the evening just as I would have had she not been in the audience. When the evening's events drew to a close, I gave my final comments and exited the stage. I decided to approach her. I knelt down beside her.

"I'm glad to see you. I just wanted to thank you for coming and tell you that I'm sorry for everything that happened all of those years ago," I said. She smiled at me.

"Oh, I think you both are much happier. You are doing such a wonderful job," she said.

"I hear that Jackson had a child recently?"

"Yes," she beamed. "Twin girls."

"Wow, that's great. Please tell him that I said 'hi.'"

"I will."

"Take care. It was good seeing you," I walked away, feeling relieved. And I felt a tremendous sense of closure. I felt as if I was tying up all of my loose ends and that surely that meant that I would be leaving Front Royal soon.

At least for now, with the sale of the house, I was going to have more money than I had ever had in my life. Not enough to be considered rich or even well off -but enough to keep us from worrying for a while and enough to provide a fresh start. We anticipated renting for a while in order to avoid the hassle of a mortgage.

We looked around for rentals in town and found nothing to meet the standard to which we were accustomed. A chance call to a local landlord put me in touch with a board member, who also happened to have a house she was willing to sell us. We decided to buy again. The money in the bank helped us to qualify for a loan that we may not have given our recent credit problems.

An older couple was currently renting the house while theirs was being built. Until their house was finished, we couldn't move in -- which would leave us essentially homeless for at least two months. We considered renting a log cabin, but the prices were too high due to the fall leaf season of tourism. We decided to move into the top of my mother-in-law's garage.

Bessie had once prepared the top of her garage for weekend visitors. It resembled a cabin and had a large carpeted room where we set up livingroom and bedroom areas. To use the bathroom or eat, we had to go inside the house. For a time, it was adventurous -- sometimes in a fun way and sometimes not.

I developed a urinary tract infection and rather than bother my in-laws by going in their house several times in the middle of the night, I chose to urinate by moonlight outside of the garage. When I went to the doctor to receive medication to relieve my symptoms, I was greeted by one of Jackson's sisters, who now worked as a nurse at the practice. This was the sister who had snatched her children up at the festival many years again. But today, she treated me and Gerald (who was with me) with kindness.

Gerald began to come out of his shell as he was able to spend time playing with his cousins and visit with his grandparents. He still had terrible separation issues and he was having difficulty behaviorally. Warren and I were both frustrated, but I hoped that when we moved to our next house, I would be able to provide him with more stability and attention. I knew that since my grandmother's death, I had been short, inattentive, and frustrated. I wanted to be somewhere -- but I didn't know where. I was trying to break from my life and it seemed that the harder I tried to go in a different direction, the more I was pushed in the same direction I had always been going.

Then tragedy struck the nation. By now, Jenny had returned to teaching school and asked me to come to her class as a guest speaker. On my way to the school, I obtained a speeding ticket, failing to recognize a speed change near the school. If it had been a couple of hours later, no one would have bothered to be checking the speed. It was September 11th. As the first period ended, other teachers began coming in the class urging us to turn on the television. The twin towers had been hit. All day at the school was chaotic as several children indicated worry for their parents who worked in the Nation's capital.

Like the rest of America, it took time to process the tragedy of what happened. For a brief period, I felt exceptionally patriotic and supportive of the President. When I saw flags or heard songs about America, I cried. Just as most of America, I was glued to the Internet and the television -- trying to sort out what was happening and what would be the future for our country. My father-in-law said,

"I guess the safest place for all of us would be in the bottom of the garage."

What would have seemed to be a bit of an exaggerated response now seemed plausible. Would we have to hide out? No one knew what would happen -- but we all were frightened at what the future held. I applied for another job with FEMA -- but didn't get the job. That was probably a blessing given that in the instance of a national incident, a FEMA worker has to be prepared to work around the clock for several days without going home. That would not be conducive for a person with a small child. I did find one blessing in 9/11, though - that my grandmother didn't live to see it.

My relatives in New York did, however. My cousin

was in Manhattan that day and her mother, Teresa, called to tell her,

"The United States is being attacked."

"Who's attacking us, Mom?" Julietta asked.

"I don't know, but they're bombing the twin towers."

"Whatever," Julietta replied. She thought that her mother had finally lost her mind and hung up the phone. Later, as she tried to cross town on the subway, she quickly realized the reality of the situation. As time went on, Julietta became heavily involved in working on the memorial project and for local and state political leaders. I was often jealous of the exciting life she led, her confidence, and her straightforward style.

I took a hiatus from the job hunt for a while -- I felt like given the uncertainty of the world, I was in no position to move at the moment. We settled in to our new home, which was in one of the nicest subdivisions in town. But I felt stifled -- I had gone from a home on 5 acres with fairly consistent privacy to a home with less than a quarter acre and neighbors were everywhere.

I felt like I was on display just walking to the car. However, that was balanced by the fact that now I was living in town and I could pick up Grandpa anytime I wanted to. We were able to move into the new house before Christmas and when our annual Christmas Eve dinner event arrived, Grandpa had Aunt Cathy drop him off at the front of our house.

It had now been a year and a half that Warren and I

had undergone the stressful arrangement of switching off with childcare duties. Warren had contemplated going into real estate and for the first time, we had the means to support the effort. I decided to put Gerald in a local daycare. I knew the owner through a board we had both served on and felt fairly confident that she was a good person.

I tried to warm Gerald to the idea of "school" (*i.e.,* daycare), but as I left him for the first time, he clinged onto me and cried hysterically. I walked out, having a flashback to the first time I had been left in the pre-school program at a local church. I could still see my mother as she backed down the hall, smiling, waving, and telling me "Bye, Bye!" while I gasped and shuddered for air between an endless flood of tears. And now I was doing the same thing to my son. He calmed later that day, but each day I received a report that he had been "sad" at daycare and spent much of his day quietly crying.

CHAPTER 27

Work was going well, but I remained unhappy. I needed to leave this town that trapped me with its memories. After the incident with Jane, I had taken a hiatus from the Community Council meetings. When I found that she was no longer attending them, I started attending again on a casual basis. At the meeting, one of the hospital personnel was there. He had been friends with my parents long ago and recognized me.

"Meredith, how did your parents' 25th anniversary party go? I was out of town and couldn't make it," he said.

"I don't know," I said casually. "I didn't go." I didn't offer explanation, but tried to convey no emotion as I answered.

To keep myself motivated in the work, I continued to be heavily involved in statewide activities and attended conferences often. In February 2002, Sandy and I attended a conference that would change my life.

Sandy and I had become very close in the three years we had worked together. She was a very spiritual woman who had a knack for being able to look into a person's eyes and "read" their soul. She could read my mood and give me just what I needed. She was ten years older than me and her children were grown. Her wisdom often helped me as I struggled through parenting. Sometimes, we even had similar dreams.

As we embarked upon the road to Northern Virginia, we shared stories and laughed that we were going to a "Dream Conference." The Dream Conference was a one-day event that was supposed to give people insight on how to understand and interpret dreams. We found the conference in a nice hotel and began to listen to the facilitator. Just before lunch, he facilitated an activity where we were to identify something that we had been questioning in our lives, or something we were struggling with. We had to write it in the workbook that we were provided for the conference.

What direction am I headed? I wrote in the workbook. The facilitator then directed us to write what we would be willing to give up as an "offering" for the information that would be provided through our dream. *I will try to lose weight and be a nicer person,* I wrote in the workbook. I knew that I had been neglecting my family (my husband and son) and felt disconnected and aggravated with them.

The facilitator dimmed the lights and sat by the podium, where he turned on the small desk lamp attached to the podium. He led us through a process of relaxing and then told us to close our eyes as he began to describe what would happen when we went to sleep tonight. We were going to sleep -- deeper and more restful than we had slept in years. We were going to dream the answer to our questions. When we awoke, we would be able to recall all of the details of our dream and we would record it immediately on paper. He kept repeating the phrase "Sleep-Dream-Recall-Record."

He began to count up to 10 -- taking our minds to a different journey. Suddenly, I realized that my eyes were in rapid eye movement. *Oh my God,* I thought, *I'm being hypnotized.*

"What do you want in your life?" he asked.

For a brief moment, I thought, *I want to leave Warren.* And then, just as quickly, I thought, *No, I don't. I don't want to leave Warren.*

In my mind, the facilitator's voice seemed as if it were coming from the end of a tunnel. I could see him sitting there with the little light shining. I couldn't hear anything or anyone else in the room. Occasionally a noise from outside would be loud enough to penetrate -- but even then it was dulled by my mind.

"Sleep-Dream-Recall-Record."

He began to count back from 10 and as each number changed, the noises in the room became more apparent. Little rustlings, breathing, coughs, and sighs became noticeable. When we were all back in the present, we broke for lunch.

Sandy and I found a little Deli nearby and discussed the events of the conference. We were both very surprised that we had been hypnotized. It was nothing like I would have imagined -- I felt quite present during hypnosis and was relatively confident that we hadn't been slipped any strange post-hypnotic suggestions.

When we returned to the conference after lunch, the facilitator had already returned. He walked out of the room with his microphone and we could hear him talking in the hall and then in a room that echoed as he opened the door and walked in. Suddenly, we heard the loud sound of liquid gushing into more liquid. He was urinating and as people were returning from lunch, they were privy to what he thought was a private moment. As he returned to the room, I struggled with letting him know so that he didn't make the same mistake again, but decided not to. The rest of the conference was not as exciting, but still useful in helping us to develop activities and skills to explore dreams.

That night, I looked forward to sleeping. I had told Sandy on the way home that I had asked for help with direction. "Watch me dream about a map!" I laughed.

The first dream I had was just that -- a picture in my mind of a map. The shape looked like an inverted Virginia - but I knew the state to be Kentucky and the location it was pointing to was between routes 39 and 40.

The next dream I had was a series of images. In the first part of the dream, I saw a bright light on my niece, who was being sexually assaulted. I saw a rock with a constantly changing phone number. I saw other victims of sexual violence. I dreamed of three directors in the field and the person in the middle -- a person from a stand-alone domestic violence program -- was not smiling. I dreamt that I took a job that seemed to be below a horse race track. It was supposed to be a progressive place, but in actuality, they were making posters with magic markers as part of their public awareness activities. I saw flashes of many people I knew who had been victims of sexual violence.

The last part of the dream was quite disturbing. There was a mansion with many rooms and a murky pool, where a man with gills and a fish with lungs swam together. It was dark and disturbing. I knew that this had something to do with Warren and I worried that something would happen to Gerald, but then he was o.k. At the end of the dream, I saw a tornado blowing in.

I woke up and Gerald was still sleeping in the bed beside me. I had set out a notebook the night before so that I could be ready to record my dream. The room was sunny with the morning light and I pulled out the notebook and frantically began to write down the words describing my dream. I was bursting with energy and knew what nearly the entire dream meant.

As Gerald arose and we began our day, I shared excitedly with Warren all about my dream and what it meant. Beyond interpretation, I could feel a miracle. Whether it was because of the suggestion that I would have a restful sleep or because of the relief of knowing the answer to my questions, I felt like years of weight had been removed from me. I called Katie and Jenny -- sharing with them my good news. I felt that I had been healed. Suddenly, I knew answers to more than I had ever known.

The dream had led me to understand that I wished to work with the issue of sexual abuse, but no longer domestic violence.

"Honey, you knew that anyway. You have been telling me that for a while, now," Warren pointed out to me.

"No, it's different. I can't describe it. This dream helped me to understand that my whole life has been a sort of preparation for what I'm doing now. All of those experiences that I've had -- all the people I've known who have been sexually abused, all of the sexual abuse I've experienced - have led me to where I am today. Me being abused was actually some sort of Divine gift that helps me to help others."

"I feel like calling my parents and thanking them for the abuse and telling them that it was a gift," I told Jenny.

"I don't think you should do that," Jenny said. "They wouldn't understand."

"You're right. This would probably just feed into their thoughts that I am crazy," I said.

The dream also helped me to understand that perhaps I had been trying too hard to go a different direction and that I should just let things happen as they are meant to happen. And another very rewarding message I received from the dream was the understanding of why I was with Warren. He protected me and because he didn't abuse me, taught me how to be healthy sexually, and helped me commit to the relationship, I was able to heal and grow and understand myself. He also connected me with so many people who had been victims -- helping me understand the subject even more.

I began to have a deep belief in the philosophy put forward in one of my favorite movies, *Forrest Gump:* that we simultaneously appear to be floating in the wind random-like and also have a destiny. I also had heard somewhere that you can't be confused by the wake that the boat leaves -- the wake shows where the boat has been, but it is not what drives the boat. I felt deep in my heart that my experiences had led me and for the first time in my life, all of the craziness had a wonderful spiritual purpose.

The next couple of nights, I continued to have vivid dreams. I had more energy than I had had in a long time and I was enthusiastic as I played with Gerald and interacted with Warren. I was excited as I went in and shared my experience with Sandy and others at work. Sandy's dream had been simpler, but she also felt good about the experience.

CHAPTER 28

Work also helped me reframe thinking of Linden as "Hell Town". I had to accompany a client to Charlottesville. As she shared with me the difficulties of her life, she reflected that she had grown up in Linden and those were some of the happiest days of her life. Her simple words that day helped me to realize that not everyone who lived there was somehow a victim of abuse or neglect -- some people actually were happy with their upbringing there.

On another occasion, I had a visit from a grant monitor. Before she came, she asked me if we could take a ride out to Linden. She had lived there when she was a toddler and wanted to see the house where she was born. There had been many times that I would ride near the area after returning from a conference or meeting. But I had not ventured past the highway. As I turned by the old post office, I noticed that the bridge was now concrete.

The bridge had once been completely wooden and as vehicles would travel across it, it would play out a rolling familiar beat of boards. It was covered with tar and in the summer, I would run barefoot across the hot tar, risking its burns to my feet so that I could then run across the highway to the little store where I could buy a candy bar.

For a short period of time in Junior High, I tried to display toughness with boys on the bus by hitting them. My second altercation was with the same boy I had prank called under the alias of Gloria Vanderbilt. This fight resulted in a call to the office, where I was informed that I was banned from the bus for 24 hours.

I decided it would be better to run away rather than convey this information to my mother. I decided that I would begin my journey by staying under the bridge for a few hours, using it as a shelter. My plan was to wait until evening and then go to Katie's house, where I could set up residence in her pig pen and she could sneak me food after dinner. My plan was short-lived.

After I didn't return home, my mother called Katie's house and her brother informed my mother where I was. I can still see my mother walking up the railroad tracks with my 3 year-old brother resting on her hip. Her stern "Get home" motivated me to rise and leave just as the tar was beginning to drip down onto my light blue pants.

Today we crossed over the bridge and my eyes wondered in the direction of my childhood home as we passed it. Then I refocused and drove her back to her childhood home. We passed several homes and landmarks that I remembered. Katie, myself, my mother, and Katie's mother had spent many spring and summer evenings taking walks back this winding country road. Now there was a mix of abandoned homes and new homes spattered between empty pastures and woods.

"Turn here," she indicated.

"It's smaller than I remember it," she said. She shared that her memories here had all been happy at this first home of her memories. I was glad to be able to make that connection for her, and further strengthen the knowledge that Linden was not hell to everyone.

As spring approached, one of my newer staff, Anita, introduced me to her mother, Betsy, who was moving here from Texas. Anita didn't want her mother to be at her house all day without anything to do, and thought that perhaps her mother could work as a nanny at my house. I took Gerald out of daycare and I began to enjoy the luxury and security of having Betsy at my house. I began to consider her as a surrogate grandmother and Warren enjoyed her company, also.

Warren prepared to take the national and state real estate exams and passed. At work, we had moved to a new building and I felt relieved that I had been able to see the organization through this transition. It was an exciting time. However, I had not abandoned the idea of moving. The type of tests Warren had taken allowed him opportunity to move to a large number of states. I was still fascinated by the idea of moving to the west coast, but because of my transformative dream, I knew that I needed to stay in the field to find success.

In the spring, I received a notice for a "Finding Your Destiny" workshop. I decided that I was going to use this as a birthday present to myself. As I communicated with the hosts of the workshop, I found out that the facilitator was a psychic from another state who was visiting here. The workshop began with a Friday evening session and resumed for an all-day Saturday session.

As I walked in the door, the psychic, Anna, greeted me with a hug. She was a lovely young woman with soft brown hair which fell to her shoulders. She was dressed in brown pants and boots, with a flowing blouse that fell into wide sleeves over her petite body. As I stood to sign in after our greeting, I noticed out of the corner of my eye that she was staring at my wedding ring. I wondered if she was getting some sort of vibe from it, but didn't question her about it.

That evening, we exchanged introductions with the group. I only knew two people there -- one of them the host and her partner, who happened to be one of my physicians in childhood (as well as my step-father's physician). I hoped that the physician wouldn't recognize me. As we exchanged introductions, we were to tell who we were, why we were here, and whether or not we felt we had led any past lives.

Many people felt they had lived other lives and some of them knew a lot of details about their past lives. Anna pointed out that she thought one person had actually been a wood sprite in another life! I wasn't sure. Anna asked the group what they thought -- many of them felt that me and another girl -— Lisa -- had not lived other lives and were in fact, angels, who had been sent to earth for a purpose.

"This just made it worth the $150," I joked. Everyone laughed.

"Can you see it in each other?" Anna asked. I looked over at Lisa, whose bright and kind face hosted large bright brown eyes that seemed to emit a halo. She looked like she could sprout wings any second.

"I think so," I said. And Lisa said she saw it in me, also. "But I'm not sweet," I said.

"I know you aren't!" said Anna. "But tough love is o.k." One of the group members pointed out what I did for a living. When I went home to tell Warren, he was not so understanding. He thought $150 to see a psychic was an extravagant waste of money and didn't want to discuss it. I had told the group members of his resistance to my attendance.

That night, my dreams were tortured. I dreamed of Atlantis, the fallen city. There were large rock plateaus that were going higher and higher and on each of the plateaus was a plague of mankind - AIDS, violence, etc. I dreamed of fire and of a book that showed all the prayers that Sandy had prayed for me. I knew that the dream was transformative, but unfortunately, I no longer had the sleep-dream-recall-record ability as the effects of hypnosis had worn off long ago.

The next day, we had to share how we had felt after the previous night's session. I told how I had gone home and noticed that I had angels throughout my home -- from the magnet on the refrigerator, to pictures on the wall, to dozens of statuettes. I told how my grandmother used to call me "cherub." The psychic pointed out that cherubs actually were the protectors and had been used at the Garden of Eden. She told me that angels were not of any one sex. This fit me because most of the time I don't feel necessarily masculine or feminine. She offered that cherubs typically come to earth to work for a purpose. I panicked slightly -- hoping that my "purpose" wasn't to help us all through Armageddon.

She also told us that angels tend to have their own brood -- people who protect them. I realized then that more than likely, my grandmother was my angel who had protected me in this life so that I could do the things I needed to do. Warren did, also, but it was hard for me to imagine that he was an angel. I could see other angels in my life -- my childhood friend Katie, who had spent her career in nursing and had a special caring about people. And my mother-in-law, who was the family caregiver -- she was another person who had angels in many different forms posted throughout her home.

Anna said that some people are aliens who get trapped within the Earth's realm and continue here. Evil people like Hitler come from an evil realm beyond our Earth. It was then that I began to ponder that my step-father might be one of these. He had a special enjoyment for Star Trek and outer space movies. As I explored the sex offender web-site, it seemed that many of the Caucasian child molesters had similar features -- short men with glasses, just like my stepfather.

She also told me that self-validation was one of the lessons I was trying to learn in this life -- learning to do what I thought and felt what was best. That seemed very in tune with my life -- I have had to self-validate everywhere in my life.

I knew that to most people, the things she was saying would seem far out, but I felt in my soul they were right. And unlike other people, these beliefs didn't conflict with my sense of Christianity or God. I believe that under God, all things are possible -- including all of the religions. And to ponder all of these ideas helped me make sense out of the craziness of life -- a sense that also satisfied my need for creativity and gave me a few smiles.

I also told the group that for a while, my husband would continue to be distant and avoid conversation about my attendance. But eventually, curiosity would get to him and one day when we were traveling or having time to talk, he would listen. If nothing else, the idea that I was an angel who had not lived maybe more than one other life gave me energy and motivation to live this life well and to do what I could to be a more helpful and better person.

As my high school reunion approached again, I spent a lot of time organizing and preparing for it. Betsy had now been watching Gerald for several weeks and as she became closer to us, she insisted upon doing laundry for us, making dinner, and anything else she could do around the house. I felt an enormous sense of trust with her.

Then she began to engage in an interesting game of triangulation. She told her daughter that we were taking advantage of her and told us that her daughter was being abusive to her. One morning, it all culminated in her arriving at my house to work in tears, saying that she couldn't take it anymore. I encouraged her to go to the hospital and called her daughter. When she casually told the doctors that she wished she was dead, I don't believe she realized that there was a consequence with that. They committed her to the Winchester hospital psychiatric ward.

When Anita and I sorted it all out, we realized that her mother had a lifetime of perpetuating drama and that the best thing for Betsy to do was to move in with her son -- who lived in another state. I was devastated and once again worried over what to do. At least now, Betsy's efforts had better prepared Gerald for potty-training (he had been very delayed in being fully potty-trained) and with that obstacle out of the way, our options were more open. Although now, there was one more in our family - a small bichon frise puppy we named Geronimo. It had been Warren's gift to Gerald for becoming potty trained. For a short time, the daughter of the family that sold us the bichon babysat Gerald. Then I put him in another local daycare. Once again, he struggled with separation, but eventually he became better.

Over the summer, I felt as if I had another baby. I was tired all of the time. The puppy was very high maintenance and I noticed myself being very overprotective over it. Somehow, I was triggered by it and found myself having frequent flashbacks of my stepfather's cruelty to the animals in our home. Eventually, I adjusted to the addition to our family and felt great success as I crate-trained him.

One day, I received a phone call at work from a community member. "Meredith, this is Marvin Stover. I know your grandfather from the lodge. I was talking with him on the phone just now and I don't know if something happened to him or he just fell asleep, but the phone dropped and the line is still open."

I raced out to my car and up to my grandfather's house. I went through the door and found him awake in the T.V. room.

"Well, hello," he said.

"Marvin Stover called me. He said that you dropped the phone and wanted me to check on you."

Grandpa laughed. "Oh, yeah, I was wondering what happened. I must have fallen asleep. When I woke up, I had the phone in my hand and no one was on the line. So I just hung up the phone. I meant to call him back, but I forgot."

This wasn't the first scare. On another occasion, the Meals-on-Wheels attendants had tried to contact me because I was listed as a back-up contact with them. When they couldn't reach me, they reached Warren on his cell phone. They said that they had been to the house, but Grandpa had not answered the door and they had not been notified that he was going to be gone that day. Warren went to the house, but no one answered the door. He tried to peer in the windows, but didn't see anything. Finally, he decided to contact the police, who entered the house to do a wellness check. Grandpa wasn't there. Warren left a note that he had been there checking on him.

In response, Warren received an ungrateful call from Aunt Cathy, who explained that they had been to a doctor's appointment. She told Warren that he had no right to go in the house and that she was going to remove our names as the contact people. Warren argued briefly with her and finally told her, "Whatever, Cathy," and hung up with her. I let my grandfather know about the situation. He was angered at her behavior, but I told him there was no use in addressing it with her.

In the fall, another high school reunion came and went - this one essentially without incident. Although, Warren was slightly bothered as I buzzed around the entire evening selling 50/50 tickets to a rather eager crowd of former male former classmates. Five years had heightened his maturity, though, and I found him to be less jealous this time.

Our evening was interrupted briefly as someone announced that there had been another sniper attack -- a sniper had been on the loose not far from us and the random victimization had us all concerned. For several months, local events were cancelled out of fear. A common misconception was that the perpetrator drove a white van. One day I stopped in Manassas following a meeting and observed a white van drive down Rt. 234. I practically ran into the restaurant out of panic.

I entered Gerald in the local Montessori School. I found myself butting heads with the teacher, who promoted the true Montessori lifestyle that minimized "unnatural" activities such as television. She thought I was horrible to have let him watch the "Wizard of Oz." I argued respectfully with her, but didn't want to go into too many details defending television.

The reality was that I had learned a lot of my values from television -- besides books, television was a vehicle which took my mind beyond the confines of my town and my family. Thank goodness that I liked shows like "Little House on the Prairie" and other shows that depicted good and healthy families. In many ways, I was grateful to T.V. for showing me what the world could be for me.

CHAPTER 29

A job in Charlottesville at a sexual violence agency came open. It had been open before after the long time director resigned/retired, but the timing wasn't right at that time for me to transition there. I applied this time. I was contacted for an interview, but didn't hear anything for several months.

At a meeting, I had opportunity to interact with the former director. I decided to risk my privacy and told her that I had applied.

"You are the dark horse candidate!" she exclaimed.

I know that ultimately her behind-the-scenes influence, along with the ultimate withdrawal of the top candidate (who desired a larger salary), helped me to get the job and through that process, I reaffirmed another important life lesson. Relationships were what this world was about -- and I had to depend upon others to be able to move toward my own individual dreams.

I was given the job just in time. Warren and I had decided that perhaps we should buy another house and just settle in. As I accepted the job, I said a prayer that our home would sell in 6 weeks or less, because anything else would create too much of a commute. I gave my one month notice.

It was hard leaving the relationships that I had developed, but I also felt that I had nothing left to offer the organization and it needed fresh leadership. I asked Sandy to watch the papers for me and let me know if anything happened to my grandfather.

Warren, Gerald, and I spent our weekends searching for a house and put ours on the market. Everything fell into place -our house sold in a few days. We had looked all around the Charlottesville area and kept ignoring one home that was blatantly in our price range. One Sunday, we took my mother-in-law with us and we decided to brave the melting snow and take a closer look at this home, which had remained on the market. Once there, we realized that the advertisements had not adequately captured the beauty and unique features of this modern Victorian. We put a contract on the home and moved in within 6 weeks, just as I hoped. I knew that the transition was right and learned another life lesson -- when you are on the right path, things move smoothly and fall into place easily.

At my going-away party at work, I had an interesting conversation with the local batterer intervention program coordinator. I had noticed through our office notification that my cousin Randy Jr. had been charged with domestic violence, placed into batterer intervention, and eventually was kicked out of the program. When I told her that Randy Jr. was my cousin, she was surprised. I shared with her some of the knowledge I had about him -- how he used to threaten us with knives, that there was apparently domestic violence in the home, etc.

She felt very validated and told me that he was one of the worst cases she had seen -- that his views that included hatred of women were so ingrained within him that they couldn't make any progress. In fact, other members of the group (also batterers court-ordered to the program) tried to confront him on things that he was saying. I found this validating that an outsider could see the dysfunction. Then she made me feel better as she said that every family has members who have problems -- and that's why some of us do the work we do.

I commuted for several weeks - spending nearly 3 or more hours on the road everyday. Gerald finished up Montessori school. As we went to the closing ceremonies, Gerald's teacher made a point of telling me how well he had done during the last several weeks.

"He's done really well during the time that you've lived in Charlottesville," she said. She had thought that I had moved to Charlottesville and left Gerald with Warren. It implied that she thought he did better without me.

"Oh, we haven't moved yet. I've been commuting," I said. Despite the face that I was offended that she thought Gerald would do better without me, I also was happy because he was doing better. To me, it meant that probably the resolution of knowing where we were going, combined with the impact this had on my own state of mind, was having a positive impact on him.

One afternoon, I had left work early and stopped by Kmart in Charlottesville on the way home. I needed a pair of pantyhose. I had never been in the store before and had a hard time locating the pantyhose. When I finally found the racks of hose, I couldn't locate my size. I was beginning to feel stressed -- my heart was starting to beat fast and I felt out of breath. I saw a worker and asked her if she knew where my size was.

"It should be right there," she indicated, offering no further guidance or assistance. Suddenly I was overwhelmed. I felt like I needed to get out of there. I left immediately and calmed down as I drove up the road. *Another panic attack,* I deduced.

The day Warren brought the moving truck to the home, we had a misunderstanding that escalated out of stress and exhaustion to a temporary shouting match. As we moved to a local motel for the evening, retrieved Gerald from school, calmed, and forgave, we talked about how we wanted to make this move a fresh start.

Before long, we had settled into our Victorian and I settled into my new work. I immediately found that I knew exactly why I had been brought there. While the center was very progressive in its programs, it had lacked administratively for quite some time.

When I moved to Charlottesville, I made a commitment to get my health in order. I asked one of my new staff where she went to the doctor. She referred me to the Falcon Practice not far from where I worked. As I entered the practice, I began to wonder at the referral.

The office was quite different than what I had been accustomed to. The waiting room was decorated very simply. There were cracks running down the walls and the carpet looked worn and slightly dirty. When I was transferred into one of the clinic rooms, I observed more interesting sites. The doctor's rolling chair had a split in the vinyl, as did the patient chair. *Maybe it's just that doctors*

here put more effort into their service than their facility, I
hoped.

A short young woman with light brown hair entered
the room. I confided in her that I wished to have a pap
smear, address my depression and panic attacks, get
something for the rash on my skin, and lose weight. After
the procedure, she came back with a prescription for skin
cream and gave me a sample of Prozac.

"Prozac! Wait a minute, I've heard a lot of concerns
about that,"I said.

"Prozac's been given a bad name. It can be very
effective and it is one of the few antidepressants that won't
make you gain weight. I'm not going to give you anything
for your weight. If you want, I can refer you to Weight
Watcher's or a nutritionist and we can go from there."

And so, I began my prescription. And just in time.
At my new job, I discovered that the previous bookkeeper
had committed embezzlement and I helped lead the process
of discovery to uncover all of the evidence that we could. I
connected somewhat with staff, but found that they had
functioned well without a leader and despite my best
efforts, I found it very difficult to team build (which I
considered one of my specialties). But I noticed that I was
handling everything exceptionally well, and at follow-up
appointments, the doctor conceded to my requests to up the
dosage.

For the first time in my life, I was having lasting
moments of happiness, peace, and euphoria. I wasn't losing
much weight, but was feeling good about my life and the

decisions I had made. We had money from the sale of the house and Warren was doing well in real estate. I began to take time for myself and enjoyed shopping, treating myself to regular manicures and pedicures for the first time in my life, and settling into the borders of this new rural city which that year had been named the best place to live in the United States.

In the summer, I placed Gerald in the after-school program offered through our county. One day, he came home and seemed very upset and out of sorts. I continually asked him what was wrong and finally, my desperation penetrated him.

"He asked me to touch it, but I didn't want to," he said. My heart stopped.

"What?" I pressed him for more information. He began to walk around in circles on the bed.

"This boy at school asked me if I wanted to see him and touch his privates."

"Where were you?"

"In the bathroom."

"What did you say?"

"I told him 'No, I don't want to.'"

"Then what did you do?"

"I left the bathroom. I didn't go. Well, the bathroom doesn't have doors in it anyway and I don't want to go in there."

When I told Warren about it, he told me that either I needed to go in and say something, or he would. Deep down, I was afraid of the response I would get. Somehow I still had that little girl inside of me who wasn't believed, wasn't listened to, and wasn't helped. I didn't want Gerald, who still had problems with separation anxiety, to be retaliated against. But I mustered up the courage to address the issue with the childcare leader.

"I'm not sure what happened, but Gerald told me was approached in the bathroom by another boy who was trying to get Gerald to look at him or touch him. Gerald says that he told him 'no', so I'm pretty sure nothing happened. But I'm wondering what we can do. He told me there are no doors on the bathrooms?"

"That's right. They're planning to fix them, but they just haven't yet. I'll tell you what, there is another bathroom that the teachers use. He can use that instead. That is a private bathroom right near the gym."

She was very helpful and I felt good that we had come to a resolution that was going to quickly help Gerald. When I told one of my co-workers about the incident, she offered me a few books about good touch and bad touch. With one book, nearly everyone in the book was naked. It was too much for me and I wasn't comfortable with it. She reassured me that I should use materials that I felt comfortable with. I took the *good touch bad touch* book home and read it to Gerald.

"Mommy, are you reading this because of what happened in the bathroom?" he asked. I laughed at his intelligence.

"Yes, I am."

Although I know that incidents like this can happen

anywhere, I thought it might be more helpful to put him in one of the city schools so that he would be closer to my work. Once again, I found that the facility was under renovation and had a lot of run-down features, but the service was good. Gerald's Kindergarten teacher was wonderful and worked well with him to get him beyond his anxiety. He made friends with a few of the children at school and thrived in his new environment.

At work, one of my co-workers had arranged an in-service with another area counselor to introduce us all to a new form of therapy. I offered to be the guinea pig.

Commonly referred to as "tapping" therapy, the practice involved the client (in this case, me) disclosing a traumatic experience, event, or situation and during the disclosure, the counselor would tap on key points of the body -under the nose, under the lip, at various points around the head, on the back, on the chest, at the wrist, on the upper arms. It was meant to release the trauma that the body had trapped and to teach the client to relax as they encountered the memories or thoughts of the trauma.

Of course, I began to disclose the situation of my abuse and how it was approaching the anniversary of my grandmother's death. Until that moment, I hadn't realized that I was beginning to feel the trauma again and suddenly realized that the anniversary date of her death was the next day. For a few moments, the counselor talked softly to me in comforting terms and I closed my eyes. And then I could feel my eyes begin rapid eye movement.

"You're hypnotizing me, aren't you?" I asked. I was

surprised again with the ease at which I entered a hypnotic state. She continued with the process and I worked through sadness. As we worked through this issue and I began to let the grief go, she asked me,

"What do you feel now?"

"Nothing," I said. In my mind, it was like I was clear and emotionally, I felt nothing particular. And then waves came over me.

"I feel anger," I said. "At who?" she said.

"At my mother and my aunt -- she's a real bitch," I said. I could feel the tenseness in my body rise up and I was almost clenching my teeth in anger as I spoke. She helped me work through this and then she brought me out of my hypnotic state.

"How do you feel?" she asked.

"I feel great," I said. Just as those words left my lips, I felt as if I were floating up. I experienced a head rush of dizziness and energy and I felt like I needed to run.

"Whoa!" I said. "I'm dizzy! I feel weird."

"You need to ground yourself," said Kris, my co-worker. "You know, feel your feet on the floor, be present in your body." After a moment, I felt grounded again. The counselor explained that trauma had sort of built a "forest" of issues in my mind and body -- it had planted grief, pain, anger, etc. The "tapping" therapy helped to clear areas of this "forest" and essentially cleared more issues and emotions for me in an hour and a half than the years of working through my issues on my own and with other methods. Once again, I felt I had been blessed by another dramatic healing event.

CHAPTER 30

On an average sunny afternoon at work, my
secretary handed me a manila envelope with a small post-it.
Meredith, I'm sorry about this, the post-it read.

I emptied the contents of the envelope. In it were
several newsletters that I had sent out, as well as a letter
from my Aunt Cathy.

> *To Whom It May Concern:*
>
> *Please remove me from your mailing list, as well as
> my aunt in Florida, Maggie Troudoe. Our names are from
> Meredith Pearson's personal mailing list and should never
> have been used for your business mailings. We have no
> interest in your organization. Please remove us
> immediately or I will take further action.*
>
> *Cathy Funkhouser*

I explained some of the situation to my secretary,
who confirmed that my aunt must be a real bitch to send
something like that. I had hoped that somehow by keeping
her on the mailing list, she would eventually read some of
the material and come to an understanding of the situation.
But she had not. I removed their names from the list, but
chose to keep my grandfather's and my mother's names on
it until such time as they asked to be removed. I wasn't sure
what had sparked this impromptu mailing -- perhaps it was
a recent solicitation or perhaps even a poignant article
about sexual violence. No matter what the reason, it
solidified that she was not interested in mending any
fences. I had sent her and my mother pictures over the
years, as well as occasional cards or copies of the holiday

letters that we sent out to all of our family and friends. Now I knew without hesitancy that there was no point.

Following the receipt of this note, I felt compelled to go back to "tapping" therapy. I called the counselor.

"I'd like to set up an appointment with you."

"Is it an emergency?"

"No."

She thought I said yes and responded, "Can you come this afternoon, then?"

"No, I said it *wasn't* an emergency."

"Oh, o.k., let's do next Friday afternoon then."

The following Friday afternoon, I found her office in downtown Charlottesville. She led me back to a small office and she sat beside me. I felt a little more uncomfortable than when we had a room full of people. I told her about the letter and refreshed her memory on my situation - most of which she remembered. She asked me,

"Do you want to go there?"-- meaning did I want to address the abuse. She began to lean toward me as I disclosed more specific information about my abuse. She was tapping on me, but also whispering negative messages in a sinister voice. I suppose she was trying to mock what she thought would be messages my step-father gave me so that I could feel the trauma and work through it. I wasn't feeling safe or relieved. And I wasn't feeling the level of hypnosis that I had felt before -- I felt awake and nervous. But at a key moment, she told me I was o.k.

"You think I'm o.k., that I'm normal?" I asked.

She stopped tapping me and said, "Are you kidding

me? Of course you are o.k. You are better than normal. You have done quite well for yourself."

"Thank you, Thank you," I whispered. I had tried so hard to overcome all of the craziness of my childhood and to distance myself from it - and it was still important to me that other people saw this and thought of me as good and normal. I was still working on self-validation.

I had visited Grandpa on a few occasions when I made it up to Front Royal. He was now living in an apartment. I had been to visit him one day at his house and he didn't come to the door. When I looked inside the octagonal window on the front door, I saw that the chair and telephone stand were missing from the foyer. I called his number from my cell phone and he answered.

"Where are you?" I asked.

"I'm at home. Where are you?"

"I'm outside. You didn't answer the door."

"I've moved!" He gave me the new address. He had taken out a reverse mortgage on his house and had been struggling financially. The life insurance policy on my grandmother had been paid for in full in 1966 and netted less than $1500 - not even enough to pay for the funeral. Christy and Cathy convinced him to sell his house. He put it for sale in the *Vintage Finds,* a local publication that primarily was used to buy, trade, or sell used items and to advertise for yard sales. When it didn't sell, Christy went to a local realtor and offered to sell it for $200,000 -- well below market price. If they had gone to Warren, who had built himself up into one of the top agents in town at that time, they probably would have gotten $50,000 to $100,000 more. Instead, that money went in another realtor's pocket as he slightly renovated it and sold it for a hefty profit. I didn't completely blame my grandfather -- I knew that he was still somewhat dependent upon them and either felt obligated or intimidated to take their advice.

His new apartment was a nice set-up with two bedrooms, a kitchen, livingroom, and bathroom. He was hard of hearing now and kept the television on close captioning so that he wouldn't disturb the neighbors. He was continuing to receive cleaning services and Meals-on-Wheels -- which provided important connections for him with the outside world. He had bruises from falling, though. He was having problems regulating his medications and as a result, he was experiencing dizziness and unsteadiness on his feet.

I continued to offer that he could live with me, but he continued to tell me that he didn't want to be a burden. I tried to explain that he would just be another addition to an already busy family, but I knew that now that I moved out of town, he would never move in with me. Moving in with me would limit visits with the other side of the family, and he wasn't prepared to do that.

On my next birthday, Warren and I spent the night at the Hotel Strasburg. Gerald stayed with Warren's mother. While dining out, I saw one of my former board members from Front Royal. She expressed to me some of the problems that they were having with the director who had replaced me and I began to ponder returning to my old job.

Because of the embezzlement issue, as well as some of the other organizational issues at my job in Charlottesville, I was contemplating going to law school. I wanted to be more active politically and legislatively and felt that law school would help me obtain my goals. But most of the law schools that would accept part-time students were located in Northern Virginia -- too far from Charlottesville. I needed to move back toward that area. I also was missing the small town life and was feeling the pull of being closer to my grandfather.

I applied for the job when it came available and interviewed. But during the interview, I realized that the board was a little divisive and my return to the job would not move them forward -- we had too much history together. They needed a fresh perspective. I withdrew my application. At the same time, another position became available in Culpeper.

Terry and Justin, my step-sons, were living there now with their mother. Culpeper wouldn't have been somewhere I would have gone directly to from Front Royal, but now that I had been in Charlottesville and learned new skills, I felt like I had something to offer a shelter program again.

Once again, everything fell rapidly in place. I interviewed once and got the job rather quickly, gave notice, put my house on the market (it sold quickly), and put a contract on a new house to be built. Again, I found a program that needed the skills I had -- once again a sort of divine message that I was in the right place. I was in the fortunate position of building an almost entirely new staffing team. I had a good board with rational, nice people who actually could provide me with good guidance. And I found Culpeper to be the twin town of Front Royal -- almost everything was familiar to me. But what I loved most was that I was building all new relationships -- it was like having a hometown again without all of the baggage.

We were able to move into our new house just before Christmas. After the holidays, we took off to New Orleans. As usual, we explored the city and on one of the streets, we noticed a long line of street psychics seated and ready to deliver prophecy to the tourists. Warren was walking more slowly than usual. He caught the eye of one of the psychics. She had painted one side of her face white and had a blue star bordering her eye.

"Can I help you, sir?" she asked.

"I don't know. Could you tell if someone is going to die or not?" he asked. I was surprised.

"You have a long time to live. What's worrying you?" she asked.

"I've been having a pain at the back of my head," he responded, rubbing the back of his head and neck.

"It's stress," she said.

"Are you sure?" he asked.

"Yes, why don't you sit down?" She proceeded to look at his hand and accurately tell him that he was having a struggle at work, but that it would be resolved. She told him that he would live into his late 70's or perhaps even 80. She offered to read me and I accepted.

"You are an angel," she said.

"I've been told that before," I said.

"Well, you have the mark," she said. "You've also had a lot of heartbreaks -- most of which were before you turned 18. And I see one more," she said.

I looked at Warren. "It better not be you," I told him. The psychic proceeded to tell me that she saw that I had some psychic ability with dreams, saw me doing more through writing, and that I could work on my compassion. Warren and I both were happy with our readings. But I kept wondering at what would be my other heartache.

CHAPTER 31

In January, Warren and I attended the annual
Coldwell Banker gala in Winchester. I dropped Gerald off
with Warren's mother and then drove down the mountain.
As I passed the little store, I noticed a sheriff's car there that
began to follow me as I continued along the mountain road.
He turned his lights over and soon I pulled over.

"Do you know why I stopped you?" he asked. And
this time, I really didn't.

"There's a stop sign back there that you didn't stop
for."

"I didn't see it," I said.

"A lot of people don't. That's why I come up here.
Are you from around here?"

"No, I live in Culpeper. But I used to live here.
How long has the stop sign been there?" I asked.

"About 15 years," he said. That basically meant that
I had probably been running that stop sign for the entire
time -- typical for me who sometimes just blocked out key
things in my environment.

I drove in the snow to meet Warren at the hotel, but
went to the wrong hotel (the right chain, the wrong side of
the city). I knocked repeatedly on the door to what I
thought was our room, but received no answer. Finally, I
called his cell phone and discovered my blunder. I made it
to the hotel. The gala was good and we took one more
chance with my luck for the weekend. We decided to forgo
birth control for the evening.

A couple of weeks later, I decided to make a visit to

the local pregnancy center. Gerald went with me. The urine test gave the result that I was not pregnant. Gerald told me that he was glad -- he didn't want a sister or another brother. I was sad. But by the end of the week and no period, I decided that we should go to an urgent care center and take a blood test. We drove to Fredericksburg and Warren dropped me off.

Unfortunately, they would not have the results until Monday. I had purchased a pregnancy test with two testing kits. One of them I had tried earlier in the week and again received a negative result. I had one left and used it on Sunday. I decided that I would try it anyway until I got the results back from the blood test. As one pink line was shadowed by another pink line, I took the display out to Warren.

"Oh my God!" I said as I showed him the test applicator. He shook his head.

"I don't know why you're excited -- it's going to be hard, Meredith," he said. He was 45 years old and now that Terry was in college and Justin was getting ready to graduate, he was not as thrilled to have another child. He had told me before that he might like to have a girl, but he just wasn't enthusiastic about having another child.

I felt like my life was already busy and if I organized it properly, it would be fairly easy to introduce a baby into the mix. And deep down, I had always wanted another child. I had been to two psychics prior to the one in New Orleans -- they both had told me that I was destined to have three children. Although I didn't feel a need to have three (even though with my ex-husband Jackson, we had planned to have 10), I felt like one wasn't enough.

I let my work know right away. Everyone was happy for me. One of my board members asked about law school.

"I've gotten rejected for nearly every one of them. So it seems like the message was 'No, no, no, and you're pregnant' -- which leads me to believe law school isn't the right path for right now."

I did know that I was going to do things differently this time. I wasn't going to worry as much. I wasn't going to bother with all of the prenatal tests -- especially the ones dealing with Down's and the other birth defects. It was irrelevant to me -- I was going to keep the baby no matter what. Unlike my first pregnancy, the gynecologist in Culpeper didn't set up my first appointment until 8 weeks and didn't offer me an ultrasound. I decided early on that I wasn't going to take Warren to any appointments except the ultrasounds. He didn't need the added worry.

I cut out caffeine and began to alter my diet. I began having morning sickness -- especially aversions to anything tomato-oriented. Gerald began to become accustomed to the idea of a baby and warmed up to the idea. All was right in his world as he had settled well into Culpeper schools. My secretary moved next door with her husband and 7-year-old blonde-haired blue-eyed daughter, Brittany. Gerald and Brittany had become instant companions from the moment they met and now that Brittany would be there every other week (her father had joint custody), they would be able to have great doses of playtime.

We took a springtime trip to New York and Connecticut to attend the First Holy Communion of Maria's daughter. I had a chance to interact with all of my aunts, but my father didn't come. He had called me a couple of times to make sure I was coming and always begged for me to visit. So I was a little miffed that he didn't come. Although in my mind, I know that he is mentally ill, there is still a part of me that just wants to be a daughter whose parents take the time to include her in their lives and support her in her life. I hope that one day I am able to fully move beyond this desire that will never be satisfied.

A few weeks later, I took Gerald and Warren to the ultrasound appointment with me. As the doctor pulled the baby's image onto the screen, he looked and it and then went back to the chart, saying nothing. He flipped the pages in my file rather hastily.

"How many weeks did you say you were?" he asked.

"20 -- almost 21," I replied. Finally, he indicated the problem.

"The baby has fluid around its heart. I'd like for you to see a specialist." He tried to find positive things to say, such as that the heart appeared to be beating strongly. He couldn't tell the sex of the baby yet. He wanted me to see the specialist right away.

The specialist was able to get me in the next day. Warren and I drove to Charlottesville and met with Dr. Hitenback. Once again, I lied down on the ultrasound table.

As he began to talk, I really couldn't digest all of the information. I felt tears begin to drain from my eyes and as he finished and we began to walk down the hall, I began to cry profusely. He took my hand and led me to his office.

The baby had fluid around its heart, stomach, and neck at the base of the brain. They could give me an amniocentesis to determine if the baby had a genetic defect. If it did, the prognosis was not good. A genetic defect couldn't be changed and whatever problems it was creating would remain. The other possibility was that I had been exposed to human parvovirus, or 5th Disease. In that case, they could potentially treat the condition through fetal blood transfusions.

"In your experience, what would you say is the prognosis for a baby that looks like this with all of the fluid?" Warren asked. "Is it lethal?"

"Yes," Dr. Hitenback replied.

I decided to have the amniocentesis done immediately and had my blood drawn to facilitate another test that could detect human parvovirus. I met with the genetic counselor, who helped us again explore our disturbing family tree. She tried to reassure us that she didn't see any indications that we would be particularly prone to genetic defects.

Warren put his arm around me as we left the doctor's office. We were both in shock. I apologized to him for putting him through this.

"It's not your fault," he said. "You don't need to apologize to me." On the way home, he made a call to his manager and to his mother so that they could spread the word without us having to do it. I called one of the ladies from my work. In my mind, all I could think about was the psychic in New Orleans. I now knew what my next heartbreak was.

I struggled that weekend, wondering what to do. I wondered if I should get an abortion. I didn't want to have an abortion, but I also didn't want the baby to be slowly dying inside of me, drowning to death on its own fluid. I cried constantly. And then finally, I came to a decision. I was not going to have an abortion. I was just going to let the situation go its own course and I said the equivalent of "thy will be done" to God, hoping that God wouldn't let me down.

Within a week, we had some hope. The baby didn't have a genetic defect. I had been exposed to human parvovirus. At first, I had difficulty finding information on this and was reassured that I didn't get it from my dog. I began to wonder where or how I could have been exposed to it. Apparently, you could have it and not even know it. It merely caused a flushed appearance to the cheeks in adults and was spread typical to how other viruses are spread.

I picked Gerald up at day care. I interacted with the public and shelter clients all of the time. I had taken the trip to New York. It could have been any number of a thousand ways that I caught this. Early on in the pregnancy, I had been very sick with terrible ear and sinus infections. I remember going to a Home Interior party and people asking me if I felt o.k. because my cheeks were flushed.

Dr. Hitenback also told me that the baby was a girl. I knew then that we were in for a good fight. Girls are survivors and by being a girl, I knew that this baby would have a great chance at recovering.

Dr. Hitenback had worked at Georgetown University, where he had learned to do fetal blood transfusions. But they had never been done at Martha Jefferson Hospital, where he operated. He had to gain permission from the hospital, schedule the procedure, and train his assistants. He did all of this in three days.

When we arrived for the first procedure, the nurse asked what we were there for.

"A fetal blood transfusion," I responded.

"Really? How do you suppose they do that?" she asked. I was not feeling confident with that response. We were placed in a warmly decorated maternity room that had a very cold temperature. The nurses kindly set me up with a large hospital gown and warm blankets. I started watching "A Baby Story" on T.V., but had to shut it off as the story covered involved a difficult pregnancy.

The virus had caused the baby to develop severe anemia, causing fluid to swell around the baby's organs and lowering the oxygen count in the blood. The baby's heart had tried to compensate by pumping more blood through the body at a faster rate. Before the procedure, Dr. Hitenback wanted us all "to be on the same page" and handed me a sheet that provided the outlook of the procedure.

The chances of miscarriage or death for the baby

were high, even with the procedure. He had listed "heart failure" as the diagnosis for the baby. The whole situation was a rarity. The process would involve inserting a 0.5 mm needle into the umbilical vein, which at 20 weeks, is only 2.5 mm in diameter. The umbilical cord had only one vein -- if it collapsed during the procedure, the umbilical cord would no longer function and the baby would die.

For two hours, the medical personnel coordinated the entire process. I went for two more procedures over the next several weeks. During the last two procedures, we experimented with various pain medications as my anxiety rose with each procedure in anticipation of the pain. During one procedure, blood was not able to be successfully entered directly into the cord, but was inserted into the baby's stomach.

The baby's condition improved. I also believed this was due to the hundreds of prayers that were sent out throughout our community and the state. Finally, the baby's blood showed that she was developing antibodies on her own through her bone marrow. Often, this didn't happen until after birth. Now she was going to be o.k.

CHAPTER 32

Warren sent me flowers at work. *Thanks for all you have been through, Love, Warren,* read the card. Later, he called me and had a question for me.

"I've been thinking. How would you like to name the baby after Mom? No one else has done it and I can't imagine a better person to name the baby after."

"I agree," I said. I wasn't completely sold on the name, but completely agreed with the logic. And then I began to utilize my baby name book. I found that "Bessie" means "consecrated to God" in Hebrew. And I chose "Olexa" as a middle name. A Greek name, "Olexa" meant "defender of mankind" -the equivalent of Gerald's middle name. Her initials would be B.O.P. -- which lent to the nickname of Bessie Bop. I decided to choose Betty Boop as a theme for the nursery. As I chose the theme, I was very aware that Betty Boop had been one of my Aunt Cathy's favorite characters. I had thought about her whenever I saw the character, but now, I would more than likely think of my own child.

We decided to hold the baby shower at my house. A good collection of Warren's family, a few of my co-workers and friends, and Justin and Terry enjoyed the festivities. It was a happy time and I felt like the pregnancy was going smoothly now. The next day, we went out for dinner and when we returned, I found a message on the machine.

"Meredith and Warren, I'm sorry to tell you this. But after we got home last night, Helen broke out in a rash.

I think it's chicken pox, but I'm taking her to the doctor to find out for sure," said Jenny.

I called the doctor immediately and went in the next day. At this stage of pregnancy, there was nothing to be done. The baby could be born with chicken pox -which could be fatal in a newborn. Or it might be protected with enough of my antibodies to ward off the disease. Helen had been vaccinated against the disease and had a mild dose of it.

Even if the baby didn't get chicken pox from this exposure, Gerald could also develop chicken pox and transmit it to the baby. We were frantic and worried again. We knew logically that we couldn't blame Jenny, but I felt tremendous anger and guilt over the situation.

On top of that, the doctors were having difficulty with my due date. I knew that my due date was correct because I had the blood test, but the measurements of the baby were showing that it was lagging by 3 weeks. We couldn't just wait an extra three weeks -- going too long was just as dangerous as having the baby too early. I had to track down my test results from the clinic where I had had the blood test.

The Culpeper gynecologist was not as concerned -- he felt that if the baby were on time, the lungs would be developed and even if they were not, there was ways to determine and address that prior to the birth. I no longer had to see Dr. Hitenback, the specialist. We had grown attached to him and Dr. Tiagara, who was assisting him during the procedure. But as specialists, they tried to keep good boundaries about not delivering babies. The experience had been so intimate with them both -- they had saved my baby -- and I felt a special attachment to them. I was going to miss them. Warren and I both agreed that we would try to give them some good press as a thank you to them.

I scheduled Bessie to be delivered by C-Section on October 12, 2005. I didn't want to take any chances with a vaginal delivery. The date held great significance for me. My grandmother had died on October 11th. Now, I would no longer view the anniversary dates of her death with sadness, but with anticipation for the next day -- the birthday of my daughter. Her birthday also was going to be the eve of Yom Kippur -- a day of atonement that I read was considered the holiest of Jewish holidays. From what I read, the Book of Life was closed on this day and it was an important day to lay aside feuds with other people. Interestingly, I had recently viewed a documentary which indicated that the date of Gerald's birthday – August 22nd – was estimated to be the true birthday of Jesus.

When I met the doctor in the operating room, I told him that it was the Eve of Yom Kippur and that people observing the holiday were supposed to fast, not wear make-up, and not have sex. I joked with him that I thought I would be in full compliance. The anesthesiologist was wonderful about explaining everything to me step-by-step as they decided to administer the epidural to me. This did not take away the pain, however. It took quite a few times before the tube was inserted in the proper location within my back. Once there, however, I began to feel the joy of numbness.

Warren came in dressed in blue scrubs and sat beside me. The procedure of opening me went rather quickly, but somehow Bessie was lodged underneath my ribs and wouldn't descend to come out. I had fully expected that she would want to get out of there as soon as possible, so I was surprised when the doctor began to ascend the table to tug her out with forceps. Finally, she was delivered and they lay the tiny 5 lb. 5 oz. baby on my chest. I began to cry.

Unlike my experience with Gerald, I kept Bessie with me in the room nearly all of the time except when she had to submit to tests in the nursery. The hospital personnel were very attentive and kind and I was walking around by the next day. Within a couple of days, I was ready to go home. I didn't even try to breastfeed. Bessie established a routine early on and only cried if she needed to eat, sleep, or have a diaper change.

Gerald did contract chicken pox and we segregated the family for over a week. Bessie and I lived downstairs and Warren stayed with Gerald upstairs. Bessie never contracted the illness. I returned back to work after 6 weeks and began taking Bessie to work with me until daycare was available. I had the office equipped with a play yard, a mobile, and a swing – all of the devices I had so resisted with Gerald. She adapted with ease. Often I would put rest her tiny body on my arms just in front of my keyboard as I typed. On one rare occasion, she began crying when the phone rang. It was a social service worker and hearing the baby, she laughed, "Can't you keep that baby quiet?" I knew that it was only a matter of time before Bessie needed a different environment where she could make more noise and have more mobility.

I explored the idea of hiring a nanny. I viewed pages and pages of online advertisements, but the pictures often revealed young girls from other countries donning heavy make-up and sexy clothing. It was clear that they were being promoted for more than childcare. One on occasion, I found an advertisement for an older woman. As she came to the door, I realized she would not be selected.

In her late 50's, she had a stocky build and strong dark hair cut into a bob. She proceeded to tell me that her experience had been with military families. Children needed to be on a tight schedule. She would have Bessie potty trained by 6 months. Every day she would provide me a sheet with detailed information regarding times of all activities, including bowel movements. Out of politeness, Warren asked her what her charges would be. I quickly responded that I didn't think we were going to be able to do this and politely rushed her out the door. Warren laughed at me. "She would get you all straight," he said, knowing that I would never submit to such rigid structure in my home.

After four months, I found a reputable public daycare close to home. In the infant room were two older grandmotherly women and I felt good that Bessie was experiencing this level of mature and kindly care within this environment.

We all visited my grandfather near the holidays. He thought Bessie was beautiful and he looked much better. He was finally getting his medical needs attended to. He still had stories of the other family members that I patiently listened and responded to just as I would with anyone who was talking about their family.

I tried not to call him often. Once he handed my stepfather the phone and told him "There's somebody that wants to talk to you." I told him I had wanted to talk to Grandpa. On another occasion, my mother answered the phone. When I asked for Grandpa, she merely said, "Hold on," and didn't offer any small talk.

I knew I would be at my work for a while now with the birth of Bessie. My children needed stability and though occasionally I could still feel a calling to move to a remote, isolated wilderness, I had learned to put it aside and try to focus on the present. Work continued to go well and I felt good that I had neighbors with whom we had developed a friendship -- we laughed often, related to each other given that we had come from similarly dysfunctional families and experiences, and supported each other through life. Together, we testified about our abuse experiences at the General Assembly budget hearings and joined a survivor caucus, where survivors in the field of domestic and sexual violence met periodically to support each other in the movement.

Warren was diagnosed with prostate cancer in February. He opted to have his prostrate removed. It was a trying time as we explored how I might survive without him -- financially, emotionally, etc. I was ignorant on how to be supportive to him. As I looked at him being wheeled into surgery, his large body enveloped with worry, I could only think about my children.

I didn't want to have Gerald experience another loss -- it had taken him so long to recover from my grandmother. And I didn't want Bessie to experience what Gerald had. When you are in that situation, you can only move day to day doing your typical mundane tasks -- the only way to move is forward. The surgery was successful, but only time would tell for the ultimate prognosis.

In May, I receive information on a rather unique event at Montpelier. The hospice in our area facilitated an annual "Butterfly Release" during which you could donate to the hospice and a butterfly would be dedicated to the person you indicate. I decided to donate a butterfly in the name of my grandmother.

Gerald and I walked up to the gardens just as the ceremony was convening. In between the sculpted hedges was a small area where tiny butterfly cages held flapping congregations of multi-colored butterflies. The chaplain began to say a few words, including words from Gandhi about being the change you wish to see in the world. I felt tears well up in my eyes.

I wished that my grandmother would somehow know that I was honoring her in this way. She would have felt good that there was such a beautiful ceremony on the grounds of a Presidential mansion and that this ceremony included her. It didn't matter that this wasn't the hospice that had served her. I viewed hospice workers as angels who brought so much care to the world as they helped people transition out of it.

It didn't matter that I was choosing this as my memorial ceremony that I would like to continue from time to time. I never felt compelled to visit the gravesite -- I knew she wasn't there. But I could believe that her spirit was with me wherever I was.

Because my mind was wandering, I actually missed when the facilitator called out her name. Although I was a little disappointed, I realized that the program had her name printed -- which was more of a memoriam than what was in my memory. They called the children forward to help release the butterflies. Gerald preferred to observe.

I watched the butterflies leave their cages -- some leaping to the air, some slowly making the ascent, and some struggling. I felt the warmth from the sun on my cheeks and smelled the fresh air filled with the garden fragrances of flowers and bushes. I knew that in my life, I had gone through several stages in leaving my cages and that there had been many spirits that had helped me along. I believed that even following her death, my grandmother was still finding ways to protect me and help me move forward in life.

My father had disconnected his phone. My mother and aunt, as well as most of my family, weren't speaking to me. My children didn't know their grandmother. To change my life, I had to cut away the roots of my family tree. It had been a sad and painfully educational journey.

But today, I was walking through the President's gardens and home, where great people who had framed a great nation had once walked. I was walking with my beloved son while my treasured daughter was home safely with her father. I was thinking about all of the wonderful possibilities of our future.

I fully expected that life would continue to have ups and downs, but over time, I knew I had developed the strength, skills, understanding, and support system to sustain me along my life's journey. The butterflies were still flitting through the crowd, releasing themselves from the ceremony. And as my eyes followed them toward the sky, I was releasing me.

Made in the USA
Monee, IL
16 April 2021